THE
NIGHT
OUT

BOOKS BY WENDY CLARKE

THE
NIGHT
OUT

WENDY CLARKE

bookouture

Published by Bookouture in 2023

An imprint of Storyfire Ltd.
Carmelite House
50 Victoria Embankment
London EC4Y 0DZ

www.bookouture.com

ISBN: 978-1-83790-465-5
eBook ISBN: 978-1-83790-463-1

For Eve (who sowed the seed)

PROLOGUE

I stand outside your house, my head tipped to the window, watching as you move across the bright room, your baby in your arms. Night has descended and I'm thankful for the darkness that has closed in on me, giving me a cloak of obscurity.

There are some people who look as though they are born to be mothers and you are one of them. I misjudged you, but I can't let that distract me. Deter me. As I watch you with your child, the age Megan was when she was taken from me, I tell myself that I have no choice.

Above my head, stars glitter, metallic and distant. You move out of view and the light at the window goes out. The glass now black and empty, forcing me to use my imagination.

You'll be laying the baby in her cot.

Kissing her good night.

Whispering you love her.

The last thing you'll be thinking, as you turn off the light, is that soon she'll be taken away from you. Why would you? I didn't. But life happens. It can be cruel and that's a lesson some people need to learn. It's just the way it is. Karma.

Behind me, I hear the pulse of the waves as they edge ever closer on the incoming tide. The foam they leave in their wake, froths and fizzes on the smooth stones.

The gate is padlocked. It would be easy to pick, but I have no need. There's a better way. Before my resolve weakens, I step back, my fingers caressing the cold steel of the handcuffs in my pocket.

An eye for an eye.

These are the words that drive me. The words that brought me to your house. To your window.

You don't know it now, but they are also the words that will bring me back into your life.

ONE

ELISE

Now

It's after eleven and the boardwalk that separates the back of our patio from the stony beach is empty as you would expect. My heel catches in one of the grooves in the wood, and Sean catches my arm. Pulls me to him, laughing.

'Maybe you shouldn't have had that final glass of Prosecco.' He kisses my hair. 'Can't take you anywhere.'

I laugh and slip my arm around my husband's waist. It's been a good night. A very good night. In fact, I've only thought about Kitty a couple of times during the evening. Wondering if Megan has managed to get her to sleep okay. Whether our baby has settled all right without my goodnight kiss.

Tonight, the sea is calm. Just a soft whisper in the darkness. Moonlight casts sea diamonds over the water's surface, and I have to admit it's wonderfully romantic.

'Thank you,' I say, giving Sean a squeeze.

'What for?'

'For suggesting our night out. For persuading me. I didn't realise I needed it until I had my first mouthful of risotto and it hit me that I could eat the whole thing while it was still hot. That I wouldn't have to get up halfway through the meal and check on Kitty.'

I close my eyes and remember the taste of it. The cream and garlic. The sweetness of the prawns. Reaching up, I kiss Sean on the lips.

He slides a hand into the back pocket of my jeans. Smiles into the darkness. 'If I knew something as simple as a night out was going to have this effect on you, I'd have suggested it sooner.'

A cloud has slipped over the moon, but I can still see the glint in Sean's eyes. I laugh and we carry on walking. Our feet taking us ever closer to our house.

Somewhere in the distance, a police car's siren wails and pulses its warning. I try not to think of it, try to block it out, but the rhythm of my feet alters. My body stiffening as the warmth and happiness I'd so recently felt drains away.

'You all right?' There's concern in Sean's voice. Puzzlement too.

'Yes, I'm fine. Just a bit cold, that's all.'

Not wanting to give in to my panic, I take a deep slow breath as I was taught in the meditation classes I used to take. Then two more. Slowly, oh so slowly, my heart rate begins to return to normal.

It's been worse recently, trivial things setting me off, and I don't know why. Don't know what makes the small hairs on my arms raise sometimes when I'm not cold, causing me to check and double-check the locks on the doors and windows before I go up to bed. Or what makes me think I see people from my past in the turn of someone's head. The tone of a voice.

Even tonight, as I'd laid down my spoon and told Sean it had been the best panna cotta I'd ever eaten, I'd felt eyes on me. But when I'd looked up, the only person left in the room was the waiter who was totting up our bill at the desk. The place having emptied whilst we'd been enjoying our food and each other's company. Our happy faces reflected in the restaurant's window.

'You're right. It is a bit nippy.' Sean takes my hand and tucks it under his arm. Walks a little faster.

The boardwalk looks different at night when there's no one here. In the daytime, especially in summer, it's a thoroughfare from the busier part of the beach to the old fort by the harbour. Dog walkers, families, couples – you name it – enjoying the exercise and the ozone smell of the sea. Stopping sometimes, heads turned to our row of expensive houses, eyes skimming the valerian-studded stones in front of the low wall that separates the properties from the beach. Soon, those same eyes will rise and settle on the vast windows, hoping to catch a glimpse of the lucky buggers who live there. The ones who swim in the shimmering water of the pool they can just see between the leaves of the potted palms.

It makes me realise how lucky I am to live in the five-bedroom house we call home. The sliding patio doors opening onto the large veranda. The spiral staircase leading down to the pool area where on hot days we'll swim and read on the curved loungers arranged between the spiky yuccas and cordylines Sean and I bought at great expense. Glasses of chilled wine within easy reach on the glass-topped table.

Our house is striking, its huge space full of light, and Sean is rightly proud of the contrasting texture of the materials that make up its structure: the smoothness of the glass, the rough surface of the concrete, the cold chill of steel and marble and tile. I, in turn, love the room on the first floor that Sean turned into my art studio. The light perfect for the wide seascapes I paint on commission or which hang in the gallery in town.

I see it now up ahead, standing proud in its row. A little taller than the others. Its windows wider. And, as we get nearer, a feeling comes over me again, one I've never admitted to Sean, that despite everything, I sometimes wish I lived someplace else. A house down a quiet country lane, maybe, the trees in the garden shading dark windows, or an unmemorable street in a large city. Any place where heads won't turn as people walk by as there'll be nothing to see. Nothing to wonder at. A place where I can be invisible.

But I know I'm safe here. I must remember that.

'Nearly home.' Sean sounds almost sad, and I know it's because he's missed nights out like this one, these perfect snatches of time when we can be alone, as much as I have.

Ahead of us is the dark empty space of the property next door to ours. The new build that's taken an age for the developers to complete. Sean stops, squints through one of the gaps in the fence that's been erected around the site, though he'll not see much at this time of night.

He scratches the side of his neck. 'Got a long way to go still. Hear they've run out of money.'

'Really?'

Not that I care. With the builders absent, it's been a blessed relief from the banging, the constant churning of the mixers and the reverberating strikes of the jackhammer they used to break up the paving on the patio. It's made me realise how much I value the quiet. How it helps me concentrate on my painting.

Next door to the dark site, the lit windows of our house are a guiding light. Sean pushes himself from the fence. Takes my hand again.

'Come on, Cinderella. Time to go home.'

As we reach the gate in the low wall that leads onto the back patio, I look up. See my daughter Megan silhouetted in the window. I wave, but she can't see us. I hope everything's been okay.

'Damn. I forgot the padlock key.' I hear change jingle in Sean's pocket as he hunts for it. 'You didn't pick it up, did you, El?'

I shake my head. 'No, I presumed you had.'

'No probs. We'll have to go round to the front instead.' He sighs. 'Good job it's a nice night.'

'Famous last words,' I say, looking up at the sky. The stars, that had been so bright earlier, have all but disappeared and there are spots of rain in the air. 'I don't think we should hang about.'

We link arms and run. Retracing our steps along the board-walk, giggling like teenagers. At the first opportunity, we cut back onto the road. Breathless. Giddy with laughter. The perfect ending to the first proper night out we've been on since having Kitty.

But the feeling doesn't last. My feet falter and I stop.

Sean is behind me. Nearly bumps into me. 'What is it?'

Something shifts in my stomach. 'Look.'

The street is quiet, but outside our drive is a police car, its blue lights flashing into the night. Two police officers are standing at our front door, and, as I watch, my throat tightening, one of them lifts their finger to the buzzer and rings it.

'Oh my God!'

Breaking away from Sean, I run up the road. Something's happened. Something terrible. I feel it in my stomach. In my bones. In my heart. In every part of my being.

TWO

ELISE

Now

The female officer turns at the sound of my footsteps, but I don't give her the chance to speak.

'Has something happened? Please, you have to tell me.' I'm breathless, my voice coming in gasps.

Sean has caught up with me now. He puts an arm around my shoulders. 'I'm Sean Bailey. This is my wife, Elise. How can we help?'

The female officer jots this down in her notebook. 'I'm PC Simons.' She stops writing and turns to her colleague. 'And this is PC Jacks. You're the owners of this property?'

'Yes, this is our house,' I say, frustrated that we still have no idea why they're here. 'Please, what's going on?'

She puts her notebook away. Scans the street. 'I'm sorry to bother you so late, but we've come in response to a call we received. I wonder if we might come in.'

'Of course.' Sean gets out his key and slips it into the lock. Megan hasn't opened the door yet, and I wonder why.

'Thank you.'

Sean opens the door, and they follow him into the wide downstairs lobby. I bring up the rear, my nails pressing four perfect crescents into my palm as Sean leads the way up the staircase to the first floor. Our house is what we like to call an upside-down house. A bedroom and a sunroom on the ground floor. Megan's bedroom and the guest room on the floor above on the road side. My studio and the huge kitchen living area making the most of the light and sea view at the back. At the top of the house is our bedroom and the one that will be Kitty's when she moves into it.

As I reach the top of the stairs, my heart is thumping out a rhythm in my chest. I can't get the thought out of my head. Someone sent the police here.

The living area opens out in front of us and, as with all our visitors, I can see from PC Simons's face that she's impressed, although she quickly hides it.

Sean gestures to one of the settees. 'Please, have a seat.'

If he's worried, he's not showing it, but that's Sean all over. *Don't stress over what you can't control* is his motto. If only I could be more like him.

PC Simons sits, but PC Jacks remains standing.

'Is it just the two of you living here?' he asks.

I shake my head. 'No, we have two daughters. Megan's fifteen. She's been babysitting our baby, Kitty, and she's upstairs. Look, could you tell me what this is about? You said you'd had a call.'

'Yes, we did, Mrs...' – PC Simons checks her notes – 'Bailey. And it wasn't you who rang?'

My brow creases in confusion. 'No, I didn't ring you. As I said, we've been out.'

She flips through her notebook. 'It was a female caller. They didn't give their name but said they lived at this address. You're absolutely sure it wasn't you?'

'Of course I'm sure. What was I supposed to have said?'

She raises her eyes to me. 'The caller was very distraught. She said a baby from this address had been taken from the playground. She'd left her for a moment and when she'd come back, the baby was gone.'

I don't wait to hear anything else. Can't think about anything except Kitty. Leaving them in the living room, I race to the stairs that lead up to the second floor, taking them two at a time. When I reach the landing, I scream out to Megan.

'Where's Kitty? Where's the baby?'

Megan appears at the door to my bedroom, taking her AirPods out of her ears – the reason she hadn't heard the buzzer. She rolls her eyes at me as though I've just said the most ridiculous thing, bringing back memories of Alex that I quickly force away. There's no reason why any of his vileness would have been passed down to her.

'She's in here with me, still asleep. Jesus, Mum, stop yelling. Do you *want* to wake her?'

'Let me see?' I push past her into my bedroom. Kitty is lying on her back in her cot, arms raised above her head, her cheeks flushed pink with sleep. I feel a rush of love. A rush of relief.

'What's going on? Who's here?' Megan's on the landing now, hands on her hips.

'It's the police. There's been a misunderstanding. Stay up here, I'll explain once they've gone.'

'But I want to—'

'Please, Megan. For once just do as I ask.'

'All right. Keep your hair on.'

'Thank you.'

I rest my elbows on the banister, my forehead pressing against the heels of my hands. The relief at having found Kitty safe and well has changed to something darker. The phone call, the officers arriving like they have. It's like the past has overlaid the present and I'm terrified. I need a moment to collect myself.

I breathe in deeply, count to ten, then lean over the banister.

Call down. 'My baby is upstairs asleep. She's fine. I don't know who it was who called you, but they've clearly got it wrong.'

'Would you mind if we take a look?' PC Jacks smiles apologetically. 'Just to be certain. We have to take these things seriously.'

'It's okay, I'll bring her down. She's a good sleeper. I doubt she'll wake.'

Ignoring Megan, who's gone back into my bedroom and is now sitting at the dressing-table mirror twisting her thick dark hair into a ponytail, I bend to my baby and lift her out of the cot. Holding her close to my chest, I take the stairs back down.

'This is Kitty. You see she's fine. I've no idea what's going on here, but whoever phoned must have given the wrong address.'

'It seems so.' PC Jacks comes over to us. Takes in Kitty's sleeping form and nods his satisfaction that she's okay. 'And you say everything's all right here?'

'Yes, of course.'

'That's good.' He hesitates. 'If we could just speak to your daughter.'

'Megan?'

'Yes, it wouldn't be unreasonable to think she was the one who made that call. It shouldn't take long to check.'

I hesitate. I'd not expected the question. 'She won't know anything about this.'

He smiles an apology. 'Just to be sure.'

'Okay.' I walk over to the stairs. 'Megs. Can you come here a minute?'

There's a pause of a second or two, then Megan's face appears over the top of the curved banister. 'Yeah?'

'The officers would like to have a word with you.'

PC Jacks smiles. 'Down here, if that's all right.'

Megan comes down, the tie of her towelling dressing gown trailing behind her, her long, dark ponytail swinging. When she reaches the bottom, she leans against the wall. 'What is it?'

'We were just wondering whether you might have made a phone call to the police this evening. Around ten fifteen.'

Megan's bottom lip catches between her teeth in that way it does when she's confused. 'Why would I do that?'

'We had a call from someone saying that a child from this address has gone missing.' PC Simons looks at Kitty who's sucking on a strand of my hair. 'A baby.'

'That's mad.' Megan scratches at her arm. 'Kitty's been here all the time. In her cot. Mum, what's going on?'

'I'm sure it's nothing.' I'm almost frightened to ask but have to. 'Do you have the caller's number?'

'The call was made from a pay-as-you-go phone, so it doesn't tell us much.' PC Simons looks at me, head on one side. 'And you can't think of anyone who would do this as a prank?'

'A prank? Bloody hell.' Sean runs his fingers through his hair. 'What kind of idiot would find that funny?'

'Who knows?' The officer's eyes move from Sean to my daughter. 'What about you, Megan? Anyone you've fallen out with recently?'

Megan frowns. 'No, but like Sean said, it was a pretty sick trick, if that's what it was.'

PC Simons gives a slight raise of her eyebrows at the use of his Christian name, and I help her out.

'Sean's Megan's stepdad. She's *my* daughter. Kitty is both of ours.'

'I see. Thank you for clearing that up.' She writes something in her notebook. 'So no one has any ideas where this phone call has come from?'

I long to shout out the truth. But I can't. I mustn't. I've learnt this the hard way. Because if I told them what I feared and was wrong, Pandora's box would look like a palace compared to the can of worms I'd be opening.

PC Simons looks down at her notebook. 'I'm sure you

understand that we'll need you to run us through your movements this evening.'

I look down at the smart jeans I put on earlier, the flimsy blouse beneath my best coat, the silver bangle on my wrist that my husband bought me last birthday. 'Sean and I went out at about a quarter to eight. We had a reservation at Tosca.'

'And, before that? Did you take the baby out at all? To the park or anything?'

'No.' I feel sweat collecting under my armpits even though I haven't done anything wrong. 'Why do you ask?' What do they know that they're not telling me? 'I took Kitty for a walk in her pushchair along the boardwalk this morning. Other than that, we've been in.'

'We have a description of the pushchair from which she was taken. Could I just ask what colour your daughter's pushchair is?'

'It's red. We keep it downstairs. You would have passed it on your way up.'

PC Simons looks at her colleague. The small shake of her head tells me it's not the same one. Maybe that's all they'll need to realise they've made a mistake.

Sean's been looking out of the window. Now he turns. 'Look, my wife has told you all there is to know. She didn't make the call and neither did Megan. Our baby's fine. Someone's given this address in error.'

'More than likely.' She smiles and looks around her. 'You have a lovely house here. I'm very envious. Could I ask you about your neighbours? Any of them have young kids around your baby's age?'

I shake my head. 'Not that I know of. I don't know anyone that well as people are quite private – it's why we choose to live here. There are a few families in the row, but I can't say I've seen any with young babies. Some of the properties are rented out by management companies, and some are empty, like the one next door.' I stop, a frown creasing my brow. 'Should I be worried?'

PC Simons gives a reassuring smile. 'Please don't be. As you say, the most likely explanation is that it's been a simple mistake. A mix-up with the address.' She tucks her notebook into one of the pockets of her stab vest. 'Thank you for your time. If there's anything else, we'll let you know. Sorry to have bothered you.'

I nod and press my chin to Kitty's head. She's starting to wake up, squirming in my arms. She'll need a nappy change before I put her back to bed.

PC Simons nods to her colleague, a signal that it's time to go. 'I can see you've got your hands full, so we'll see ourselves out. If you think of anything in relation to our visit, just give the station a ring.'

'I will.'

'We'll say good night then.'

They take their leave, and I wait until I hear the front door close before letting out my breath. The horror of something happening to Kitty had been so strong that the bitter taste of it is still with me.

'So, what was *that* all about? Mum?'

I drag myself out of my dark thoughts. Fight the urge to crush my daughter to me. 'It was nothing. They'd got the wrong house, that's all.'

'So that's *it*?'

'What else is there? It was a mistake.'

'And there was me thinking something exciting was going to happen for the first time in my bloody boring life.' Megan pulls the neck of the oversized pink T-shirt she wears to bed over her chin and narrows her eyes. 'Stupid me.'

She turns and stomps to her bedroom. I know I should have called her out for her rudeness, but recently our relationship has been difficult and I'm afraid to demand too much from her or push back too hard in case I lose her entirely.

Sean takes Kitty from me. 'Come on. Let me deal with Kitty. You go to bed. You look done in.'

I feel sorry for him, his carefully planned evening's now in tatters. It's been months since we've had time to ourselves and now this. Whatever *this* is.

Megan's banging about in her room, and as I listen, realisation grips me. However much I want to believe what I told her – that the caller made a mistake and what happened just now has nothing to do with me or the family – I can't. I *do* know someone who could want me to know what it feels like to lose a child. Someone who could send the police round in an instant.

I know who is behind what just happened, and it's a warning.

What he wants me to know is simple.

He's found me.

THREE

ELISE

Then

I hadn't been sure I believed in love at first sight. Not really. Yet, there was this man sitting across the table from me, his chair pushed back, his legs crossed at the ankle. A man whose obvious appraisal of me should have felt awkward but somehow hadn't.

Quite the opposite, in fact.

For at that moment, as I sipped my second glass of Chablis, the lazy confidence with which his eyes scanned my face was doing something ridiculous to my insides. Love or simply lust? It was difficult to know as it wasn't something I'd felt before. Something I'd fought against this last year.

Anyway, whatever it was, I couldn't help wondering what he saw as his mouth curved into a smile. It could hardly be the girl who often struggled to get out of bed in the morning, despite two alarm clocks, who had to force a brush through her thick hair to tame it into submission. No, it couldn't be that one as he'd never seen her. The smile he gave, as he tilted his head and looked at me, was for the girl whose face had been painted on by her best friend Phoebe, especially for this date. Her lips a shade of red to match her nails. The thin line of pencil above her top lids, winged into a flick at the edges. Feline. Sexy.

'You're very pretty, you know.'

His voice was lower than I'd expected when I'd first seen him enter the bar, leather jacket hooked over his finger. Throwing the door open as though he owned the place, even though he'd told me he'd never been here before. As he'd stood, rubbing at his stubble with his free hand, looking at each table in turn to find me, I'd taken as much of him in as I could. Thankful I'd chosen a booth at the back of the bar to give myself more time to compose my face – to stop the admiration from showing. For it was clear he hadn't fallen for the cliché of posting a photo of himself from five years earlier. Or one taken on a beach to show off muscles that were no longer firm. He hadn't needed to. As he'd moved around the bar, his eyes eventually alighting on me, I'd known there wasn't anything about him I'd change.

Not then anyway.

'Thank you.' I realised it had taken me longer than it should to answer. Would he think me rude? Heat rose to my already flushed cheeks, and I wondered whether the glass of wine I'd drunk to give me confidence before he got there had been a good idea.

His smile broadened, shifted from mouth to eyes, deepening the fan of creases at the corners. 'I can see you're not used to compliments. I can't think why. I'd imagine you get them all the time.' The fingers of his right hand slipped to the leather twist of bracelet at his wrist and my eyes moved to it too, taking in the fine, dark hair covering a tan that hinted of foreign holidays.

'No, not really.'

'I can't believe that. You're too modest.'

He leant forward and took a strand of my hair between finger and thumb. Smoothing it as though it was something to be treasured, and I could feel it – the slow burn of desire. Unexpected and shocking. Even though my head was shouting a warning. Telling me I didn't even know him. That touching someone's hair wasn't the usual thing for a man to do so soon into a first date.

Eventually, my brain kicked in and I moved back, my hair slipping through his fingers, and took a sip of my drink. Wanting to hide whatever it was that was happening from him.

'I'm sorry.' He sounded amused. 'I didn't mean to make you feel uncomfortable.'

'You didn't.' It was a lie that I knew he didn't believe. The small movement away from him enough to give me away.

He gave a short nod. 'That's good then.'

In the space left by his words, he raised his glass, his eyes still watching me as he tipped his head back to drink.

My heartbeat quickened under his gaze.

'So you're a police officer.' It was an attempt, unimaginative I know, to move us on from where we were – an older man and a girl a little out of her depth, or that's how it felt at the time – to something more equal. I faltered, unsure of what else to say. 'That must be really interesting.'

I stopped, embarrassed by my lack of ingenuity.

A flash of amusement crossed his face. He sat back. 'You could say that.'

The pause that followed took up too much space and I rushed to fill it. 'Tell me about it. I'd like to know.'

The beer he'd been drinking was half gone, and he turned the glass around on the beer mat, his brown eyes still on mine. '*What* do you want to know?'

'I don't know. Anything. A typical day.'

'There *is* no typical day.'

I tried to hide my foolishness by taking a sip of my drink. An action that gave me thinking space.

'Well, what did you do today?' I said, as I placed the glass back on the mat.

It was hard to picture him in uniform. In his jeans and smart patterned shirt, sleeves rolled halfway up his forearms, he resembled a footballer or one of the better-looking bouncers you often saw outside one of the clubs in Broad Street on a Friday night. High cheekbones. Strong jaw. Someone who looked as likely to cross a line themselves on a night out as enforce it.

'What did I do today?' He tapped his fingers on the glass, his eyes following a couple of students who had drifted in off the street. All white trainers and ripped jeans. The taller one's hair was caught and twisted into a scruffy bun, her friend's hung down the back of her denim jacket in a bleached white curtain. They were in the middle of a conversation, something about it cracking them up, their laughter loud as they dipped their heads to the taller girl's phone.

He watched them until they reached the bar, then turned back to me, his head cocked on one side. 'I prevented a murder, unarmed a gunman holding up a building society, then organised my team to thwart a drug heist.'

My wine glass stopped at my lips, and I stared at him wide-eyed before realising he was joking. 'Very funny. You don't have to tell me if you don't want to, Alex.'

His name felt strange on my lips, like I was trying it out for size. It was a good name, I thought. A solid name. It suited him.

'I shouldn't tease you. It's very bad manners. You asked a perfectly reasonable question, and you deserve a better answer. I was on early shift today, so I got up at five.' He pointed to the skin under his eye. 'You can probably tell by the bags. When I got to the station, I got my kit out of the locker and got changed, then went to the cells as a guy in custody was kicking off and the poor sods on the late shift wanted to get off home. After that, I looked at some emails, then saw the sergeant from the night shift for a handover briefing. So far so boring?'

'It's not boring. It's interesting.' It was true. There was

something about Alex that made me want to know as much as I could about his life. As though it would bring me closer to him.

'Then I had a briefing meeting with my own team, to get them up to speed.' Alex linked his fingers behind his head and closed his eyes as though transported back to the room full of officers. 'When we were done, I allocated crews to vehicles and vehicles to areas. I wasn't lying about the drug heist. Well, not a heist exactly, we'd had a tip-off about a crack den.' He opened his eyes again and locked them with mine. 'I joined them for that one in case it got messy.'

'You don't always then?'

He shook his head. 'Nah. The constables get all the fun. Mine is as much a supervisory role as anything else. Planning, overseeing, co-ordinating.' He pulls a face. 'Babysitting.'

'What do you mean?'

'Part of what I do is mentoring. Helping the team members "achieve their goals".' He drew quotes in the air with his fingers. 'I'm there for the good stuff though – the special operations.' His eyes lit up when he said this. 'It's what keeps me interested. Just wish there was more of it.'

As he told me more, I studied his face in between sips of my drink. I knew he was in his late thirties, and he looked good on it. The lines that were starting to show around his forehead and eyes added character, texture, to his face. Roughing up what might otherwise be too perfect.

He could do better than me, I thought. Someone taller. Slimmer. An edgy, feisty blonde like the girl at the bar. Or someone his own age with their own flat and a job that was worth talking about.

'Elise?'

'Sorry. What?'

His lips were moving, but I hadn't been listening. I'd been too caught up in wondering what I would do if he kissed me.

'I was asking you about your art. Whether it's just a hobby or whether you plan to do something with it.'

On the dating app, I'd put art as my hobby as well as my occupation, neither of which were actually a lie – just a blurring of the truth. I'd done the art and design foundation year at Birmingham City University and then the first year of a BA. Not long into my second year, I'd left.

I pushed the memory aside, not wanting to go there. Not sure why that memory was so strong today. 'I'm not sure what I want to do. I suppose I'm at a bit of a crossroads. At the moment, I do a few bits and pieces, mostly commissions for friends and family – pets, illustrations for special cards, paintings done from people's holiday photos. That sort of thing. It's not enough to live on, though. To be honest, I don't know what I'd do if it wasn't for Mum.'

'You live with her?'

I dipped my head to my drink to cover my blush. 'Yes.'

'That's nice.'

I imagined him to be making fun of me, but when I lifted my eyes, his expression was sincere.

'It's all right,' I said, wishing we could get off the subject.

'And your dad?'

'He died when I was young. I don't really remember him.' The only thing I had of him were the photographs in the album Mum kept in the sideboard and a distant memory of sitting on his lap, my cheek pressed against his. The scratch of whiskers against baby skin. He was a good man, Mum had always told me. A very good man. It was said so often I sometimes wondered if she was trying to convince herself of the truth of it.

'Did she remarry?'

'No, she said he was the love of her life. That no one would be able to match him.'

'Romantic.' Alex slid his hand across the table and ran a

finger down the back of my hand, making me shiver. 'Pretty awesome. I lost my dad ten years ago to drink.'

He looked up for my reaction.

'I'm sorry. That must be hard for you.' It was all I could think of to say. 'For your mum too.'

Alex's face tightened. 'Don't waste your sympathy. He was a bastard. And as for my mother, well, she pissed off soon after and married my stepdad. Seems things had been going on for a while.'

He pulled a face before tipping back his glass and emptying what was left into his mouth.

'You don't sound very happy about it.'

He gave me a sideways look. 'I don't give a shit. He's no better than my dad was, and if my mother was too stupid to realise that before marrying him, then that's her problem. One day I'll pin something on him and see how he wriggles out of that one.'

I was shocked. 'You don't mean that.'

His stubble rasped as he rubbed the side of his face. 'Unfortunately not. More than my job's worth, more's the pity. Anyway, let's not waste time talking about him. What about you? What made you sign up to the dating app?'

'A friend suggested it.'

Phoebe. Soon to move in with her boyfriend of four years, Josh, and desperate to set me up before that happened. Desperate for me to be as happy as she was.

He looked amused. 'I see. And do you do everything this friend tells you?'

'No, of course not. I just thought that it might be a bit of fun.'

'And is it?' He leant forward, the edge of the table pressing into his chest. 'A bit of fun?'

The last three words were said slowly, giving them a weight they didn't deserve. I was about to answer, but his attention had left me, taken by a group of young guys sitting at a table on the opposite side of the bar. One of them was laughing loudly, his thin face reddened with drink. His jeans hanging off his skinny hips. As he got up and placed his glass on the bar, he turned. Caught Alex looking at him.

The laughter dropped from his lips. His face hardened.

'Is everything all right?' I was careful to keep my voice light. I didn't like the look of him. Or his friends.

'Yeah, of course.' But it was impossible not to notice how Alex's body had stiffened. Muscles tensed. Senses sharpened. If he was a dog, his hackles would have been raised.

'You know him?'

Reluctantly, he forced his attention away from the group of youths. 'You could say that. Piece of shit.'

'Do you want to go?'

'No, of course not.' It was clear how hard he was trying to make his body relax. To appear normal. 'Problem is, Elise, in my job, you're never off duty. Not really.'

I glanced back at the guy with the red face who was still looking our way. When he raised his glass, I quickly looked away again. 'I suppose not.'

'I knew you'd understand.' He gave a wide, quick smile, one that didn't quite make his eyes this time but did something ridiculous to my insides, nonetheless.

Sliding his hand into his pocket, he drew out something metal, then pushed it back once he knew I'd seen it. It took me a moment to realise what it was.

'You have handcuffs with you? Even though you're off duty?'

His eyes flicked to the guy then back to me. 'You never know.' He smiled, tapped a finger to his nose. 'An officer's best friend.'

Taking my hand, he placed it on his thigh, covered it with

his own. I felt his thumb slide across the bony projection of my wrist, gave a shiver I couldn't hide.

He smiled. 'The cuffs should be tight enough to prevent them from rising up above the bone but not so tight they can cause nerve damage. Not unless you want them to, of course.' With a grin, he lifted my wrist to his lips and kissed the soft underside where my pulse throbbed. 'Did I mention you were beautiful?'

I laughed. Colour rising to my cheeks. 'Yes, as it happens you did.'

And the way he was looking at me made me wonder if maybe I was. If all the time the mirror had been lying. The plump ugly duckling with her father's untamed hair and her mother's heavy features turned into a swan.

It was the way he'd wanted me to feel. Of course it was.

'I want to make love to you,' he whispered in my ear. 'Not now, but when you're ready. We have chemistry... you must feel it.' He placed my hand on the leather seat beside us and leant back, looking sheepish. 'Tell me to fuck off if I'm wrong. If I'm coming on too strong. It's just that when I know something's right, I'm terrified of losing it. Please tell me you feel the same, Elise.'

I was still reeling from the shock of what he'd said. Scared of agreeing yet equally scared of doing what my brain was telling me to do. Pull back a bit. Say I wanted to take things slow. That I didn't know him. Not really.

Yet, he was right. There *was* a chemistry. It wouldn't be the same as before. He was a police officer. Responsible. Safe. Wasn't that what my mum had always told me when I was little. *If you get lost, find a policeman.* As though there would be one on every street corner.

It was how I persuaded myself it was okay.

I looked at Alex and slowly nodded. Feeling the warmth

flood through my body as he took my hand again and circled the palm with his thumb.

'Thank you.' Two simple words as though I'd given him a present.

And so it began.

FOUR

ELISE

Then

I'd never have admitted, not to Phoebe, not to my mother, least of all to myself, that I'd been waiting for Alex to call. In fact, I would have said that in the weeks following our meeting in the pub, I'd been busier than usual. Getting on with my life with a decisiveness and energy that was out of character. But now, looking back, I see that waiting was all I'd really been doing. The long days with my sketchbook or camera a way of covering up my increasing anxiety that he hadn't phoned. Believing I didn't care, when in fact my hand would keep slipping to my mobile whenever my mind wasn't occupied. My senses on high alert for the ping of a text, the trill of a call.

But there'd been nothing, and as the days turned into weeks, I berated myself for my stupidity. Asking myself why someone like Alex would be interested in a girl like me. What false vanity had led me to imagine he'd want to see me again. He was probably, at this moment, sitting across the table from some smart young thing who worked in accountancy or PR. Someone with something interesting to say. With a body or face that would turn heads. A confidence in themselves, and in their self-worth, which would have Alex punching their mobile number the next day for fear that someone else might muscle in. Snatch what he wanted from under his nose while he'd been dithering.

I'd imagined all this and more. Much more.

Which is why when, finally, he made the call – to me, not that fictitious girl in my head – I'd answered it without a racing heart. Without the rush of adrenaline that would have accompanied the act had I stopped to read the number on the screen. So sure I was that he'd given up on me.

'Why did you think I wouldn't call?'

Alex was holding open the door for me, waiting for me to go through to the foyer of the cinema before following me in. At the ticket counter, he didn't let me pay for my own ticket but opened his wallet with a flourish, flicking his credit card out like a conjurer. I liked it back then, that old-fashioned chivalry, his desire to treat me. It made me feel special. Wanted. Only later would I wonder if this simple act of purchasing a ticket for a film I can no longer remember, or have wiped from my mind, should have given me some clue as to what was to come.

The girl behind the ticket booth smiled up at Alex through her spider-dark lashes as he pressed his card to the machine, and I wondered if she knew him or whether she just liked the look of his face. I couldn't blame her if she did.

'Well? You didn't answer my question.'

I took the ticket from him. Thanked him. 'I just thought...'

'I never took you to be impatient.' He placed the flat of his hand on my back and steered me across the shiny atrium towards the bar. 'Fancy a drink before we go in? A proper one, not the blue muck in plastic bottles they sell at the sweet counter.'

He didn't wait for me to reply but took my hand and led me over to the counter. I didn't really want a drink, knowing that alcohol, along with the dark interior of the cinema might send me to sleep, but he clearly did.

'Just a small glass of wine.'

'Good choice. I'll join you. Two glasses of white, mate.'

The guy behind the bar looked up. 'Hi, Alex. How's things?'

Alex pulled a face. 'You know. Some fucker messes up, we pull him in. Same old story.' It was said with nonchalance, but I heard a sliver of something else. Satisfaction? Pride? I'm not sure which.

I waited for him to introduce me, but he didn't.

'Any trouble here since—?'

He let the question hang.

The bartender leant his elbows on the counter and looked across the atrium to the ticket counter. There were other people waiting to be served, but he didn't seem in any hurry to accommodate them. 'Nah, all good.'

Alex nodded and took the drinks. He got out his wallet, but the barman waved it away.

'Sure?'

'Of course, mate.'

I felt uncomfortable. Surely, it wasn't his place to stand Alex free drinks, but what did I know? Maybe they had some arrangement with the police that I didn't know about.

'Cheers.' Alex handed me my drink, and I could already tell from the glass that it would be too warm. 'We can take it in if you like. Screen four I think it was.'

He led the way and I followed, noticing how he looked around him as he went, eyes flicking past the couples to the groups of teenagers. Keeping them in his sights, as though daring them to misbehave. Wanting it, maybe. Even though he was no longer in uniform.

The auditorium was dark after the brightness of the hall, the only illumination coming from the small lights set into the walls either side of the steps and the emergency exit sign. It was still early and there were only a handful of people sitting in the beige plastic-covered seats.

Alex led us to the back row and gestured for me to go in front. I stopped halfway along the row, putting my wine in the holder before sitting down. Surprised when after doing the same, Alex slid an arm across my shoulder and pulled me to him.

'Mmm. You smell like lemons.'

I put my hand to my hair. 'It's my shampoo.'

'I like it. It makes me horny.'

I hadn't expected him to kiss me there, not in the cinema like a teenager, but it didn't take long for me to forget where I was. To blot out the stickiness of the seats. The piped music. The rustle of a sweet wrapper from somewhere in the front. His kiss was soft, lingering. His hand on the back of my head, fingers laced in my hair. It had been a long time since anyone had kissed me like that, as though I was something precious, and to my surprise, I found myself responding.

At last, he pulled away. 'I hope you didn't mind.'

It was a pattern I would come to recognise over the next few months. Taking action first, asking later. I liked it then. Of course I didn't mind.

'I thought maybe you'd changed your mind.' My lips were still numb from the kiss. 'About us.'

He looked genuinely surprised. 'Why would you think that? I thought I made it obvious in the bar the other night.'

The way he said it was as if it had only been a day or two ago, not several weeks, and I wasn't sure how to react.

'It's been a while.'

'Not really.'

Even though the lighting was subdued, I saw his frown. Wished I hadn't said it.

But, to my relief, his face softened. 'I'm a police officer,

Elise. That has to take precedence over everything else.' He tucked a strand of hair behind my ear. 'You see that, don't you?'

'Yes, of course I do. It's just—'

He stopped me with another kiss, and when at last it ended, the lights had dimmed further and the safety curtain had risen.

All through the film, the one I no longer remember, he held my hand so tenderly it made my heart ache. Held it through to the bitter end.

The bitter, bitter end.

FIVE
ELISE

Then

My mum liked Alex at first, just as everyone did. He was smart. Thoughtful. Always made an effort with her when he came to pick me up. A compliment. Flowers from M&S, not something garish from the local garage. To be honest, I think she was just a little in awe. We both were.

At first, we saw each other once a week – arrangements made once he knew his shifts. But, as the months went by, he'd turn up out of the blue. Leaning against our brick porch with a present for Mum and a smile. It didn't matter that it might be inconvenient, that I'd just washed my hair or had planned an early night. The confidence with which he walked into Mum's small hallway and called up the stairs made it difficult to say no. Not that I wanted to. I loved that he wanted to see me. That he couldn't wait until the next date we'd arranged in our diaries.

I'd close the door behind us, but, instead of going straight to his car, he'd pull me into the narrow alleyway that led past the bins to our small back garden. Pushing me up against the cold bricks and telling me how much he wanted me. Like teenagers hiding from their parents. Now I see how odd that was.

Not that we'd slept together yet. I'd made it clear I wasn't ready, and he'd respected that. Told me it was refreshing after the behaviour of some of the slags he'd met in bars and pubs in the city. Instead, we'd lie on the settee in his first-floor flat after a night out, and he'd trace a finger down my neck, my shoulder, my breasts. Making me shiver. Giving me hope that soon I'd be able to go through with it. That I'd be able to push away the memories of the night, a year earlier, in my student accommodation. A night that had changed me.

'Do you want to talk about it?'

It was several months into our relationship, and by this time I was mad about Alex. Counting down the days until I would see him again. Desperately disappointed when he'd call to say his shift had changed and he'd have to cancel. More so when he simply wouldn't turn up. No text. No call. Presuming an apology the next time he saw me would be all that was needed to keep me from leaving him.

How well he knew me back then. That other Elise. That other me.

Recently, though, he'd been more attentive. More reliable. And now he was asking me to confide in him. Could I do it?

The television was on, but neither of us were watching it. Instead, he had been telling me about the lad who had been sentenced in court that morning. He'd mentioned him before – a cocky young dealer who'd evaded arrest many times. Who'd clearly injured Alex's pride. I remembered how elated he'd been when they'd eventually caught him. How wired. Telling me he'd be sure to see the bastard went down.

The boy had only been eighteen and the sentence had been long, making me query its harshness. My head had been on Alex's lap, and the fingers that had been in my hair had stopped their stroking. *An eye for an eye, Elise,* he'd said. *An eye for an eye. Can't you understand that?*

If only I'd been paying more attention.

Now, though, the question Alex had just asked me was going round in my head. I'd never told anyone about that night. Not my mum. Not Phoebe. But Alex was a police officer. I wasn't sure why that made things different, but somehow it did. He was used to being told terrible things. He wouldn't drag emotion into it.

'Don't if it's difficult. The last thing I want is to put pressure on you or to make you feel uncomfortable.' He bent his head and kissed my forehead. 'I love you, you know.'

I *did* know. He'd told me many times.

'I love you too, Alex.'

And I did. More than I could say. Maybe if I told him about that night, he'd understand why I'd kept him at arm's length, despite being mad for him whenever we kissed. Whenever his hand slipped under my T-shirt. He wouldn't wait for ever, I knew, and I was terrified of losing him. Maybe telling him what happened would buy me time until I was ready.

The only way I could relive it was to tell it as if it had happened to someone else. Make my voice flat. Emotionless.

'It was the second year of my degree, and I'd moved from the halls of residence into a shared house near the city centre. Two girls, three guys. I didn't know them all that well.'

Alex's fingers moved through my hair, drawing it away from the temple. 'I'm listening.'

I turned my head away, my eyes fixed on some comedy show on the TV. Not wanting him to see my face as I told him my story.

'The girl in our house share, Jules, had gone home for the weekend and the others had gone out clubbing. They'd asked if I'd wanted to go too, but it wasn't really my scene. To be honest, I liked the idea of the house to myself. I'd planned to sketch out some ideas for an assignment due in the following week, then have a bath and an early night.'

Alex was silent, and I pictured him in an interview room, nodding his encouragement as some victim of crime poured out their heart.

'I was in my dressing gown, drying my hair, when I heard the front door open. I was surprised. Hadn't expected them back so soon.'

Alex's fingers stopped. 'Go on.'

I drew a breath to steady my voice. 'There was a knock on my door, and when I opened it, one of my flatmates, Ethan, was standing there with a bottle of wine in his hand.' It was hard to go on, knowing what was to come, but I had to. 'He said the club had been rubbish, that he'd left the others there and come home.' I swallowed. Seeing his face again – the flop of fair hair across his forehead. The way he'd leant against the doorframe to steady himself as he held out the bottle and asked if I wanted to join him in a glass.

'He was pretty drunk,' I continued. 'But he was a nice enough guy, and I couldn't see the harm in it. He was my flat-mate, after all. Not a stranger. Not someone who follows you through an unlit park at night.'

'What happened?' Alex's voice had changed. There was a gravity to it that hadn't been there before, and I worried that I'd made a mistake in telling him.

'I said I'd get dressed and join him in the living room, but he told me not to bother. To come as I was as it was only him. It wasn't as though we were entertaining or anything. So I put a hoodie over my dressing gown and went into the living room. We had a glass of the wine, and he told me about his bad evening. The argument he'd got into with the doorman at the club. The girls who'd seen it and laughed at him.' I forced my eyes shut in the hope that I could say the words without a picture forming. 'I was sympathetic. I felt sorry for him. But when he suggested having another drink, I told him I was tired. That I wanted to go to bed.'

Alex's arm tightened around me. 'You don't have to tell me any more, Elise. Not if you don't want to.'

'No, it's all right.' I said it even though there was a sickness lying heavy at the bottom of my stomach. Fighting through the pain, I carried on. 'We were on the settee. I got up to go to my room, but he reached out a hand and pulled me back down. Said it was early yet, not even midnight. That I shouldn't be a party pooper.'

I leant forward. Covered my face with my hands. 'Maybe I encouraged him. I don't know.'

Alex took my hands in his. Lowered them to my lap.

'Don't ever say that, Elise. Do you hear me? Never, ever say that. I've heard enough. The bastard! The fucking bastard! You went to the police, right? Please tell me you did that.'

I hung my head. My dark hair falling around my face, covering my shame. 'No.'

'Jesus. Why not?'

The tears were falling now. Hot, angry tears that I allowed to flow, take me over until there was nothing left inside. 'I don't know. I just couldn't. I felt so helpless. So *dirty*.'

I didn't know how I'd got through the night. All I did know was I lay curled up on my bed, my knees drawn in, listening to the sound of male voices as the rest of my flatmates returned. Hearing the clatter of mugs in the kitchen. Their laughter. Sleep impossible as I was scared of the dreams I might have if I gave in to it. Terrified it would be a rerun of what had happened. His hands. His lips. His body. Over and over.

'I went home the next morning. Told Mum the course wasn't for me, after all. She didn't question it, but I suspected she didn't believe me.' I turned to face Alex at last. Needing his comfort. His strength. 'It's why I haven't been able to... Why I haven't let you—'

'Hush.' He leant forward and touched his forehead to mine. 'You don't need to say any more. I understand. You know that you could give me his name, Elise. I'd make sure he never walks the streets again.'

'No, it's over. I don't want to think of it again. Drag it all up. I wouldn't have said anything now if it wasn't for the fact that I wanted you to know. I had to explain why I've been like I am with you. That it's not because I don't love you.'

He dropped a kiss on my head. 'I'm glad you did. There's no hurry, sweetheart. We have all the time in the world.'

I laid my head on his shoulder. 'Thank you.'

'You don't need to thank me.' I felt Alex's eyes on me. Assessing me. 'You did right to tell me. What happened to you wasn't your fault. I'm sure you did nothing wrong.'

Maybe it was the relief at having told someone at last. The feeling of a weight being lifted. Whatever it was, it was a long time later before I thought about that remark.

How the first two words *I'm sure* had changed its meaning.

Turned it on its head.

Made me doubt.

SIX

MEGAN

Now

Megan slides the door of the living area open and steps out onto the wide veranda. A glance behind her shows a bank of windows set into the flat wooden façade of their home. Sunlight glinting off the glass. Through the patio door on the left, she can see her mum at her easel, her dungarees already smeared with paint. Her hair twisted into a knot and secured with a paintbrush.

Moving slowly so as not to draw attention to herself, she slips past her mum's studio and down the twisting metal staircase to the patio below where the pool shimmers. Enticing her to swim. But it's not the chlorinated water of the pool she craves, it's the sea. Not just because the sometimes bone-chilling water centres her but because of its nature. The waves, the tides, the sheer vastness of it, reflecting all her moods. Wild and tragic some days when the grey clouds gather. At other times, flat and calm like the stone Buddha that sits cross-legged in the shadows, half-hidden by the fronds of the yucca. Mirroring a lethargy she cannot shake off.

She smiles as she removes her shoe and dips a toe in the water of the pool, making it shiver. It's how she likes it. A way to ensure her mum won't know from one day to the next what mood she'll be in. Unable to settle to her painting until she finds out. Fussing. Hovering in the doorway of her room, asking stupid questions.

Megan puts her shoe back on and protected by the spikes of the yucca, the fronds of the palms, looks up at the glass doors. Watching as her mum stands back from her painting, lifts the pencil she keeps behind her ear and holds it vertically in front of her to measure the size of whatever it is she's looking at – a yacht, a windsurfer, a dog playing at the edge of the sea, maybe.

Another boring painting to add to the others stacked up against the stark white studio wall.

As she watches, her mum lowers her hand. She comes closer to the window and stares out, her face white and pinched. Her head turning one way then the other, eyes scanning the boardwalk as though looking for someone. The visit from the police last night has rattled her, she can see that. But why? When it's clearly been a misunderstanding?

She shakes her head. Bloody parents. Or, rather, bloody parent singular as Sean's okay. It's just her mum who acts crazy sometimes.

Megan skirts the pool and opens the gate at the back of the patio, letting herself through. The stones move under her trainers as she crunches through them, zigzagging between the swathes of valerian that create their own reddish-pink ocean.

At the boardwalk, she stops. Tips her head to the sky and feels the wind on her face. Her eyes dip to the sea, taking in the rows of waves that run into the shore. Turning the shingle at the shoreline before peeling back with a fizz. She thinks of Sean's paddleboard angled against the wall of the sunroom. She wants to be out there on those waves, would be out there, if it wasn't for her mum. *The sea's dangerous. Haven't you read how many people die out there? Wait until you're older.*

Megan gives a huff of impatience. Jesus Christ. She's not a flipping kid.

She scans the blue for Sean's sail. Thinks she sees it. Sean's great. She'll work on him, get him on her side so that, together, they can persuade her mum she's old enough to learn. She's fifteen, for Christ's sake. Sixteen in a few months.

Megan turns, her hands wedged into the back pockets of her denim shorts, and takes in the row of detached buildings that stretch all the way to the fort. Each one different, their only similarity the wide glass eyes reflecting the waves. She's the envy of all her classmates living here, yet, even so, she can't help feeling as though something is missing. That she and her mum are just biding time. Treading water until...

She frowns. Until what?

She has no idea. It's just a feeling she gets sometimes that things aren't quite right. That their lives don't add up. Something in her mum's overprotectiveness. Her refusal to talk about her father. She knows the basics: that he was a one-night stand and that her mum brought her up on her own. But when she presses for details, she clams up. As if her daughter doesn't matter. As if *her* needs aren't important.

Just a nameless man. One she's never met and is not allowed to ask about.

A breeze blows her hair, and she holds it back with one hand. There are so many things she'd like to know about the man whose genes she shares. Like whether she resembles him in any way. What he thought of her mum and, more importantly, what he would have thought about *her* had he stuck around.

Swallowing down the hot, hard lump that's risen in her throat, and angry with herself for letting her emotion push through her indifference, Megan steps off the boardwalk onto the beach. She keeps on walking, and, when she reaches the wet stones at the edge of the sea, takes off her trainers and stands in the shallows, the incoming tide licking at her feet. The taste of salt on her lips. Unaware of the wave that washes up, looping a trail of seaweed around her ankle before retreating again.

The vastness of the ocean makes Megan feel small. Insignificant. Lonely.

She catches another glimpse of Sean's red and yellow sail amongst the other windsurfers who are skimming the white crests whipped up by the wind and the tide. Her stepdad's great, but when she sees him with Kitty, his own flesh and blood, it makes her crave more. Makes her want to know who her father was and what he was like. Whether he wishes, now he's older, that he'd met her.

When she gets back, she'll do some digging, and since her mum won't answer any of her questions, the obvious place to start is with Sean. Her mum tells him everything... he *must* know.

Megan pinches at the soft skin either side of her nose. Swallows hard before angrily wiping her face with the heel of her hand.

Wind tears, she tells herself. That's all.

SEVEN

ELISE

Now

If you saw me through the window of my studio, you'd presume I was painting, but I'm not. I'm watching the boys on the beach watching Megan. Hating the way they jostle each other. Making obscene gestures with their hand when she's no longer looking at them. Just kids, I know, but still. Boys like that turn into men, and though most will turn out good, there will be one or two who will take that disrespect into adulthood.

I know that only too well.

Megan doesn't know I watch her. Doesn't even know that I'm aware of when she leaves the house. But I *do* know. I always know. It's like some magnetic force draws me to her, forcing my head to turn to the window when she creeps by. Thinking I haven't seen.

It's always been like that, but when she was a child, it had seemed more natural. Something every mother did... or should do. Who wouldn't look out for their young child? Be keenly aware of their surroundings and all who travel through them? A lioness with her cubs – a cliché I know, but true all the same. And Megan used to like it too. Slept better when I scooped her up and lay her in my bed, my body curled around her like a shield.

But now?

Now Megan is fifteen and no longer wants that buffer to the world. No longer needs it. Not knowing, or not caring, that it's me who wants it.

I watch her crouch at the water's edge and pick up a stone, or that's what I think it is as I'm too far away to see. The sun is shining, the sky a silky blue, and I have everything I want: a beautiful home, two beautiful daughters, the love of a good man.

I don't know what's wrong with me today. I should be content. Thankful that I'm living this perfect life. That Sean wants me to be happy and does everything he can to make me so.

Besides, it's been fifteen years. What happened was a lifetime ago, and there's nothing for me to be anxious about. Except for that visit from the police, of course. Since then, I've been on edge, my mind constantly turning back to the past. Had that phone call about the missing child been just a mistake? Or had it been Alex's way of unnerving me? Reminding me of what I'd done... how I'd robbed him of his daughter.

Since the police officers' visit, I've found myself obsessively checking the baby monitor whenever Kitty's been having a nap. Not leaving it more than ten minutes before walking back and staring at Kitty's image on the screen again. Telling myself she's fine. That there's nothing to be worried about.

A door slams downstairs – Sean must have come back from his morning windsurf. I'd been so wrapped up in thoughts of Megan that I totally missed him coming back along the beach. Though he must have looked up and seen me. Must have waved.

'Sean?' I hear footsteps climbing the stairs from the sunroom on the ground floor. Move to the coffee machine to make him the cappuccino he likes when he's been out on the water. Pop some seeded bread into the toaster.

He pushes into the room. Wide smile. Sea-wet hair. Still in his wetsuit. Larger than life. Just his presence warming me, calming me, as it did the first time I met him. Sean is even-tempered. Rational. Liking, when he's not out on the water, to fix things: cars, watches, computers. I know he'd fix me if he could. If I'd let him.

He switches on the radio; Dolly Parton's voice fills the room hoping that Jolene won't take her man. 'Weren't expecting anyone else, were you? Brad Pitt? Hugh Grant... or is he a bit past it now?'

I force a laugh and hand him his coffee. Change the channel to something else as I try to control the tightening in my stomach the song has brought on. 'Just a bit. I was thinking more along the lines of Tom Hardy.'

He comes over to me and presses his lips against mine. 'Typical. Bloody typical.' He moves away and cocks his head at the wall. 'John messaged me from Dubai. Apparently, the rental's fallen through. Government's proper buggered things up for him. With the cost-of-living crashing through the roof, no one wants to pay the sort of rent he's asking, and he's not prepared to lower it. Same problem as with the other side. Developers overstretched themselves, and I can't see the place being finished for a good while.'

'Good. Having no neighbours suits me just fine. I prefer my own company.'

Sean laughs.

I wrap my arms around him and hug him tight as though I don't want to let him go. He looks down at me. 'Still thinking about that police visit?'

'Not really.'

But I've never been a good liar. Picking up on something in my voice, Sean pulls me closer. 'I heard you get up last night to check the locks on the sliding doors. I'm sure there's nothing to worry about. It must have been a mistake... like you said.'

'You're probably right.'

I want to share my worries about Alex, but I can't. Not when I've never told Sean about him. Not much anyway and certainly not the truth. Just his name. He'd like to know more, I know, but I've never been one for indulging in emotions, still less for showing them, preferring to keep them tamped down where they can do no harm. I know, although he hides it well, that it frustrates Sean at times, but there's nothing I can do about it. I've learnt the hard way. Opening up to Sean would be no different to exposing an open wound. A wound that will heal better the less it's probed.

Wanting to reassure him, I give him my best smile. 'I'm fine, Sean, honestly.'

He looks at me a fraction longer than he should, then takes his coffee to the window. 'Seen Megan this morning? She up yet?'

'Yes, she went out earlier. She's down on the beach. I'm surprised you didn't pass her.'

He walks over to the window and shields his eyes against the glare.

'Can't see her.'

'What do you mean?'

'What I said. I can't see her. Probably gone into town or something.'

I stiffen. 'She never said.'

Sean turns, walks back to me, and rubs the tops of my arms where goose pimples have risen. 'She's fifteen, Elise. You've got to cut those apron strings sometime. When I was fifteen, I never told my folks anything. And even when I did, it was often a lie. Something they wanted to hear to get them off my back.'

'Oh, Sean. You didn't?'

'Course I did. It's what kids do.' He grins. 'Normal kids anyway. Let her grow up. Give her some space. Some slack.'

Something in me hardens. 'You think I mollycoddle her?'

He shrugs. 'Just a bit. Look, I know why you do it, who wouldn't after bringing her up on your own... but that's in the past. You're with me now and I'll never let anything happen to you or the kids. Speaking of which, is Kitty still asleep?'

As if on cue, the baby monitor springs into life and we both look at it, smiling as we hear our baby's coo. A sound that will soon turn into an angry cry if I don't go and get her up.

'I think that answers your question. Shall I get her? You need to get changed.'

It's a rhetorical question really as I already know the answer. Wetsuit or no wetsuit, Sean will be the one to go. He'd pick her up after every sleep if he could. If it wasn't for the inconvenience of him having to go to work. And if, on a week-day, she wakes before he leaves, he'll drop his toast back onto his plate, climb the spiral staircase to our bedroom at the top of the house, its wide French doors stretching across the entire length of the second floor, and gently lift her out of her cot.

Through half-closed eyes, I'll see him cradle her in his arms, kissing her sweet head before bringing her to me for her morning feed. Lingering in the doorway before going back down to the kitchen area and slurping the last of his coffee. Giving a last wistful look up at the ceiling before descending to the garage where his Mercedes waits in the darkness. Or that's what I imagine anyway.

Such a gentle, sweet love he has for the child who is the product of our own love. And even though I know I should be anxious about our baby, more so than I am for Megan – as she's so small, so defenceless – I'm not. For, mad though it sounds, and impossible to explain, it's as if I know nothing bad will happen to her.

Maybe it's because I know she's nothing to do with Alex. That it's not Kitty he'd come searching for – a child he knows nothing about, would care nothing about – but Megan.

The child I took away from him. *His* child. His baby daughter.

Sean has disappeared up the stairs. A few moments later, he reappears, one hand on the metal handrail, Kitty on his hip. Her cheeks are pink from sleep. Her Babygro bulging with the wet nappy he'll change without me having to ask.

He takes Kitty to the window, pressing kisses to her hair, and points. 'Look there's your sister. There's Megs.'

And I see Megan now. Her shoes in her hand. Weaving through the clumps of white sea kale and red valerian to reach the boardwalk. Immediately, my shoulders relax, and I let out a breath I hadn't realised I'd been holding. It's been the same for fifteen years. It's how I am and probably always will be.

There are things that will never change. The past in my case, and I'm a prisoner to it.

'Oh, there was some post for you. I left it on the side.' Sean swings round and points vaguely in the direction of the landing. A large open space in the centre of the house that Megan's bedroom opens onto, not wanting to sleep on the same floor as us but not wanting to be alone on the ground floor either.

I frown. 'That's early.' Recently, the post hasn't been arriving until after lunch.

'Probably just junk mail.'

Sean slides a finger down Kitty's cheek. 'Don't think so. It had your name and address on the envelope. Where's the change bag? I should have changed her nappy before I came down.'

'It's on the landing where I dumped it yesterday. I'll get it.'

I cross the living area to the wide atrium that separates the

front of the house from the back, noticing that my daughter's
bedroom door is resolutely closed, as it always seems to be now.
I walk past it, wanting to take a peek at her young adult life yet
knowing I have to respect her privacy. With effort, I resist the
urge to look in, telling myself I should be glad that her mess is
shut off from the rest of the house. Remembering the number of
times I've berated her for the unmade bed, the makeup left spilt
on the bedside table, the clothes strewn on the seagrass floor for
anyone to see. *For goodness' sake, tidy up or shut your door!*

But this new bid for privacy is disconcerting, and although I
know it's a natural part of growing up, I miss the sight of that
messy teenage life. I'm not ready to be shut out of either her
room or the heart of the young girl I know as well as I once
knew myself. Better even.

Or did.

'Where?' I call to Sean.

'Where what?'

'The letter. Where did you put it?'

'Oh, I left it on the table by the couch.'

I see it now, half-hidden by the tubular steel arm of the
white leather settee Sean bought from a furniture-designer
friend, along with most of the other seating, when the house was
completed. A house that after hiring a top Brighton architect,
bears no resemblance to the small, old-fashioned chalet
bungalow that used to stand in its place.

Opposite the settee, two matching chairs are angled against
the other wall and between them hangs one of my paintings: a
giant seascape in acrylic. A wide expanse of white canvas with
just a hint of cloud, only the bottom third showing a restless sea
that, even to my biased eye, appears to be moving. Surging onto
a shore rendered invisible beyond the frameless edge.

I sit on the settee and reach over to the envelope. My eyes
still on the painting as I slide my thumb under the seal to open
it, then pull the page out. Only looking down when it snags on

the envelope and I see it's not a letter at all, but something torn from a newspaper.

There's no way to know that this simple act will be the end of something: the calm and safe chapters of my life with Sean. Even as I release the cutting from the envelope and place it on my lap, smoothing it with my hand, all I'm thinking about is that I wish I'd added a red and yellow sail to that vast seascape on the wall. To relieve the monotony. A little part of Sean.

But, when, finally, I look at the article and my eyes pull to the photograph in the top right-hand corner. When my blood leaves my body, taking with it every atom of warmth, its sledge-hammer-impact knocking out the bricks from the wall of security I've built up over fifteen years. When I look at the headline I STILL MISS HER the shock is so great that I don't even register the front door slamming and the sound of Megan's feet on the stairs. Then, yes, only then, does it sink in.

Someone knows where I live, but, worse than that, someone knows what I did. Cares enough to send me this. The hairs on the back of my arms raise as the eyes in the photograph stare back at me. Desperate. Accusing.

It brings it all back. How fifteen years ago, I'd left Alex. Fled with Megan. But what else could I have done? I'd had no other choice. Staying was no longer an option. It had changed my life forever. Changed *me*.

It has to be Alex who sent this. Who else would it be? All this time I'd underestimated him, the man I'd run from, the man I'd thought I'd escaped, but this is a wake-up call.

I haven't seen this news article before, avoided the papers in the early days, but I know, even without looking, that the other photo, the one of the baby, will have Megan's dark hair. Megan's eyes. Kitty's too.

I'd thought the trail had gone cold years ago, that he'd stopped looking for us, but Alex is a policeman and only a fool would think he'd give up.

I am that fool.

The article is old, but it's meaning is clear. Something must have happened that has made him search for us again after all this time and he knows where I am.

An eye for an eye. Alex's words come back to me. His motto. I used to think he was joking, but now I fear he isn't.

EIGHT

ELISE

Then

I adjusted the position of the vase of flowers and stood back. Trying to decide if the way I'd set the table was right. What Alex wanted. It was our first dinner party as a couple, and I was determined everything would be perfect. I wanted him to be proud of me.

Alex's flat wasn't big, but it was comfortable, the table in the living-dining area looking out across the city rooftops. We'd never discussed me moving in, it had just happened. After all, what was the point of getting a taxi back to mine after a night out when Alex's place was so central. Or that's what Alex had liked to tell me, and I couldn't disagree. Though as I tapped out the ever more regular messages to Mum: *Staying at Alex's. See you tomorrow,* I'd feel guilty.

Not that she seemed to mind as, over the weeks, she'd become one of Alex's biggest fans. If she hadn't, then I might have taken a step back. Thought more about what I was doing and let my head rule my heart instead of the other way round.

But it's not fair to put the blame on her. She was as blind as I was. To start with, anyway.

Usually, if Alex was on an early shift, I'd wake with his alarm. Liking the feel of his freshly shaved face as he bent to kiss me, loving the words he whispered in my ear. Then, a month or so ago, I'd woken late to find he'd already left for work. I'd slept through the alarm, and it had only been when I'd pushed myself up on my pillow and squinted at the clock that I'd noticed the key on my reading book. A note beside it.

For you! My home is now your home.

A fait accompli.

We'd never discussed it, and he'd given no hint that he'd been thinking this way. Yet, the excitement I felt as I turned the key over in my hand proved I didn't care. Alex wanted to be with me, and despite the suddenness of it, deep down it was what I'd been hoping for. Or that's what I told myself.

I hadn't waited for him to come home but phoned Phoebe straight away. Asked if she'd pick me up in her lunch break and drive me back to Mum's to get my things. Of course she'd agreed, but on the way back to Alex's, she'd turned to me when we'd stopped at a traffic light, a slight frown on her face.

'Are you sure it's what you want? It's all very sudden.'

'Of course it's what I want,' I'd replied.

She'd looked away. Stared out of the windscreen at the car in front, her finger tapping a rhythm on the steering wheel. 'You don't think it would be better to buy something together? Something you can both put your own stamp on?'

'Like I'd ever be able to afford that, Phoebs.'

I remember how surprised I'd been – how offended. Yet, the question was one that would come back to haunt me later. *Are you sure it's what you want?* A question Alex should have asked but hadn't.

But it was early days. I was in love, and it was way too soon to be looking out for clues to the future. Alex wanted to be with me, and this was his way of proving it. Why would I want to question it? And so I'd told Phoebe I knew what I was doing.

'I thought you'd be getting ready.' I hadn't heard Alex come into the room.

I turned and smiled. 'What do you think?'

'Of what?'

I waved a hand at the table. 'This.'

He moved closer. Finished doing up the button on his cuff. 'It looks great.' He turned me to him, hands on my shoulders. 'Everything you do is great.'

'I'm glad. I wanted it to be right for your friends.'

He laughed. 'It's only Simon and a few of the others from the station. They won't care what the table looks like as long as there are a few bottles on it.'

'I know but still—'

'I said it looks fine. You worry too much.' He stood with his hands in the back pockets of his jeans, his attention drawn to the vase of flowers I'd just been arranging. 'We need to get rid of that, though. Cathy gets hay fever.'

'Oh, you never said.' I'd bought the flowers in a florist's near the flat, thinking the bright yellow sunflowers and deep blue delphiniums would brighten up the room. The vase was one Mum had given me when I moved out. One I'd always liked.

'Not to worry. I'll get rid of them.' Reaching across the table, he picked up the vase, not looking at me as he took it across the room and into the kitchen. I couldn't see him from where I was standing, but it was impossible to miss the clang of the stainless-steel bin as the lid closed. Impossible not to picture the crushed stems. Those beautiful yellow flower heads pressed into the remains of my lunch.

There was the sound of the fridge opening, and Alex came back in, a bottle of white wine in his hands. 'You didn't know.

No harm done.' Pushing back his shirtsleeve, he looked at his watch. 'Ten minutes until the delivery arrives. Time for a quick one. You joining me?'

'Just a small one.'

I didn't want to start too early, afraid of how I'd appear if my words and thoughts became dulled by the alcohol. But, equally, I needed the liquid courage.

At least nothing could go wrong with the meal, though I had to admit to feeling disappointed that there was no smell of cooking coming from the kitchen. For me, the dinner party was a pretty big deal. I'd had visions of the two of us standing side by side at the long worktop. Maybe cooking something from one of the recipe books Mum had given me. Jamie Oliver or Rick Stein. Laughing as we mucked up a step in the recipe or forgot to wash our hands after chopping a chilli. Silly things. Things I'd seen in films or read in books.

But Alex hadn't wanted to cook. Hadn't wanted me to either. *It's why they invented Deliveroo. We've got nothing to prove.*

I'd laughed. Covered up my disappointment. I'd wanted to show Alex I wasn't just a university dropout. That there were things I could do besides paint a decent portrait of someone's dog or pen and ink drawings of St Philip's Cathedral and the old buildings around the canal.

Alex's arm was heavy around my shoulder. 'Tonight's going to be fun,' he said, giving me a squeeze. 'I haven't had the chance to properly let my hair down in ages.'

I smiled. 'What are they like? These friends?'

I'd never met any of them, though Alex mentioned them often.

'A great laugh. You'll love them... and they'll love you.' He added it as if it were an afterthought. 'Just make sure you join in. Don't sit there like a lemon.'

His words stung, but I didn't pull him up on it. 'I'm not likely to do that. I want to get to know them.'

'Of course you do.' His hand left my shoulder. Slid down my hip until it rested on the curve of my backside. 'Wear the dress I bought you. The black one that shows off your beautiful arse. Though I might not be able to keep my hands off you.'

Since the night I'd opened up to him about what happened in my student house, things had moved on in our relationship. For weeks after, Alex had been patient, loving. Not putting any pressure on me when I made it clear I didn't want things to go any further for the moment. That I wasn't ready. It wasn't that I didn't want Alex, far from it... how else could I explain the way my body had responded on our first meeting in the bar? It had simply been that I was scared. Worried that if we slept together, it would bring back memories of that night. That he and the guy who'd assaulted me might merge into one and I wouldn't be able to distinguish between the hands... the lips.

But Alex had hung in there, and, one night, after we'd been out for dinner, we'd returned happy and relaxed from the wine we'd drunk and made love. An experience that had left me crying with happiness, not fear. Amazed that not for one moment had my mind taken me back to that place. My only awareness being Alex and what he was doing. What I was doing in return.

'The dress I bought you, Elise. Why don't you put it on?' Alex's face was slightly flushed from the wine. He was waiting for my reply.

I wasn't sure how to answer as the last thing I wanted to do was to hurt his feelings. I could hardly tell him that I hated it. That it was not like anything I'd choose myself as the thick black jersey clung to my curves in a way I didn't like, and the neckline was so low I had to keep pulling at it. I'd been planning on taking it back but hadn't yet got around to it.

'I thought I'd wear my green trousers tonight. You said it would be informal.'

'I want you to wear the dress. It was why I bought it.'

'I know, but it's a bit tight and I was going to see if they had it in a bigger size.' I'd seen how his face had changed, his muscles tightening, and knew the lie was better than the truth.

He frowned. 'You're wrong. You look amazing in it.'

'It's too small,' I said again. 'It makes me feel like a prostitute.'

His face darkened and he stepped back from me as though I disgusted him.

'You don't know what you're saying, throwing out comments like that as though you're some ignorant child. Those girls... those women... you have no idea what they have to contend with.' He drew in a breath. 'Do you know how many times we've been called to Soho Road this month? Had to talk to some sleaze in a car and show them, teach them, how to be respectful? Calling at the apartments where the girls live to try and persuade them to leave even though they're fucking terrified of their pimps.'

I was shocked at what he'd said. 'I know all that and it's terrible, but you're blowing things out of proportion. I'm sorry if what I said was thoughtless, but the fact is, the dress is too small.'

He drew himself up. 'So what you're saying is you don't like it. That you'd rather I didn't give you presents.'

'No, I'm not saying that. Why are you twisting my words?' I was near to tears. 'Why are you being like this?'

'Why am *I* being like this?' He snorted. 'Give me strength.'

'Please, Alex. Let's not spoil the evening before it's begun. Let's not argue.'

He looked at me for a moment, then rested his hands on my shoulders, his face softening. 'You've heard of body dysmorphia? Well, that's what you've got. The mirror is lying to you, but I'm not. You looked fucking amazing in it.'

It was an argument I knew I'd never win. Besides, the minutes were ticking by, and I didn't want our guests to arrive while I was still in my jeans. 'Okay. I'll put it on if that's what you want. If it makes you happy.'

'It does.' He pulled me to him then. Pressed a gentle kiss on my lips. 'Really. I wouldn't say it if I didn't mean it.'

But of course he would. Back then, he said a lot of things he didn't mean.

Alex's friends arrived at eight. Simon, a constable in the response unit and his wife Cathy; Peter, a detective sergeant whose girlfriend hadn't been able to make it and Corinne, who Alex introduced as his right-hand woman which she accepted with the ghost of a smile.

I'd wanted to be the one to open the door to them, but Alex got there first, leaving me hovering in the doorway, fighting the urge to tug down the hem of my dress.

'Come in. Grab a beer or wine if you'd prefer. Make yourselves at home. We ordered from the Vietnamese Street Kitchen, so it's ready to go when you are. But look how rude I am. I haven't introduced you to Elise. Elise, this is everyone. Everyone, this is Elise.' His laugh was hearty, and I smiled, trying to remember everyone's names from when he'd told me earlier.

Peter was nearest to me. Around Alex's age but a little taller. Fair hair cropped close to his head. He introduced himself, then moved away to the settee where he lounged, feet on the coffee table, in a way that suggested he had once been a regular visitor here.

Simon was next. He bent and kissed me on the cheek, and I tried not to notice when his eyes dropped to my neckline as he leant in. 'Good to meet you, Elise. Heard a lot about you.'

He winked at Alex, leaving me wondering what exactly it was that he'd been told, but I made myself smile back at him. 'Thank you. Good to meet you too.'

His wife stood back, assessing me. Short black hair pushed behind her ears. Leather jacket. Blood-red lipstick. 'I'm Cathy. What Simon's trying to say is we've been wondering who it was who'd taken our Alex off the market.' She gave a cackling laugh. 'Not that it was for want of anyone trying. The women were practically lined up... gagging for it, by all accounts.'

Her words were faintly distasteful, and I wasn't sure how to reply to them, but, thankfully, I was saved by the girl Alex had described as his right-hand woman. She pushed past Cathy and embraced me. 'Ignore Cath. I'm Corinne. Alex clearly couldn't be bothered to introduce me properly. I like your dress, by the way. It suits you.'

I glanced at Alex, wondering if he'd primed her, but he was busying himself with the drinks.

'Thank you.' I pulled at the neckline. 'It's a bit tight, but Alex bought it for me.' I stopped, realising how feeble it sounded. Hoped Alex hadn't heard.

She grinned. Her teeth perfectly even. 'Now why doesn't that surprise me.'

Simon leered. 'Yeah, you've always been a tits and bums man, haven't you, Alex?'

'What's that?' Alex thrust a beer into Simon's hand. 'Come on 'fess up? What was that, mate?'

'Nothing.' He smirked and took a swig of his beer, and I knew, at that moment, that I didn't like him.

'Ignore him, Elise. He's an idiot.' Corinne took my glass from my hand. 'Look, you're empty. Let's get you some more wine. Waiter!' She clicked her fingers in Alex's direction, and I couldn't help laughing.

Corinne was petite, with a heart-shaped face and wide brown eyes. Her fair, poker-straight hair, falling loose to her shoulders. I tried to imagine her with it tied back, her officer's hat framing her face, and failed. She looked too slight to be a police officer and yet there was something about the way she held herself, a confidence, which made me suspect she'd be good to have around in a crisis.

I watched as she took the bottle from Alex's hand and filled our glasses. She handed mine back to me and raised hers.

'Here's to you... for putting up with misery guts over there.' She inclined her head in Alex's direction, then dropped her voice. 'For being the chosen one.'

I raised my glass in return. At the time it sounded like a good thing, something to be proud of. Only later would I truly understand the meaning of that statement.

NINE

ELISE

Then

I had the beginnings of a headache, my dress was sticking to my thighs and an overwhelming tiredness had come over me. Talk had been mostly of work and any attempt I'd made to change the subject had been met with little enthusiasm by Alex. It wasn't yet ten, but still I wished everyone would go home.

If I thought I'd drunk too much, it was nothing compared to Simon. He was sitting across the table from me, his round face florid, a glint of saliva on his lower lip. As I was wondering how much longer the evening was going to go on for, and whether it would be rude to get up and start clearing the table, he tipped back his chair, reached behind his wife and slapped Alex on the back.

'Like family,' he slurred. 'The response team. We look out for each other. Support each other. Ain't that right, Sarge?'

His lips were stained red with the wine he'd been drinking and his eyes were glazed.

'Fucking hell, Simon. How many times do I have to tell you not to call me that when we're off duty.' Despite his words, I could see that Alex was pleased. He cracked open another beer and put the can to his mouth, tipping back his head and taking long, slow gulps. His Adam's apple bobbing. He'd drunk nearly as much as Simon but could hold it better.

Straightening his chair, Simon took his serviette from beside his empty plate, screwed it into a ball and lobbed it at Peter. 'Hey, Pete. Wake up. The night's still young.'

'Watch it,' Alex said, as the balled-up paper made contact with Pete's wine glass. 'This table cost a bloody fortune.'

It was true. He'd found it in an antique shop, loving the solidity, the heaviness, of the teak it was made from. Insisting we have it even though it would clearly need someone stronger than me to help him carry it up to his flat.

Peter yawned, steadied the glass, then picked up the phone that was next to his plate and put it in his pocket. 'Sorry. With overtime, I racked up nearly fifty hours this week. I'm knackered, to be honest with you. That woman who was found in the canal.' He stretched back in his chair. Linked his hands behind his head. 'The one who was identified a couple of days ago. Had a suspicion it was something to do with that domestic violence case you were looking into in Moseley, and I was right.'

Alex nodded. 'Yeah. The husband was brought in yesterday. Claimed he had nothing to do with it. Then again, he said the same the night he gave her a split lip.'

Across the table, Cathy pulled a face and took a drag of her cigarette. 'They all say that.' She blew out a plume of smoke and tapped the ash from her cigarette onto her side plate. 'Though from what Simon was saying, she sounds like she'd given as good as she got.'

Simon laughed. 'You're not wrong. She had a right gob on her and gave me an earful when I tried to read her husband the riot act. From the filth that came out of her mouth, you'd have thought it was me who'd given her that shiner not her husband.

Don't you just hate the ones who call and then change their minds once you're there. Fucking waste of everyone's time.'

Corinne twisted round in her chair. 'What are you trying to say?'

'I'm not trying to say anything. It's just that if we didn't have to spend half our time interfering in domestics, we could get on with catching the proper criminals.'

Corinne tutted. 'For God's sake, Si, you should listen to yourself sometime. Don't let the super hear you say stuff like that.'

I sat back and listened as they continued to discuss it. Ashamed to be a witness to what I was hearing. Although no one had actually said it, it was clear from the way they were talking that they considered the poor woman had been asking for it. That if her husband was to blame for her murder, she'd somehow driven him to it.

I pushed back my chair, unable to hear any more. 'Has everyone finished?'

'Sit down, Elise. We're still talking.' Reaching out a hand, Alex pulled me back into my seat.

Corinne shot him a disapproving look, then wiped her mouth with her serviette and smiled at me across the table. 'Actually, I need to be going soon. I'm on earlies tomorrow.'

'Me too.' Pete downed the last of his wine. 'Can I cadge a lift back with you? Save me calling a cab.'

'No problem.' Corinne got up and started to collect the plates.

I stood as well. 'Please leave them. I'll do it after everyone's gone. No early shifts for me. Thank you so much for coming. It was nice to meet you.'

'Thank *you*. That crispy pork belly was to die for. It's not often we all get the chance to see each other outside of the station.' She pulled a rueful face. 'If you and Alex stay together, you'll find out soon enough that plans are hard to stick to. Emergencies. Shift changes. It's something you'll have to get used to. Sadly, my husband didn't. That's why he's now my ex.'

Alex finished his beer, crushed the can in his hand and dropped it onto his plate. 'She's right. Cold dinners are a regular thing in our line of work. Sorry we didn't do anything special tonight, Corinne, but cooking isn't really El's forte. Didn't think they'd be impressed down at the station if half of us were missing with food poisoning. It's why we decided on a takeout.'

I couldn't ignore what he'd just said. The injustice of it. 'It wasn't that at all, Alex. You said—'

Pushing back his chair, he came over to my side and kissed the top of my head. 'Only joking, babe. Forgive me.'

He might have been expecting to be absolved, but with the wine I'd drunk, I was in no mood to be placated. 'It didn't sound much like a joke.'

'Okay, okay. No need to snap my head off. Jesus! Women!'

Simon gave a bark of laughter. 'You said it, mate. Can't live with them. Can't live without them. What do you say, Cath?'

Cathy pursed her red lips. 'I say you're an idiot and it's time to go. Are you driving, or am I?'

Simon squinted at her through half-closed eyes. 'What do you think?'

'I can call you a taxi,' I said quickly. They'd both been drinking, and I couldn't believe they were even having this conversation.

'It's all right. I'll drop them home. Just promise not to throw up in my car. We're not teenagers.' Corinne to the rescue again. After the first glass of white, she'd stuck to soft drinks. The only one who had. 'You can collect your car in the morning. That okay?'

Simon shrugged, beyond caring. 'If you want.'

I picked up coats and scarves from the back of the settee and handed them to Alex's friends. Relieved that soon the evening would be over. That soon I could take off the ridiculous dress and sleep.

Corinne kissed me on the cheek. 'No need to see us out. You relax. Like I said before, thank you for a nice evening.'

'Next time I'll cook,' I said, glancing back at Alex. 'I'm not that bad.'

'I'm sure you're not. Alex can be an arse sometimes.'

Alex hadn't told me how long they'd been working together, but I guessed from her tone it must be a while.

'He's not always like that.'

'I'm sure he isn't, Elise. Take care.' She prised Peter from his chair. 'Come on, sleepyhead. Home.'

Peter got up reluctantly and the other two followed, Simon leaning unsteadily on Cathy. At the door he raised his hand. 'Cheers.'

They jostled out into the hallway, and I waited until they had rounded the first bend in the stairs, still hearing their laughter as I shut the door. I leant my back against it and closed my eyes. Offering up thanks that the evening had ended.

'Well, ta very much for that.' Alex's voice made me open my eyes again. The words were nice, but they were laced with sarcasm.

'What's the matter, Alex?'

He was still at the table, but he'd pushed back his chair so he was facing me. His legs stretched out in front of him. Feet crossed at the ankles.

'What's the matter? I'll tell you what's the matter. You humiliated me in front of my friends. My work colleagues.'

I stood dumb. Trying to digest what he was saying. To understand.

'Well? Haven't you anything to say for yourself?'

My breathing had become shallow, and I fought to control it. 'I don't know what you want me to say. I thought the evening went well. I thought they enjoyed it. Corinne said it was the best night out she'd had in ages.'

Alex shook his head as though reprimanding a schoolkid. 'She was just being kind, Elise. You don't get it, do you?'

This change of mood was so sudden, I didn't know how to react to it. Scared to say the wrong thing in case it made him worse.

'What did I do? If you just tell me, I'll make sure it doesn't happen again.'

His eyes clouded in irritation. 'Well, if *you* don't know.'

I was tired and no longer had the patience for this. 'If you won't talk to me, if you won't tell me what's bothering you, then I'm going to bed. I'll clear up in the morning.'

My tone seemed to surprise him. 'All right. I'll tell you. You sat there like a fucking stuffed toy, a face on you that made it clear what you thought of everyone.'

It wasn't true. Yes, I found his friends boorish and self-obsessed at times, but I knew I'd hidden it well. And I'd liked Corinne. Had found her engaging and clever. Alex was just saying these things to get a reaction from me. The only thing I didn't understand was why.

'Sitting there with your tits out for everyone to see. Giving Simon the come on—'

'What? Now you're being ridiculous. You bought me this dress, Alex,' I said, looking down at it. '*You* bought it. I tried to tell you that it was too tight, that I didn't want to wear it, but you made me feel bad. The only reason I wore it was because you liked it. Because you thought I looked good in it.' I hated the tears that were stinging my eyes. Hated that he was making me feel like this. 'If I'm such a disappointment to you, then why did you ask me to move in?'

'Sometimes I wonder.'

The evening was spinning out of control, and there was nothing I could do to stop it. 'Then I'll leave in the morning.'

His face was set hard, and, suddenly, I was consumed with the terrible fear that I'd have to carry out my threat. He might be behaving like an idiot, but I didn't really want to leave. For the simple reason that I loved him.

'I don't think you will.' He was smiling now, but the tightness of his tone was at odds with it. 'Come here.'

He held out his hand, and I went to him. He'd changed his position. Was sitting forward in his chair, his elbows on his knees, and when I reached him, he straightened. Moved his legs apart and pulled me into the open space between them.

'You do look fucking amazing.' Reaching out a hand, he touched the soft dip at the base of my throat, then let his fingers trail down until they reached the low neckline of my dress. With his other hand, he reached around to the back of me, sliding the zip down to my waist. 'That's better.'

In the bright light of the dining room, it felt wrong. I was tired. Upset. What I wanted was to go to bed and sleep. In the morning, we would be two different people to the ones we were tonight. We'd laugh about this. Have breakfast in bed and make love. Be better versions of ourselves.

But Alex's fingers were urgent now. Sliding the dress from my shoulders. Pulling down the lace of my bra. His hot lips on my breast.

'No, Alex. Not tonight. Not when we've argued. I've had too much to drink. You have too.'

He said nothing, but his hand was pushing my skirt up my thighs.

Something in my stomach shifted. Memories rose to the surface. Pushing his hand away, I pulled my dress back over my shoulders. 'I said no, Alex. I don't want this. Not tonight.'

The skin of his neck was flushed, and he was struggling to focus on me. A shadow crossed his face. Passed. My heartbeat was hammering in my ears. What had I done?

Panic rose in my throat, and I reached out to him. 'I'm sorry. You understand, don't you?'

'Of course.' But the look in his eyes conveyed what he was thinking.

I brushed a strand of hair from my eyes. 'Maybe in the morning.'

'Yes.'

'Thank you. You know I love you.' Bending down, I pressed my lips to his. A seal to my promise.

I felt him respond. Felt his fingers slide through my hair, wrapping the dark strands around them. Hot breath on my neck. Wanting me still. Standing now, he pressed the length of himself against me. Kissed me more urgently.

'No, Alex.'

But he hadn't heard, or that's what I told myself when I woke in his arms the next morning, my eyes sliding to the warrant card on the bedside table. Heard his peaceful breathing beside me. For the alternative didn't bear thinking about. It's what I had to believe so I could ignore my instincts, the gnawing panicked feeling that I needed to leave Alex.

And how I managed to reassure myself when, a few weeks later, I realised I was pregnant.

TEN

MEGAN

Now

When Megan reaches the top of the stairs, she's surprised to see her mum sitting on the settee in the seating area outside her bedroom. A place that's used mainly as a dumping ground when they get in. Hearing her, she turns, placing the flats of her hands over whatever it is she's been reading.

'Had a good time on the beach?' Her voice sounds forced. A little too high. A little too strained.

'It was okay. What are you doing? You'd better not have been in my room.'

'No, of course not. I'd always ask you first. You know that.'

Megan hears the hurt in her voice. Bites back the reply she wants to give. One that even *she* knows would be cruel. Something's not right. It's not usual for her mum not to tick her off when she's been rude. She also hasn't answered her question and it makes her uncomfortable. *She's* the one who's supposed to have secrets. *She's* the teenager.

Megan tries again. 'What were you reading?'

'Oh, this?' Her mum doesn't move her hands. 'It's nothing

interesting. Just a review of an exhibition I went to.' She looks
pale and Megan has the distinct impression she's lying to her.

She rubs her nose with the heel of her hand. Her mum
never lies. Skirts around the truth sometimes but never lies. She
doesn't like it. She looks like a rabbit caught in the headlights.
Pale skin. Wide eyes. Desperate to get away.

'Have you got that change bag, El.' Sean is holding the baby
under her armpits, lifting her high and frowning as he examines
the bottom of her sleepsuit. 'It's starting to come through. Jesus,
Kitty. You don't half stink.' He comes towards them. 'The bag,
Elise. It's just by where you're sitting. I'd have got it myself if I'd
known you'd get distracted. Oh, hi, Megs. I didn't hear you
come up.'

Megan gives Sean one of her rare smiles. At least he's not
acting weird like her mum.

'Nice out there?' she asks. 'I was watching you for a bit, but
you were too far out to see properly.'

Sean returns her smile with a wide one of his own. 'That's
an understatement. It was fucking amazing.' He looks sheepish.
Glances over at her mum. 'Oops, sorry. It slipped out.'

But her mum isn't reacting as she usually does. There's no
shake of the head. No raised eyebrows. No tut. She's staring
into space as though transported somewhere else.

'You okay?' It's Sean who asks.

'What?' Her mum turns to him. 'Yes, of course. I'm just a
bit... I'm just...' She shakes her head. 'Would you mind keeping
an eye on Kitty for a while? I've got a headache coming on and
need some air.'

'No, why would I mind? You have Kit all week when I'm at
work. I enjoy taking care of her at weekends.' He moves his
hand away from the brown patch that's seeped onto Kitty's
sleepsuit, creating a damp crescent around the outline of her
nappy. 'Though there are times when I could quite happily put
her up for auction with a label *Stinky child free to a good home.*'

Megan laughs, but her mum doesn't. What's wrong with her?

She watches her stuff whatever she'd been reading into her back pocket before reaching down and lifting the change bag onto her lap.

'There you are.' She gets up and hands the bag to Sean, and Megan sees how her hand is shaking. Something happened while she was out, but there's no time to ask her what as her mum is already heading for the stairs.

Megan wants to follow, but something stops her. She's got into the habit of being indifferent around her mum and it's hard to stop. The habit too engrained. When she was younger, they'd been close and she hadn't minded her fussing, her overprotectiveness, but this last year or so, it's started to get on her nerves and being rude is the only way she can think of to break that contact. Show her mum she's a person in her own right, not someone else's property.

The door closes downstairs. Her mum has gone out. She looks back at Sean who is kneeling on the floor by the change mat, Kitty's ankles gripped in one hand as he extricates the dirty nappy from under her bottom and drops it into the bag beside him.

'I'll be the first to say you're a beautiful baby, Kit, but I'll also be the first to say you're the smelliest.' He raises an eyebrow. 'Don't fancy taking over, do you, Megan?'

'You must be kidding.' Megan wanders over. Kneels next to him. 'Did you always know you wanted to have children, Sean?'

Sean looks up at her quizzically, and she's sure he's going to give one of his silly answers, but instead he puts his head on one side and thinks. 'Yes, I reckon I did.'

'Why didn't you have one before?'

'Before what?'

'Before you met Mum.'

'I dunno. I hadn't met the right person, I suppose.' He makes a face at her. 'Is this your way of telling me I'm old?'

She smiles. 'Maybe.'

Sean pulls a new nappy from the bag and opens the tabs. 'Why are you asking? Not pregnant, are you?'

'Bloody hell, Sean.' She feels herself colour. 'Of course I'm not. And don't start putting ideas into Mum's head that I am.'

'What then?'

'I don't know. I've just been thinking about things recently. I'm glad you had Kitty. It's tough being an only child.'

'Really? I'd have thought it would be rather good. I was one of five and had to fight for everything. But I've probably told you that before.'

'Only about a million times.'

'There you are then. It must be true.' Sean fastens the tabs, then picks at the lint between Kitty's tiny toes. Squints at it. 'What even is this stuff?' He flicks it away, then pushes her foot into the leg of a fresh Babygro. 'You should count yourself lucky really. You had your mum to yourself for fifteen years, well, seven if you want to discount the years after I muscled in. That makes your relationship pretty special in my book. Especially after everything...'

He trails off and busies himself with the rest of Kitty's poppers. In their house it's always been a bit of an unspoken rule that they don't discuss the past. Not in detail anyway. But suddenly there are things Megan wants to know. Things maybe Sean can tell her.

She perches on the edge of the white leather settee and watches him pop up the fasteners, holding Kitty's legs still with his large hand to avoid a bloody nose.

'How much has Mum told you? About our lives before.'

'What BS?' When Megan frowns, he qualifies. 'Before Sean.'

'Yes.' She shakes her head at his bad joke. 'Seriously, though. You've never really told me. How much do you know?'

Sean lifts Kitty and puts her on his hip. He carries her over to the window and looks out. 'Can't see Mummy, Kitty Cat. Must have gone the other way.' He comes back to Megan and sits beside her, placing Kitty on the floor and pulling over a wicker basket of her toys. Smiling when she grabs the rim and pulls it over, bricks and books and soft toys spilling onto the floor. 'I don't know much, Megs.'

He's serious now, and Megan sees, behind the good-natured face, the boy he must have once been. The one the teacher would have chosen to hand out the crayons. The one who would sit next to a crying child on the friendship bench and offer to play with them. Kind yet focussed. Eyes on the goal. Intent on working hard. Building a successful career and willing to share the spoils with a woman he barely knew. A child who wasn't his.

'She told you about Earthbound?'

'The commune?'

'Yes.'

He pushes a plastic telephone with a smiley face back and forth with his foot. Kitty gurgling every time it comes near her.

'Some. Not everything.' His eyes slide to hers. 'I know it was like a big family. That you were pretty much self-sufficient there. I don't pretend to understand places like that, bit too hippyish and out-there for me, but your mum was in a difficult place and she needed somewhere to go. It must have been hard for her giving up everything. No technology. No money of her own. Everything shared.'

'She told you about Amity?'

'Her friend there? Yeah. Sounds like they were joined at the hip.'

Megan smiles. Remembering. 'I liked it there. I hadn't known anything else, and I didn't want to leave. Mum never really explained why we did... just skirts around the subject. I had friends there too.'

He studies her. 'And you don't now?'

'I spent seven years playing with kids who, for years, I thought were my brothers and sisters. Having no toys of my own. Sharing everything. Eating together. Never seeing a TV or a mobile phone or a computer. Is it any wonder, once we left there, that the kids in school thought I was odd?'

'No. I suppose not.' He doesn't try to bluff or smooth things over. It's what Megan likes about him.

Megan doubts that Sean ever got called names or was ignored, which at times could be even worse. She doesn't comment, though. He's doing his best.

'Sometimes, I wonder why Mum didn't tell my dad about me.' Despite herself, tears spring into her eyes. 'Do you think it was because she thought he wouldn't love me?'

Sean looks uncomfortable. 'Jesus, Megs. No. You'll have to ask your mum why.'

'I have and she won't tell me.' She knows it's ridiculous as she doesn't remember him, but the absence of her father from her life is an ache she's never been able to push away.

'Knowing your mum as I do, she would have had her reasons. And I'm sure they would have been good ones.' He rubs his cheek, looks as though he's choosing his words carefully. 'It's not really my place to speculate, but my gut feeling is it would be better to let things lie. There must have been a good reason why she didn't stay with him, Megan, and even though he was your father, I have a feeling you're better off not having him in your life.'

Megan looks at him sharply. It's the first time she's heard this. 'She told you that?'

'No, it's just something I sense.'

'Do you know his name?'

'What? No.' Sean's eyes flick briefly to hers. 'Look, I've said too much already. It's your mum you should be asking, not me.'

He looks so awkward she feels sorry for him. 'Yeah, I know. Sorry.'

'You don't need to be. I just wish I...' He stops and sighs out a breath. 'I wish I could be more help, that's all. Look, you know what your mum has said. He was a one-night stand. They weren't in a relationship or anything. I'd leave it at that.'

Megan reaches down and picks up Kitty. Placing her on her lap, she scatters a dusting of kisses on her head, laughing when Kitty reaches up and grabs a handful of her hair.

'Poor Mum. Something really bad must have happened for her to want to go through with the pregnancy on her own. Knowing she'd be a single mum.'

'Yes... but that's water under the bridge and my advice to you is not to dwell on the past. Not let it interfere with your future.' Sean scratches his head. 'Someone famous said that, but I've no idea who. Anyway, you've got me now... and your little sister. Your mum's happy—'

'Is she?'

'Of course she is. Why do you think otherwise?'

Megan thinks of her mum's white face. The hand that shook as she passed Sean the change bag.

'When I came in from the beach, something was up. I know it was. She was jumpy and, whatever she had in her hand, she tried to hide from me.'

Sean turns his head. Looks back through the house to the settee where her mum had been sitting. 'A letter came for her. It was on the mat when I came in. Maybe it was bad news.'

'Then why didn't she say? Why the big secret?'

'Do *you* always tell us everything?'

'No, but that's different.'

He gives her a straight look. 'Is it? Isn't everyone entitled to a bit of privacy?'

'I suppose.'

'There you are then. She'll tell us when she's ready. And if she doesn't, then, you know, we'll just have to accept it.'

Kitty bounces up and down, her hands waving. Holding her closer, Megan nuzzles her soft cheek. 'Why do you always have to be right? Did they give lessons in it at school?'

Sean's eyes crease in amusement. 'Something like that. Don't worry about your mum. It will be something and nothing. You'll see.'

'Probably. There's something else I wanted to ask you, Sean.'

'Yeah?'

'Whether you'll take me out on the paddleboard. Show me how to do it properly. All the other kids at school have them.'

'I doubt that. They're not exactly cheap.'

Megan frowns in frustration. 'Okay not everyone, but a few. What's the point of living on the beach if I can't even use it?'

'No one's stopping you. It's a free country. A free beach.'

'You know what I mean, Sean. Windsurf, paddleboard, fun stuff.'

'It's not for me to make that decision.' He turns away, and she sees how uncomfortable the conversation is making him, hates seeing him like this, but she's fed up with being treated like a kid.

'She doesn't have to know.'

'I'm going to pretend I didn't hear that. Look, if it was up to me, we'd be down the beach now. But it's not, so please don't keep asking.'

Sean reaches out and takes Kitty from her. Lays the baby on her back on the floor and blows raspberries onto her tummy, making her squeal. Megan tries to imagine what it would have been like for Kitty if she'd never known her dad. If her mum had upped and left without telling Sean she was pregnant. Then she thinks of Sean and how empty his life would be without Kitty in it. He often jokes that his family is everything to him. That he'd fight for them. Give his life for them. But behind the laughter in his eyes there's a seriousness, a gravity, he doesn't quite manage to hide.

Megan shivers and rubs at the tops of her arms, the material of her hoodie wrinkling. It's not because the sun has gone in and the large open-plan room has grown suddenly dark. Not because she's worried about her mum. No, none of these things.

It's because she's consumed with a feeling that her mum stole her from her dad.

Took away his right to be a father.

And maybe she can undo that.

She thinks back to the letter her mum was holding. Maybe there are other things hidden away that might tell her about her father.

ELEVEN

ELISE

Now

The boardwalk creaks under my feet as I walk. Usually, I turn left in the direction of the fort, but today I go the other way. Not caring where I'll end up, knowing only that I need to get away from the house to think.

The beach is a riot of colour, clumps of pink, red and white valerian pushing up through the cracks at the edge of the boards. Yellow horned poppies vying for space with the purple mallow that's nearly as high as my knees.

Yesterday, I might have stopped to take a photograph, stood and marvelled at how lucky I am to live in this beautiful part of the Sussex coast, but not today. Now I have more urgent things on my mind.

I have Alex.

The newspaper article is in my back pocket, and my hand reaches behind to check it's still there. I stop and look over my shoulder. Is he on the beach somewhere? Watching? Waiting?

There are more people around now: a group of windsurfers who've just come in from the sea, their boards dragged onto the stones, sails rippling in the breeze. At the water's edge, a teenage girl throws a stick for her dog and, on a bench beside the boardwalk, an elderly man closes his eyes to the sun, his walking stick across his knees. None of them are Alex.

A young man jogs past me and I do a double take before realising how stupid I'm being. All the time I've been walking, I've been picturing him as he was then. The pronounced jaw, the dark hair. His body lithe and muscular beneath his clothes. But time hasn't stood still and, of course, he won't look like that now. He'll no longer be that young virile man he was when we were together, he'll be older. Fifteen years older. Will the years have been kind to him? Will he still work out or will his stomach, his jawline, have softened?

Since I've been living here, since I've been with Sean, I've tried not to think of Alex, but now he's in my head and I can't get him out. His eyes – that way he had of looking at me as though he was looking into my very soul. As though I was the only one in the world who mattered to him.

My chest tightens as I remember how those same eyes could also look at me as though I was something brought in on the bottom of his shoe.

Would I even recognise him now? This man who I'd once loved so passionately... feared so desperately.

A sharp sea breeze blows my hair across my face before I capture it in my hand. It whips the sea and flaps the edges of my cardigan against legs toned by the gym equipment we keep in the downstairs sunroom. My post-baby physique trim from running on the treadmill each morning. Bon Jovi in my ears, the sea visible through every window.

Running from him still... if only in my head.

I look down, seeing myself as Alex would see me now. A successful artist, fit and confident, and realise the question I should be asking is this: Would *he* recognise *me*?

I left the boardwalk some time ago and now I'm on the

pavement heading west. I have no plan, no idea where I'm going, but ahead of me is the Church of the Good Shepherd. When I was a child, we went to church every Sunday, but I haven't been to a service since I left home. The door is partly open, and something draws me to it. A need to confess? A need to atone? Who knows.

I can do neither of these things, but as I push open the door and see how the sunlight throws patterns on the wooden floorboards, I remember how being in a church as a child had soothed me. I take a seat at the end of a pew. Maybe it will again.

The door of the church opens, letting in the cry of a seagull. I lift my head and unclasp my hands as a middle-aged woman walks down the aisle with an armful of fresh flowers in a bucket. She smiles at me as she passes, and I stand, no longer wanting to be here. As though she's been able to hear my unspoken prayers.

I look at my watch. Sean and Megan will be starting to wonder where I am, so I leave my sanctuary and walk back home, my legs breaking into a run when I reach the boardwalk.

At the house, I look up at the wide floor-to-ceiling windows that take up almost the whole of the wooden façade, taking in the sharp lines and angles of the home that has been mine for the last few years. Behind the low wall, the swimming pool glitters in the bright sunlight, inviting me to swim, but I'm not interested. I have to go in and face my family who will be waiting, wondering why I left the house so suddenly. Knowing I'll need to show my children and Sean the face of the woman I am now not the one I was before... the one I thought I'd never have to be again.

I take a minute to compose my face, then skirt the edge of the pool and walk to the door of the sunroom. It's important I give the impression that everything is fine. That today is the same as yesterday. Hard as it will be, I need to pretend to myself it never happened – that I never received the newspaper article in its white envelope. That I haven't been forced to confront the past. It's the only way I won't fall apart.

As soon as I reach the sliding door, I see Sean on one of the exercise bikes and pull up short, my hand on the cold metal frame. He's pedalling hard, his forearms resting on the handlebars, his head bent. Kitty isn't with him, so she must be upstairs with Megan. There's a line of sweat down the ridge of his spine and his hair is still damp from earlier. It's unusual for him to be exercising after having been out on his board, so I know he's been waiting for me. He looks up when I slide open the patio door and stops pedalling.

'I wondered where you'd gone. Feeling better?'

I force a smile and step into the room. 'A bit. It must have been something I ate. The prawns last night.'

He takes his feet off the pedals and presses his hands into the small of his back. 'I don't think so.'

'What do you mean?'

He dismounts and rubs at the fronts of his legs. 'We both ate the same thing, and I haven't had any ill effects.' Coming over to me, he places a hand either side of my shoulders. 'Tell me, El. What's going on? It's got something to do with that envelope I gave you, hasn't it? You were fine until then.'

My instinct is to reach behind me to my pocket to check that the newspaper article is still there, but I force my hand to stay where it is.

'Elise. Talk to me.'

His eyes are so soft. So concerned. Would it harm to let him in? Just a little?

I breathe in deeply. 'It's Alex. Megan's father.'

Sean's hands drop to his sides. 'What about him?'

'He knows where I am.' I glance out of the patio door as

though he might be standing there next to the stone Buddha or swimming a length of the pool.

'And that's a problem?'

I chew my lip, trying to filter out the parts of my past that won't damage me. Damage us. 'Yes. He can't know.'

'Want to tell me why?' Sunlight is streaming in through the glass and there are beads of moisture on Sean's forehead. He wipes them on the back of his forearm. 'Okay. If you're not ready to tell me, that's all right. I guess you have your reasons, but unless you've got in touch with him, there's no reason to think he'd know where you live.' He thinks a moment. 'Unless someone else told him.'

'No one here knows about Alex.'

He's frowning now. 'So what was it he sent you? Let me see.'

My heart freezes. I have to think fast. 'It was personal. I tore it into pieces and threw it away. I couldn't bear to keep it.'

'Why would you do that? If you think he could cause trouble, it could be evidence. Something to show the police if you had to.'

How can I tell Sean that Alex *is* the police? That if he hadn't been in the force, none of this would have happened and my life would have been so very different. Megan's too. I wish I could, but I can't. I stop, hoping I haven't hurt him by telling him so little. I have to remember that if things had been different, I wouldn't have met Sean either.

He picks up a towel. Wipes his face. 'It might help if you shared what was in his letter.'

I think of the photograph, the headline, and wonder what to say. 'It wasn't a letter. It was a newspaper article.' I bite my bottom lip until I taste blood. A half-truth is all I can give him. 'It was horrible.'

Tears are running down my face, and Sean pulls me into his arms. 'It's okay,' he says, his voice muffled in my hair. 'It's okay.'

I feel myself tremble. Even the warmth of Sean's embrace can't stop the fear that's growing.

'Hey. *Hey.*' Sean's arms tighten around me. 'Maybe it was a mistake. Maybe it wasn't for you. The same as when the police came.'

'It was. I know it was.'

'Look.' Sean cuts me off. 'I don't pretend to have all the answers, but I think you're worrying over nothing.' He loosens his arms and kisses my forehead. 'There will be an explanation for this, and even if it *was* Megan's father, it doesn't mean he means you any harm. I just wish that you hadn't thrown the article away. If I could have read it myself, I might have had a better idea of what's what. But, honestly, El, I'm sure there's nothing for you to worry about. Fifteen years is a long time. Water under the bridge.' He takes my hand and leads me to the stairs. 'Come on, let's think about some lunch.'

I want to believe him, I really do, but Sean doesn't know the half of it. I've only told him the parts I want him to know. The bits of my life that I'm happy to reveal. It's not a way to live a proper life, I know, but it's the way it has to be if I want to keep everything the way it is. If I want Megan and Kitty to be able to live a life outside of the shadows that brought me here.

Ignoring the clues that were staring me in the face was what made the nightmare start all those years ago.

Dare I do it again?

TWELVE

ELISE

Then

I wasn't sure how Alex would react when I told him I was pregnant, but I had to convince myself everything was going to be fine.

'You're kidding, right?' He stared at my face, eyes narrowed, before seeing from my expression that I wasn't. 'Oh, my God! That's wonderful, Elise.'

We were sitting outside a pub, the one where we'd had our first date in fact, and I'd been watching a group of young mothers in floaty summer dresses, sunglasses pushed high on their heads, with their toddlers. Noticing how disjointed their conversations seemed to be. Their voices cutting off as a child took their attention. Food on the plates in front of them getting cold.

I watched as one of the women tried to persuade her child to eat the chip she offered on the end of her fork. How another bent to retrieve a toy dropped from a highchair tray before leaving her seat to chase her older child across the grass.

Scooping the boy up under her arm and bringing him back to howls of protest.

Was I doing the right thing? Ignoring the other night?

'You will be the best mother.' Alex's eyes were shining. 'My baby will have everything it could want. Everything.'

I noted his use of the word *my* but didn't question it. I was just pleased that Alex was happy. Because I wanted you, Megan. More than anything. Even though we hadn't been trying for a baby. Even though it hadn't been something I'd thought about much. Parenthood was something for the future... or so I'd thought.

Alex insisted on phoning his friends from the station, even though I was only a few weeks into the pregnancy. I'd asked him not to, but he'd waved my protest away with his hand and taken a large mouthful of his beer before jabbing at his phone.

'Si. Guess what? El's in the club... What? No, preggers, you idiot.' He stretched his legs out in front of him and smiled. 'Yeah. I knocked her up.'

I grimaced at his crude words, the schoolboy-like bragging, but decided to ignore them. I didn't think too much about that phone call, or the one he made later to Peter, but now I look back, I see it was his way of putting his stamp on our baby's head. Claiming the embryo as his own even though it was such early days and anything could happen.

'Jesus, I'm a lucky bastard.' Alex settled back in his chair, a smile on his face. 'A lucky, lucky bastard.'

A girl in black jeans and T-shirt, her hair pulled into a ponytail, stopped at our table to collect our glasses, and it was only then I realised Alex had managed to drink two pints to my one sparkling water. I held out my glass to the girl, but when she went to take Alex's, he waved her away and stood up. He'd already visited the gents, so I knew he must be going to get another. Alex was the one who'd driven here; I wasn't on his insurance so wouldn't be able to drive us back.

I put a hand on his arm. 'Is that a good idea, Alex?'

'What?' His face hardened into a new shape. The smile gone. He glanced at the girl, waited until she'd moved on to the table with the young mothers. 'Tell me what you're trying to say?'

My skin prickled with unease. 'Just that if you have a third, you won't be able to drive – probably shouldn't even now. Let's go back, Alex. To be honest, I'm feeling a bit nauseous.' I laughed nervously. 'Think I might be getting morning sickness in the middle of the day.'

But it wasn't that. It was true my stomach was churning, but it wasn't anything to do with the pregnancy – it was because the change in atmosphere was so sudden. So chilling. I didn't know it then, but I was already scared of him. The man who would be your father. The man without whom you wouldn't exist.

'Come on.' I felt his fingers grip my arm.

'Stop it, Alex, you're hurting me.'

He didn't release his grip but put his lips close to my ear. 'We're going. Isn't that what you wanted?'

'Yes, but I don't want you to drive. Maybe we could call a cab.'

'Just shut up.' He pulled me from my seat and marched me across the grass of the pub garden to the car park. When we reached the car, he opened the passenger door and, placing a hand on top of my head, pushed me into the seat. A practised move as though I was a criminal rather than his girlfriend.

How I wished now I'd let it go, but I couldn't. I turned to look at him. 'Aren't you worried you might get stopped?' I said the next sentence in my head. *Aren't you worried that you might have an accident... that you might kill someone? Kill us?*

In answer, he twisted in his seat, felt around in his pocket, then shoved his warrant card in my face. 'I don't think so, do you?'

His photograph, so close to my eyes, was distorted. So too

was the name, the rank and warrant number. But I didn't need to be able to read it. Alex was larger than life. Well known, well liked, in the force. That much I'd gleaned from the dinner party. He'd made his point. I was shocked at his arrogance. In his belief that he was above the law. That he *was* the law. But I knew he was telling the truth. Even if he'd had that third pint and he was stopped, no one would question him.

'It was only two pints. I wasn't going to have any more. Not that it's any of your fucking business.'

He forced the car into gear and reversed out of the parking space, narrowly missing a blue Audi that was parked in the space behind us. I sat with my head turned away from him, resisting the temptation to call him out. What good would it have done anyway?

'Alex, I—'

He tapped the brakes, lurching me forward. 'For the love of God, what now?'

'Nothing.' I stared ahead, terrified of what he would do next. 'I'm sorry.'

He flicked a sideways glance at me. Turned the radio on loud, Dolly Parton complaining so loudly that Jolene had taken her man that I could barely hear him. 'I should bloody well hope so.'

Despite what I feared, the rest of the drive home was uneventful though Alex's face was set hard, his fingers choking the steering wheel. He didn't speak to me again, and when we got back to the flat, his icy calmness as he shut the door behind us, made me jittery.

I should never have said anything, I told myself. Shouldn't have spoiled the lovely afternoon, my news, with my nagging.

It wasn't the first time I'd blame myself. It wasn't the first time I'd make excuses for him.

But it would be the first time he would hit me.

THIRTEEN

ELISE

Then

'You're having a baby! Oh, my God, Elise. That's amazing!'

My hand floated to my stomach, caressed the swell of it, and I knew Phoebe had heard the smile in my voice when I told her. 'I know. Brilliant, isn't it.'

'So tell me everything. When's it due? How are you feeling? It's been an age since I've seen you.' There was a hint of accusation in the sentence, which she quickly tried to cover. 'Though it works both ways. I could have made more effort too.'

'I'm sorry, Phoebs. I've just been so busy, you know? And Alex's shifts are annoyingly erratic. He does such a lot of overtime too.'

'You don't always have to come with Alex, El. Before you knew him, you were happy to pop over even when Josh was there. We'd ditch him and go to the pub for a catch-up. He never minded.'

'I know. It's just...' I stopped, not sure how to continue. Knowing what she said was true. Even when I'd turned up when Josh was there and we didn't go out, I was never made to feel a gooseberry. We'd have fun, the three of us.

Fun. Sometimes, I was scared I'd forgotten what that was.

There was a pause at the other end of the phone, and I imagined Phoebe turning to Josh. Pulling a face and mouthing to him. *She's being weird.* For some reason, it was important for me to prove to her I was the same Elise who'd scrolled through the faces on the dating website with her. Finger slowing when I saw Alex's profile. His face. Those eyes. The same Elise who'd caught her best friend's eye and giggled as she'd muttered *fit* under her breath.

'So, come on. Tell all. How far along are you?' Phoebe was making an effort and I needed to as well. Whatever Alex said, she was not annoying. She was kind and funny, and sometimes I missed her with an intensity that brought tears to my eyes.

'I'm nearly five months. I'm feeling great, Phoebs. I'm—'

'Five months?' It was impossible not to hear the hurt in her voice. 'And you've only just told me?'

I bit the inside of my cheek. 'Alex didn't want people to know too early.'

'Well, you certainly don't need to worry about that. No one would ever say calling their best friend five months into the pregnancy to tell them the good news, early.'

Guilty heat clawed up my neck as I fumbled for an excuse that would sound believable. 'I had terrible morning sickness. I wanted to wait to tell you about the baby once I was feeling better.'

Although not strictly true, it was the best I could do.

'Well, I'm happy for you. Really I am. And Josh will be too when I tell him. Was that why you didn't come to our engagement party? Because you were sick? You should have told me.' She sighed. 'I really wanted you there.'

'I'm sorry. I wish I had been.' But how could I have gone to the party with the prints of Alex's fingers on the soft skin of my upper arms. It had been a hot afternoon and long sleeves would have brought questions of their own.

There was a pause on the other end of the phone. 'You *are* happy, aren't you, El? You'd tell me if you weren't, wouldn't you?'

I pressed my mobile hard against my cheekbone, hoping the ache it elicited might stop the tears that had formed.

'Of course I'm happy. I'm going to have a baby. It's a girl.' I stopped. The sex of the baby was something Alex and I had decided to keep to ourselves, but it was too late to backtrack.

'A girl!' Phoebe's delight was evident in the timbre of her voice. 'Oh, that's wonderful. I can just imagine you with a girl. Have you thought of a name yet?'

Alex and I hadn't got around to discussing names, but, suddenly, it came to me with such certainty that it took my breath away.

'Megan.' My voice lowered to almost a whisper. 'I'm going to call her Megan.'

'Megan.' There was a pause as Phoebe ruminated on the name. 'I think it's beautiful. Hold on.' There was a clatter as she put the phone down and called to Josh. 'Get your fat arse in here, Josh. El's going to have a baby and she's calling her Megan. Chat to him for a minute, Elise. I need to check on the dinner.'

Almost immediately, Josh's deep voice came over the phone, 'Great stuff, Elise. A baby. Wow! Congrats to you... and to Alex, of course.'

Had his voice changed when he'd mentioned Alex's name? Cooled slightly? I thought so, but Josh hardly knew him.

I told myself not to worry about it. It had, most likely, been my imagination. 'Thanks, Josh. I'll pass it on.'

In the silence that followed, I heard a clatter, the distant sound of Phoebe swearing, then Josh calling out to her to check everything was all right. Phoebe replying.

'She dropped the saucepan of pasta into the sink when she was draining it. Nothing broken. Panic over.' He cleared his throat. 'You know what, El. We haven't seen much of you lately. Phoebe misses you, I know she does.' His voice lowered. 'Look, she'll probably kill me for telling you this, but she's been having a pretty shit time at work recently. There's a new manager at the office who seems to have taken a dislike to her. I know she's got me to offload onto, but I'm pretty rubbish at that sort of stuff − try to help but end up saying the wrong thing. It's a friend she needs to talk to. A good friend. Maybe you could come over sometime.'

I closed my eyes. Pained at his words. I hadn't known. How could I have when I hadn't spoken to Phoebe in months. 'Yes, of course. I wish she'd said something.'

'She tried to. She called you a few months ago, said she really needed to speak to you, and Alex said he'd get you to call back. I guess he never passed the message on.'

'No.' I shook my head although Josh couldn't see. 'No, he never did. He's been so busy. I expect he forgot.'

There was a second's beat. 'Yes, I expect that's it.'

'Tell Phoebe I'll pop round next week sometime.' This time I wouldn't let Alex put me off. 'In the evening after she's back from work.'

'Thanks, Elise. It would help, I know it would. Any idea when?'

I tried to remember Alex's shifts, but they'd been so erratic over the last few weeks it was impossible. I wedged the phone between my chin and my shoulder. 'Hang on a minute and I'll check the diary.'

I slid the kitchen drawer open, the one where we kept our junk, and took out the diary I bought to try to keep tabs on our comings and goings, but it only had my writing in it. Nothing exciting − just a hygienist appointment and a reminder to phone my mum. Alex had put his shifts in the first week we'd got it, then had clearly given up.

'I'll see what Alex says when he—'

There was a sliver of something in Josh's voice. 'You don't need to ask Alex's permission to see your best friend, El. You know that, don't you?'

'Yes, of course.' I felt hot with embarrassment. 'That wasn't what I meant.'

But it was. Without realising it, I'd got used to checking with Alex before making any plans. Checking he was all right with them before I confirmed.

That way, when I'm not on duty, we can spend as much time together as we can. It had sounded so reasonable then, and I can't believe how blind I'd been. But that's what they say about love, isn't it? It can make you see only what you want to see.

I heard the door of the flat slam, the clink of Alex's keys in the pot where he kept them.

'Look, I've got to go, Josh. Say goodbye to Phoebe for me.'

'But you haven't given me a—'

I never heard the end of the sentence, had clicked my phone off just as Alex came into the room. Slung it onto the worktop. But my guilty glance at the screen, my pink cheeks, gave me away.

'Who was that?' Although the words were said pleasantly, there was something off about him. 'I heard you talking to someone.'

He came over to me and kissed my hair. In his hand was a holdall. Placing it on the worktop, he unzipped it and pulled out a pair of his uniform trousers and a white shirt. Turning away from me, he shoved them into the washing machine but not before I'd seen the spatters of blood on one of the shirtsleeves.

Alex turned. Caught me looking. His face was guarded, and I knew from experience it was better not to ask. But as he bent to throw in the detergent pod, I found myself scrutinising his face for swelling. For bruises. Relieved when I saw neither.

'Well?' He straightened, turned and leant his back against the worktop. 'You didn't answer me.'

'It was Phoebe.' There was no point in lying. If I refused to tell him or gave a lie he didn't believe, he'd only take my phone and check it.

'What did she want?' His voice was tight with suspicion.

'Nothing much. She just hadn't heard from me for a while, that's all.'

Alex's face softened as he looked down at my belly, distracted. Wanting to change the subject. He placed an arm around my shoulders, the fingers of his other hand, stroking circles around my belly. His knuckles red and swollen. 'Our baby. Our beautiful girl.'

I leant my head against his shoulder. When he was like this, loving, attentive, when it was just me and him and our unborn child, it was easy to forget the other stuff. 'I'd like to call her Megan. It's such a pretty name.'

Alex's hand stopped its circling. 'Megan? Where the hell did that come from? She's not bleeding Welsh.'

'That's not entirely true. My grandmother was Welsh, which makes me a quarter, but that's not the point. I chose it because it's a beautiful name.'

'I don't like it.' He dropped his arm from my shoulder. Stepped away from me and reached for the kettle. As he filled it with water, he turned and smiled. 'I've been thinking about the name Anne... after my late grandmother. It would be a lovely way to remember her, don't you think? Megan can be her middle name if you really want it, but...' He flicks the switch on the kettle and lifts two mugs from the mug tree. 'Yes, Anne. Definitely.'

'All right. We'll call her Anne.' There was no point in arguing. Once Alex had got an idea in his head, there was no changing his mind.

I picked up my phone and put it in my pocket. Walking to the window, I looked down at the street. At the cars and buses. The shops with their garish window displays. The umbrellas and the rain that blackened the pavements.

What I didn't tell him was I was stubborn too. Once you were born, you might be Anne on paper, but in my heart, you would always be Megan.

To me anyway.

When you were born, you were perfect in every way, and I mean that.

Alex was by my side the whole time. Still dressed in his work shirt, the epaulettes on his shoulders incongruous in the bright lights of the birthing suite, he'd been invaluable. Pressing a cold flannel to my forehead. Breathing with me through the contractions. Telling me he loved me. Some of the hospital staff knew him and the midwife smiled indulgently at him before bending to me and whispering in my ear. *You've got a good one there.*

As your tiny fingers curled around mine, as you turned your head, your rosebud mouth searching out my breast, I vowed that I would love you more than anything that had come before. That I would cherish you. Keep you safe.

And it was like Alex noticed that too. Saw our bond. Saw that I had a new focus in life.

I think it was in that moment I realised I didn't want you to have any piece of him, and it shocked me. Giving birth to you had brought about a change. Every push, every cry that escaped my lips, had begun the process of dragging me from my stupor. Making me see how blind I'd been to everything. And, as I watched him press his lips to the soft down on your head, all the awful things he'd ever said and done came back to me, fighting against the image of the perfect father who was cradling you in his arms. The one who raised his eyes to the nurse to see if she was watching.

I saw him then as he really was. Controlling. Manipulative.

Once we were back home, my days were spent caring for you, and when you slept, I painted. I was content in those early days, but, as with all fairy tales, it didn't take long for things to change. Alex wasn't happy with the amount of time you took up... hadn't bargained on it. Every minute I spent with you was time away from him, and he was jealous of the bond we'd formed, hating how it was always me who got to wheel you around the park in your buggy. Me who took you to the health centre for your injections. Me who put you to bed most nights.

When he was home, he talked to me as though I was someone passed on to him via the desk clerk at the station. His voice clipped and formal. His smile absent. I saw then how he couldn't cope with the unpredictability of life with a baby, and it wasn't long before I started to notice other things too – a tightness around his eyes and mouth. A darkness.

And I felt the threat of him again. Knew I would have to do everything in my power to keep you safe.

FOURTEEN

MEGAN

Now

Megan sits on a rock and watches the groups of teenagers on the beach. She knows some of them from her school but doesn't join them, preferring to be on her own. They think she's standoffish, but it couldn't be further from the truth. Once, she had loads of friends. It's not her fault if she's never felt she's fitted in here.

She rubs her nose with the heel of her hand and looks away. Lies back on the rock and raises her knees, smiling as she feels the warmth of the hot stone on the bare strip of skin between her black bandeaux bikini top and frayed denim shorts. The sun is bright, and she crosses her arms over her face to block it, breathing in the sweet smell of her skin: coconut sun cream and sweat. She sticks out her tongue to taste the salt on it, filtering out the voices to her left.

It's hotter than she expected, and she doesn't want to burn like Nicky Delawney did last year. What a joke she'd looked coming into the classroom with an angry slash of red above the collar of her school shirt. She'd had to endure the boys' ribbing and jibes for days after until it had faded. Reaching out a hand to her bag, Megan pulls out a bottle of sun cream. She flips the top and squeezes some of the cream into her hand, smoothing it over a stomach still pale from winter. As she does, she takes in the freckled skin wishing she had her mum's creamy complexion.

She wrinkles her nose. Traces a finger over the pale dots, joining them. Did this come from her dad? Is it him she takes after? It's a question she's been asking herself recently: when she brushes her dark hair, when she cleans her teeth, when her blue eyes look back at her in the mirror.

High above her head, a seagull floats as if on an invisible thread. Wings spread. It's cry plaintive. She watches it, through half-closed eyes, until it's out of sight, then closes her lids fully, letting the sound of the waves wash over her. Feeling the sun on her cheeks, her stomach, her legs. It's too bright, so she pulls her khaki cap down over her eyes, the inside of her eyelids changing from pale orange to dark marmalade. She wriggles her shoulders to get more comfortable and thinks about her mum. There's something up, she knows it. Something that's spooked her. Even though he hasn't said anything, Sean's aware of it too – she's seen it in the way his brows pull together when he watches his wife. How his lips tighten. He knows more than he's saying, she's sure of it, but she's equally sure that whatever it is, and however much she badgers, she won't be able to get anything out of him. He's loyal, she'll say that for him, and however fond he is of *her*, her mum comes first. Always has. Always will.

A fly lands on her arm tickling her skin. That piece of paper her mum had in her hand when she'd acted so odd... What was it? Whatever it was, she hadn't wanted to show it to her. Megan bats the fly away irritably. She hates secrets. Always has done. If only she knew what it was that had caused her mum's face to pale. Caused her to lie.

How she wishes there was someone else she could ask. It makes her long to be back at Earthbound. When they'd been living at the commune, she'd had the feeling of never being alone. Always cared for – the centre of her mum's world. Not that she resents Kitty, not at all, she loves her. It's just that sometimes. Sometimes...

Megan rolls onto her stomach, the hard rock pressing into her hip bones, and looks back at the house. Her mum and Sean are out with Kitty. Would it harm to have a snoop around? If she could just find that envelope, things might become clearer.

She pushes herself up. Rummages through her bag until she finds her T-shirt, then pulls it on. Ignoring the group from her school, she jumps down onto the stones and walks to the boardwalk, stopping when she reaches it to make sure her mum and Sean aren't anywhere to be seen. When she's sure the coast is clear, she crosses to her back gate and lets herself in.

As she unlocks and slides open the sunroom door, late afternoon sunlight streams in. She stands amongst the gym equipment, her hand on the handlebar of the exercise bike, and looks around her. The only place her mum might hide something is the large sideboard that stands against the wall where Sean's windsurfing equipment and paddleboards are stashed. She goes to it and opens the doors. Squatting on her haunches, she rifles through the old photograph albums, flyers for windsurfing events and takeaway menus that are in there. But even as she's looking through it all, she knows she won't find anything. Most of this stuff is Sean's. Her mum had clearly not wanted him to know what was in the envelope either, so it's not going to be there.

She stands, hands on hips, thinking. It would be somewhere her mum would know neither she nor her stepdad would look. Megan chews on her bottom lip, picturing the closed door of her mum's studio. Remembering the countless times she's been told not to go in there without asking first. That there are wet paintings there that could get spoilt. Things that shouldn't be touched.

Pleased with herself for thinking of it, Megan closes the sideboard door and takes the stairs up to the first floor. She stops outside the closed door of her mum's studio feeling guilty. She knows she shouldn't go in there, that her mum would go mad if she knew she was snooping, but what choice does she have? What does she expect if she keeps secrets from her?

Megan lets herself in, shutting the door behind her. In front of her, by the window, is her mum's large table. Her easel. Finished canvases are propped up against every wall and on the desk are a collection of brushes, a tin of acrylic paints and a white plastic palette, dried paint colours bleeding into each other. An artbook is open at a page showing a stormy seascape.

Hating herself for doing it, she walks to the desk and pulls open the first drawer. In it is a collection of rubbers and marker pens. A roll of masking tape and a ruler. Megan pulls open the drawer beside it. Inside is an old wooden box filled with half-used tubes of oil paint. She's just about to close it again when she stops, her brow furrowed. She's seen her mum take paints from this box and knows it has two layers. With her heart beating loudly, she takes the box out of the drawer and lifts the wooden tray containing the top layer of paints. She stares at what's pressed into the space beneath, hardly able to breathe. It's an envelope. Unable to still the butterfly wings of anticipation, she takes it out and opens it. Slides out what's inside. It's a newspaper article, a little worse for wear but still readable.

Looking out at her is the face of a man she's never seen before. It's a head and shoulder shot, but she can clearly see epaulettes on the shoulders of his jumper. Another, smaller, photograph shows a young baby in a car seat. The headline is I STILL MISS HER.

Her hands are shaking so much, she has to put the article down on the table. Her eyes skim the words, devouring them. It was written several years ago, and, in it, the man tells how his baby was taken from him by his wife. They disappeared out of his life, and he's never understood why. There's a number to contact if anyone's seen them.

The baby's name is Anne. Megan presses her hand to her heart. Her middle name is Anne. That baby is *her*. It must be. And the man must be her father. No wonder her mum hid it from her. Has been lying to her these years. This was no one-night stand as she'd been told. The man and her mum lived together... it says so here.

None of this is important, though. Megan straightens and looks out of the window at the people on the beach, not seeing them. What *is* important is this. Her mum took her away from her dad and he missed her. Wanted her back. Maybe still does.

She clasps her hands in front of her and closes her eyes.

It must mean he loved her.

FIFTEEN

ELISE

Now

'I've got to go to Newcastle.' Sean pushes back his chair and takes his dinner things to the dishwasher.

'Newcastle? Why?' I finish the last of my wine and wait for him to answer.

'They've got a problem with one of the distributors. Come to a bit of a stalemate.'

I take a sip of my drink. 'How long will you be gone?'

'Not sure. Depends how long it takes to sort out. Have to play it by ear.'

'But does it need to be you? Can't they send Andrew?' I'm used to Sean working away from time to time and being in the house without him has never bothered me, but as much as I've tried to ignore the newspaper clipping, and Alex, now is not the time for Sean to go away.

'Not this time. They need someone senior to sort it out and I'm the only one with the knowledge to do it. When I'm dead and buried, remind me to have "troubleshooter" etched on my tombstone, will you?'

'When you're dead and buried, you won't care,' I reply, hoping the joke hasn't sounded as forced as it felt. Sean is such a big presence in our lives that I can't imagine him not being here. Not being a part of it. I can't imagine him being *dead*.

I pinch the skin of my arm under the table. I have to stop thinking like this. Have to stop imagining the worst. Since yesterday, I've let my imagination run away with me. Jumping if someone bangs a door or even if my phone pings a message.

I need to pull myself together. What am I expecting? For Alex to stride into our home with a warrant card? I watch Sean upend his mug in the rack at the top of the dishwasher and close the door, a strange fear gripping my stomach.

That's exactly what I'm expecting.

'You okay?' Sean straightens. Scratches his head. 'Why don't you take some time out? I can look after Kitty. Take the train into Brighton and see a film. Meet up with a friend...' He stops and folds his arms. He knows I don't have many of those.

'I'm fine, honestly. Why would I want to go out when I have a beautiful home? A lovely family?' I bend and lift Kitty out of her bouncy chair. Bounce her on my knee, enjoying the sound of her laugh. 'I have all I need here, Sean.'

'If you say so.' He points to the cooker. 'What time did Megan say she'd be home? Do you want me to put some foil over her plate?'

I try to remember. I know she told me, but I'd been changing Kitty's nappy and my mind had been elsewhere – something that's been happening more often recently.

'She said something about going to a friend's after school to do a homework assignment. I thought she'd be back by now, though. I know I told her dinner would be at six thirty.'

Sean shrugs. 'Perhaps she didn't hear or maybe she simply forgot. She's nearly sixteen and being deaf to her parents is par for the course.'

I look at my watch. 'Maybe I should ring her.'

'Maybe you shouldn't.' Sean's voice is firm. He opens a drawer and pulls out a box of foil. Tearing off a strip, he folds it around Megan's plate. 'Let her have some fun. We should be glad she's made some friends. The girl can't win.'

I feel myself bristle. 'What do you mean by that?'

'I mean exactly what I say. The poor kid is damned if she does and damned if she doesn't. She'll be home soon and I'm warning you, El, if you give Megan a hard time, you'll push her even further away. Choose your battles is my advice, and being half an hour late for dinner isn't one of them.'

Sean slides the plate into the oven, and as he closes the door, I force myself to remember how much he does for us. How good he's been taking on my child. Treating her as his own.

'You're right,' I say. 'I promise not to overreact when she comes in.'

Sean grins. 'Good. You'll thank me for it.' He turns the oven to its lowest heat and comes back to the table. Pulling out a chair, he sits, his face turning serious. 'You know we were having a bit of a heart-to-heart the other day.'

I raise my eyebrows. 'What you and Megan?'

'Don't look so surprised.' He puts his fingers on the coaster where his glass was, sliding it towards him then back again. 'Yeah. I don't know if I'm even supposed to be telling you this, but she was asking about her dad. About Alex.'

I feel myself grow cold.

'What did you say?'

'I told her the truth. That I don't know anything about him.' His eyes lock with mine. 'Actually, that's not quite true. I told her I didn't know his name. Followed the party line that he was a one-night stand. God, I hate lying to her.'

'You think she'd be better with the truth?'

Sean shrugs. 'How should I know? All I'm saying is it feels wrong me knowing and not her. Maybe it's time you told her about her father.'

I have to check Sean's face to make sure he's serious. He is. 'Tell her about Alex? Never.'

My ex-lover's face flashes before my eyes. The skin of his neck mottled with anger. The knuckles of his fist raw and bloody from where he'd been hammering on the bathroom door one night. The only place where I would feel safe when he was in one of his moods.

'I still don't understand why not. Give her something... We met at a club, he had brown hair, I liked his shoes. Anything to give her an idea of him. Would it really be such a bad thing?'

'Yes, it would, Sean.' I get up and put Kitty in her chair, then sit back down, watching as she bats at one of the animals on the arched frame, a gurgle escaping her.

He frowns. 'She wants to contact him. Hear his side. Maybe you should let her because one day, maybe not today or next week, but sometime in the future, she'll find him and ask him the questions you won't answer. And if she doesn't like what she hears, she might not forgive you.'

I'm hearing the words but not comprehending them. Is this really what Sean thinks?

I push back my chair so roughly it knocks into the variegated fig in its white pot that's behind me, making the silver and green leaves shiver. Sean frowns, but I don't care. I stand up and point an accusing finger at him.

'So what are you suggesting? That after fifteen years, I drive Megan to Birmingham so she can have a cosy little chat with Alex. That, after years of hiding from him, we break cover so he can give *his* side of the story. Is that what you're saying, Sean? Is that what you're really fucking saying?'

Tears of anger are streaming down my face, and I allow them to fall, unchecked. I've never sworn at Sean before, and I know it's shocked him, but I don't care. 'Can you even hear yourself? If you loved me, you'd never say those things.' I take a shuddering breath. 'Never.'

I walk away from him, but he catches my wrist. 'Don't walk away, El. You never said you were hiding from him... How can I help you if you don't talk to me?' I look down at my wrist, at his fingers circling it, and a memory bursts into my head, unbidden. Unwanted. The bite of cold steel. The metallic click of ratchets locking into place.

'Let go of me. Let go!' My voice is hysterical.

Shocked, Sean releases me, his hands dropping to his sides. He takes a step back, concern creasing his brow. 'What is it? What did I do?'

I cover my face with my hands, sobbing. Sean thinks he knows everything, but he doesn't. I've never told him the full story of my short years with Alex. He knows he was controlling, but I've never told him the extent of what he did. Never want to have to.

Kitty's eyes widen and she starts to cry. I press my hands to my ears, not ready to hear. Because now the memories have moved on... to those early days when Megan was a baby, and it makes me cry harder.

'I'm sorry,' Sean says, unable to hide his puzzlement. 'I didn't mean to upset you.'

I lower my hands and look at the man I love. So even-tempered. So rational. He doesn't deserve this. I step forward and touch his arm. 'No, Sean. It's me who should be sorry.' How I wish I could tell him everything, but I can't. Kitty's cries are getting louder, and I bend to her. But Sean stops me.

'I'll do it.' He lifts Kitty from her chair and a sick feeling creeps into my stomach. Is it because he doesn't trust me with her?

I watch him rock his daughter, his voice soft and melodic as he attempts to calm her. Apart from the children, he is all I have. My bond with Megan is being tested to its limits and, if I'm not careful, I'll be in danger of pushing him away too. I know Sean will only have said what he did because he cares about Megan. Is worried about her. But how can Megan knowing the truth be the best thing for her when, every day, every waking moment for the last fifteen years, I've been too scared to revisit it in case it consumes me? Makes me doubt myself. Sends me mad.

'You know what else Megan said?' Sean stops his rocking. Kitty's quietening now, her trusting eyes looking up at him. 'She said she was worried about you.' He runs his fingers through his hair. 'And you know what, El? I am too.' He turns away. 'I'm going to get Kitty ready for bed.'

He climbs the stairs and soon I hear his voice through the baby monitor. *Let's get you into your jimmy-jams, Kitty Cat.* Then the sound of his kisses on her plump cheeks.

Resting my elbows on the table, I drop my head into my hands, only realising Megan has come home when I hear the thump of her bag on the table in front of me.

'Jesus, Mum. What's wrong with you?'

I lift my head. See how my little girl is staring at me as though she doesn't know me. I want to say something to explain, but no words come out. With a shake of her head, she pulls her mobile from her pocket, her thumbs racing across the screen as she turns on her heel and walks away from me.

'Megan, who are you...'

But she's gone. As the door of her bedroom slams shut, I close my eyes against the tears that have formed. I haven't seen Alex for years yet he's still with me. Controlling me. My daughter is growing up. She wants to know about her father, and soon I won't be able to stop her from searching for the information she craves.

She'll be putting us both in danger and there won't be a thing I can do about it.

SIXTEEN

ELISE

Then

If it wasn't for you, Megan, I don't know how I would have gone on. I was lonely, stuck in that flat all day with no job, no self-esteem and no friends to confide in.

I'd stopped ringing Phoebe, partly because our lives had gone in different directions and partly because I couldn't stand hearing the condemnation in her voice whenever the conversation turned to Alex.

She and Josh had come to see me soon after you were born but hadn't stayed long – Alex had seen to that. I was tired. Needed time to settle with the baby and get my strength back. That was what he'd told them. And, although I'd wanted them to stay longer, had almost begged them to, they'd taken Alex at his word, handed me a present for the baby and left.

Later, when I'd messaged to thank Phoebe for her gift, her reply had caught me off guard. *We're worried about you, El. You and Alex are not one person. We'll always be here for you. You know that, don't you?*

I don't know why I'd deleted the message. Maybe it was

because, deep down, I knew there was some truth to it, and it shamed me. Over the weeks and months I'd been with him, I'd found myself taking on his views. Giving in if we disagreed about something. I told myself it was because he was older than me, knew more than me, but really it was because I was scared to argue. Didn't have the energy for it. And the more I acquiesced, the greater was his control over me.

In a strange way we *were* becoming one. It was how he wanted it.

And even though I knew it was happening, I found myself incapable of doing anything about it. I had you to think about and, although it's hard to believe now, even though I knew Alex was far from a saint, I still loved him. Any criticism of him was a criticism of me and I wasn't ready to confront that.

So, the gaps between calls with Phoebe became longer, the texts and messages shorter, until eventually they stopped altogether. It was better that way, I told myself. We had each other... We didn't need anyone else for us to be happy.

But I was wrong.

It was ten o'clock, a few months after your birth. I'd given you your final bottle and got you down for the night. Was settled on the sofa with a book. It was one I'd ordered, a thriller set on a windswept island in the North Sea, but I couldn't concentrate on it. Instead, my eyes kept sliding to the phone that was on the cushion beside me, it's face blank. Where was Alex?

His shift had started early that morning, the sky still dark when he'd got out of bed and gone for his shower. I'd expected him home hours ago. I looked down at my paperback, trying to read, but my brain wouldn't hold the words. My eyes skimming a line I'd already read three times, still not taking it in. There'd been no message, no call, to say why he was late. Was it an emergency or had he agreed to overtime? Giving up on the book, I placed it next to my phone. It wasn't the first time he'd been late and I should have been used to it, but it felt different that evening.

Too anxious to go to bed, too restless to do anything else, I got up and went to the window. The living room curtains were open, raindrops patterning the window – chasing each other in winding trails down the glass in a race to reach the sill. I looked down, watching cars and buses slide by, light from the street lamps shining on their wet roofs. Wondering if the next one would be Alex's.

As usual, on a Friday night, the road was busy: a queue of people outside the kebab shop opposite; a stag group pushing each other into the road, cans of beer in their hands; a woman in a rain mac taking her dog for a last walk. My eyes left the cars, my attention snagged by an illuminated shop sign, one letter flickering, threatening to go out. It did nothing to soothe me.

I knew how it was. Things came up. Unexpected things that couldn't be brushed aside just because Alex had a partner, a baby, waiting for him at home. I didn't want to be one of those women who constantly questioned. Pried. I'd have to be patient and, eventually, I'd hear his key in the lock. The thud of his shoes as he tossed them into the corner of the hall.

For that's what my life had become since I had you... a waiting game. After a day of nappy changes and feeds, of circuits of the kitchen, you bound tightly to me in your sling in the hope you'd sleep, I'd crave Alex's return. Like a drug, I needed him. Needed the way he managed to divert me from the monotony of my day by feeding me titbits from his own. Stories from that day's shift and others. Drugs. House raids. Car chases. Exciting things that I'd lap up, hanging on his every word as he leant against the kitchen island in his white T-shirt. The face on his warrant card, which he'd taken from his pocket and placed on the worksurface beside him, staring up at the ceiling with serious eyes. And as he talked, he'd watch me. Enjoying how much I needed this.

How much I needed *him*.

So when, later, as I was putting the bottles into the steriliser, I heard the door shut and heard Alex's heavy footsteps in the hallway, I didn't call him out for being late. For not telling me. Instead, I told my face to smile before I turned to greet him. Flicked the switch on the kettle that I'd already filled ready to pour onto the teabags that were waiting in the mugs.

But that night, things weren't as they usually were. Alex didn't come over to me as he normally did to place a hand on each shoulder and drop a proprietorial kiss on my head. Instead, he sank, heavily, onto the settee, pressing his fingertips to his forehead.

'What a fucking day.'

I brought his tea over and sat next to him. 'I'm sorry. Here, I've made you some tea.' I pushed the mug towards him, but he stopped it with the side of his hand, tea spilling onto the wooden coffee table.

'I don't want that. God, what are you like? Isn't it obvious I need a proper drink?'

He got up and went over to the sideboard. Opening the doors, he reached in and brought out a bottle of whiskey and a glass. Not asking if I'd like one, he poured himself a large measure and downed it, wiping his mouth on the back of his hand.

I sat watching him. Wondering at his calcified silence. Thinking how best to soothe him.

'The baby's just gone down,' I said, extricating a rattle that had got stuffed between the seat cushions of the settee and tossing it into the basket where we kept her things. 'Not a peep out of her since, but she may be still awake.'

You were so good, Megan. Never crying when I laid you in your cot. Happy to watch the mobile above your head until you drifted into a milky, contented sleep. I knew we were lucky –

that some babies refused to be put down or woke and screamed as soon as they were moved out of their mother's arms.

I tried again. 'Did you want to go in and see her?'

'You have to be kidding. I'm too fucking tired for *round and round the garden.*'

His words hurt, but I didn't comment on them. Instead, I got up, went over to him and put my arm around his waist. 'Did something happen at work? If you tell me, maybe I can help.'

'You?' He gave a scoff of laughter. 'How could you help? You know about policing all of a sudden, do you?'

'Of course not. I just thought—'

'No.' He pointed a finger at me. 'That's where you're wrong. You never think. I just want some fucking peace and quiet.'

I kicked myself for being so stupid as I sat down again. Corinne had told me at the dinner party that the number one rule of being a policeman's partner was to give them space after a hard day. Not to bombard them with questions or advice. I'd agreed with her, of course. It must be difficult being in a constant state of fight or flight, and being under daily public scrutiny would take its toll on the strongest of police officers. My place wasn't to question but to make our home a haven for Alex. A place for him to unwind. And if he didn't want to see the baby as soon as he got in, well, that wasn't surprising. I couldn't blame him for finding it hard to switch off when he was home. Swap from being a police officer to a father.

He refilled his glass and came to sit down next to me on the settee, then waved a hand at the large box standing in the corner of the room.

'What the hell's that?'

'It's the new washing machine. The one you ordered last week.'

'They weren't supposed to be delivering it until tomorrow. Why didn't they plumb it in?'

I looked at the space where the old machine used to be. 'I didn't know you wanted them to. I thought you said you were going to do it.'

'Jesus wept! Can't you think for yourself? When on earth did you think I'd have had the time to do that?'

I hated how his eyes had narrowed. How he was looking at me. 'I'm sorry, Alex, I presumed—'

'You presumed what? That I do nothing all day like you? That I have nothing better to do with my time when I come home than plumb in fucking washing machines?'

His voice had risen, and I looked nervously at our bedroom door. 'Don't shout, Alex. You'll wake the baby.'

'Don't tell me what I fucking can and can't do.'

He picked up his drink, tipped his head back and swallowed until the glass was empty. For one terrible moment, I thought he was going to throw it. Imagined it shattering, shards of glass flying, glinting in the light of the table lamp. But he didn't. Instead, he put down the glass and turned towards me. Smiled.

'So, tell me. What *have* you been doing today?'

I felt his scrutiny. Reddened under it. Was this some kind of test?

Sometimes, the quiet Alex, the calm one, was more menacing than the one who shouted. It was because I knew it was just the eye of the tornado. A tiny respite before the storm raged again.

'Nothing much.' I kept my head down as I answered, didn't meet his eye – something telling me it wasn't safe to do so. 'I did the online shopping order. Finished the painting of the Labrador, you know, the commission I got last week. Took the baby out for a walk in the park. The usual.'

'The usual.' His voice was mocking. Hateful. 'I wish I could spend all day strolling around the sodding park.' He got up again and fixed himself another drink. 'Do you know what I did today?' The amber liquid in his glass slopped dangerously as he waved it at me. 'I spoke to a woman who'd said she'd been raped.'

My breath caught at the irony of his words, but I knew I couldn't let him know what I was thinking.

'God, how awful. What did you do?'

'What do you think I did?' He smiled smugly. 'She was too frightened to say who it was, but I knew. He's been sniffing around her for a while, so I found the bastard and taught him a lesson. Threw him back in the gutter where he belongs. I doubt he'll be capable of trying a stunt like that again in the near future. Or the distant one for that matter.'

It was impossible to hide my shock. 'You mean you didn't arrest him?'

'Scum like that don't understand the language of the law and, even if they do, they know that, more often than not, they'll get away with it. Not enough evidence or no witnesses. The woman herself refusing to testify as she's scared she won't be believed – knows the conviction rate is low and doesn't want to take that chance.' He laughed to himself. Looked down at his hands. 'You need to talk to vermin like that in a language they'll understand.'

'And the girl?'

He shrugged. 'We tell the girls to be careful, but they don't listen... say they've got no choice. It's not how it used to be when I first came onto the force. Punters expect more for less. Think they can treat the girls as they please. Soho Road used to be okay once upon a time, but now it attracts all sorts.'

He looked at me, his glass pressed against his lips, waiting for my reaction.

'So you got a call... from the girl.'

He frowned, puzzled. 'No.'

The baby chose that moment to cry, and I watched as Alex got up and walked across the room. I thought he was going to see to her, but he didn't. Instead, he went into the kitchen area, picked up the baby monitor from the worktop by the microwave and switched it off.

Tears were pricking the back of my eyes. I didn't want to say what I was thinking, but I couldn't help myself. 'You were on early shift today. What were you doing there so late?' I heard my voice cracking. 'Why were you there at all?'

We hadn't had sex since the baby was born, and I couldn't get the image out of my head. Alex approaching one of the girls who frequented that area. A girl barely out of her teens, her face made up, waiting on the arterial road from Birmingham to the Black Country to earn petty cash from the kerb crawlers. In my head, I saw him take her hand, lead her round the back of one of the buildings. My heart thudded. What if that hadn't happened. If, instead, he'd told her to get into the back of his car. If that was what had happened, my heart would break, but, also, Alex could lose his job.

He was looking at me now. A look that chilled as I'd seen it before. One that gave out a silent signal that he'd won some game only he understood.

'So that's what you think, is it? That the father of your child would risk his career for a quick fuck in an alley.' He reached out his now empty glass towards me, his index finger pointing an accusation. 'When he's got his own slut at home?'

'To be honest, I don't know what to think.'

Slowly, deliberately, Alex put down his glass. 'No? Then why don't I show you?'

A deep chill penetrated the marrow of my bones. 'Stop it, Alex. You're frightening me. I know you've had a difficult day, but you don't need to take it out on me.'

'You think that's what this is about, do you? A difficult day.'

He picked up his warrant card, put it in his pocket. I hoped against hope he was going to take himself off to bed, but that hope was futile. Instead, he came towards me, face set, and dread tightened its hold. Getting off the settee, and wanting to keep him in my sight, I backed away from him, only stopping when my calves hit the traitorous edge of the coffee table.

'Let's go to bed, Alex. Talk about this in the morning.' I knew my voice had taken on a hysterical edge. Hated myself for it.

Alex didn't answer. He'd reached me now, his hand stretching out to take mine. I should have known what he was doing, should have stopped him, but I didn't. I couldn't. I was frozen, my brain taking longer than usual to give orders to my body, a small, ridiculous, part of me still wanting to believe that this was the Alex I loved. His fingers curled around mine, trapping them, a peace offering.

But of course it wasn't.

Releasing my hand, he circled my wrist, the fingers of his other hand reaching into the pocket of his trousers. His eyes flicked to the leg of the solid wooden dining table and then back at me. And as he pulled out the handcuffs, I felt the breath leave my body.

Outside, in the street below, a car hooted its horn. A man's voice shouted obscenities.

I'd never felt so invisible.

SEVENTEEN

ELISE

Then

The desk sergeant looked up at me, and I was relieved to see it wasn't anyone I recognised.

He smiled. 'Can I help you?'

I glanced around me, thankful there was no one else in the room. 'I'd like to speak to PC Skelton.'

A few months had passed since you were born, Megan, but instead of getting better, things had got worse. Wherever I was, whatever I did, I felt the imprint of Alex's handcuffs on my wrist. Had the strange feeling that he was behind me. Usually, he left the care of you to me, but sometimes, when I was still sleeping, he'd take you from your cot and leave the house with you. It was his way of showing me the control he had over both of us.

The sergeant put down the pen he was holding. 'Could I ask what it's in relation to?'

'I'd rather talk to her in private if you don't mind. It's...' There was the sound of a door shutting in the corridor behind me, and I looked round, dreading seeing Alex, even though he'd already told me he'd be several miles away giving a talk to teenagers at a comprehensive. It had taken a long time for me to work up the courage to be here, but I was already changing my mind.

'Yes?' The desk sergeant looked at me expectantly.

'It's delicate,' I finished. 'If you could just tell her I'm here.'

'Let me check for you.' He pointed his pen at the blue and white striped sling, where you were nestled, your heart beating against mine. 'Lovely baby you have there.'

'Thank you.' Even though I was grateful to him for saying it, impatience clawed at me. I hated being there... in Alex's territory. I needed to get out. 'So will you tell her I'm here?'

'What did you say your name was?'

'I didn't.'

How many people here knew my name? I'd only been to the station once when Alex had left his phone at home and I'd driven down to leave it in reception, guessing he'd need it. We weren't married, so there was no reason why anyone would know my surname and, apart from the colleagues he'd invited to dinner that night before you were born, I'd never met any of the people who worked with Alex.

'It's Elise James.'

He turned to his computer screen. 'I'm afraid PC Skelton hasn't come on duty yet. Would it be all right to speak to someone else?'

I hesitated, unsure now. Did it have to be her?

'I hoped she'd be here, but if she's not...' I trailed off, my mind racing. Did it matter who I saw? Wouldn't the result be the same whoever I told?

Now, I wasn't sure why I'd thought it so important I speak to Corinne. All I knew was I'd liked her – thought we had some sort of connection. There had been an integrity about her that had been lacking in the others, and I felt that if I trusted her with the truth, she'd act upon it despite the difficult situation it would put her in.

Your small cry echoed in the empty reception area, and I pressed my lips to your head, swaying from one foot to the other, hoping it would soothe you. Not wanting the attention your cry would attract if it became louder.

The desk sergeant looked at us both, tapped his pen against the wooden counter.

'What would you like to do, Ms James? PC Lang is available if you're happy to wait a moment.'

'Yes, I suppose so.'

'Give me one minute.' He pushed his chair back and walked to a room with a glass panel at the back of the reception. The door closed behind him, there were muffled voices and then, a few minutes later, he returned.

'If you'd like to take a seat, PC Lang will be with you shortly.'

'Thank you.'

I took a seat in the waiting area, pressing a hand against the back of your head and looking nervously at the door every time I heard a voice, a footstep, in the corridor. Wondering if I'd been a fool to come and what Alex would do if he found out.

When he found out.

At last, the door from the corridor opened and a male police officer with a serious face and salt and pepper hair stepped into the waiting area.

'Ms James? The desk sergeant said there was something you'd like to talk to me about.'

I stood, supporting the weight of the sling with my hands. Now it had come to it, now it was no longer in my head but happening, I was doubting myself. Could I really tell this stranger what had happened? The things Alex had done? I caught my top lip between my teeth, torn between doing what I'd come to do and fleeing.

'Maybe this isn't the best time. I could come back when—'

'Please, Ms James. I'd feel anxious too if I had to sit in this waiting room for too long. It's worse than the dentist.' Lang gave a small laugh, his pale-grey eyes travelling across my face, assessing me. 'If you'd like to come with me, there's a room free where we'll be able to talk without being interrupted. What do you say?'

'I suppose so.'

'That's good.' He smiled. 'After you.'

PC Lang held the door open, and I followed him through into the corridor, the anxiety that had been with me ever since I'd decided to come here, balling into a fist in my stomach. Taking me by surprise.

I reached out a hand. Leant against the wall. 'I'm sorry, could you give me a moment?'

'Are you all right? Do you need to sit down?' PC Lang pointed to the red plastic seat outside one of the doors that opened into the corridor, clearly worried I might faint or throw up.

'No.' I closed my eyes a second, then straightened. 'I just felt a bit faint, that's all.'

I needed to get this done because I knew that with each day that passed, it would become harder. Maybe Alex knew it too as in the last few days he'd made an effort to behave normally. He'd let me know if he was going to be late home and took more interest in you, Megan.

But the sudden change from disinterest to doting father was disconcerting, and it didn't fool me. As I watched him change your nappy or lift you out of your bouncy chair and bind you against his chest in the sling to take you out, I'd feel my stomach tighten. This new Alex wouldn't stay long. What he was doing was simply a smokescreen, some warped way of controlling me through you, and I didn't trust him. Not any more.

Your rightful place was next to *my* heart, not the man who

had done those things to me. This time, I was no longer able to convince myself that what we had was normal... that all relationships were like this. Because the reminders were there every day when I walked into the flat, or ate a meal, or sat on the settee with my book, dreading the sound of his key in the lock. Everything was there as a warning, our bed, the uniform he put away, the table leg he'd cuffed me to.

The warmth of your body against mine was keeping me strong. I had to do something. Make sure someone knew the truth about what he was like. What he was capable of.

'I'm okay now.'

'Sure?' PC Lang's pale eyes studied me. 'It's just along here then.'

I followed him to a door at the end of the corridor. Waited as he opened it, then beckoned me through.

'Please, take a seat,' he said.

As he shut the door behind us, I took the opportunity to look around me – not that there was much to see. The room was around eight feet by ten and sparsely furnished. Just a table with a recording device and two chairs. Apart from that, the room was bare. Soulless. The dark-grey epoxy flooring merging seamlessly with the paler grey walls where no clock, no pictures, broke the monotony. I'd expected it to have a view of the station car park, but the walls were blank. Windowless. There was no glass panel in the door either and my heart quickened. Had I been taken to an interrogation room rather than an interview room?

Seeing my face, PC Lang shrugged an apology. 'Sorry. It was all we had available at short notice.'

But I didn't need comfort for what I was about to do. I needed someone who would listen and take me seriously. Begin the process that would stop Alex from ever doing anything like that to me again... or anyone else. Expose him for the man he really was.

PC Lang indicated one of the chairs, but when I tried to move it away from the table, I couldn't. It was bolted to the floor.

'Sorry, that was stupid of me. I should have warned you. They're fixed so they can't be used as a weapon. Some of the people we see in here... you wouldn't believe. Good job we have this.' He pointed to the CCTV in the corner of the room. 'Saved my bacon a couple of times, that's for sure.'

I looked at the small black eye, wondering who it was who watched the interviews. I felt a pulse of anxiety. Would Alex have access to this?

I turned back. Realised there was no way I was going to be able to fit into the small space between the table and chair with you in your sling. Bending my head, I tried to untie the knot around my waist, but my hands were shaking, making it impossible.

Noticing, PC Lang put out a hand to stop me. 'Please don't wake the baby. You take this chair.'

I went round to the other side of the table and sat, expecting him to sit in the immoveable chair, but he didn't. Instead, he remained standing.

'Take your time. Start whenever you're ready.'

I lowered my lips to your soft head, breathed in the warm biscuity smell of your scalp to calm me. I was glad that PC Lang wasn't putting pressure on me to talk straightaway. Instead, he perched on the edge of the table, watching me with his pale-grey eyes.

Time ticked on. I sat in that small, windowless room with its bolted chair, staring at the hideous grey walls, the unblinking eye of the CCTV, waiting for words that refused to come. My uncertainty striking me dumb. Because now, every part of me was screaming out that this man with his unwavering stare was not the person I should be telling my story to. That I'd made a mistake.

I stood again.

'I shouldn't have come. I've been overthinking things. Over-reacting. I'm sorry for wasting your time, but I need to go home.'

PC Lang frowned. 'Are you sure?'

'Yes, I'm sure.'

Clutching you to me, I walked on unsteady legs to the door.

'Please, let me.' PC Lang released the door and let me out. Led me back through to reception. 'If you change your mind—'

'Thank you, I know.'

He looked at me thoughtfully. 'Very well then. You know where we are.'

I waited until the door closed behind him, then let out a shuddering breath. In front of me was a stand containing a variety of leaflets. One in particular caught my eye, and I pulled it out of its Perspex holder and stuffed it into my bag before leaving the building.

As I stood in the police station car park, a frigid wind bit my cheeks and blew my hair around my face. Tears of frustration blurred my vision. It had taken all of my courage to come here, and I'd let panic take control. Hating myself for my weakness, I walked to my car, but just as I was about to unlock it, I saw someone get out of the car in the row opposite. A red, woollen scarf was wrapped around her neck and her blonde hair was scraped back into a tight bun at the back of her head. After locking the door, she walked in the direction of the station building, pulling the collar of her padded jacket up against the wind.

Corinne.

Shoving my car keys back into my bag, I ran after her. Caught her before she could reach the door.

'Corinne. Wait.'

She turned, a mixture of surprise and concern on her face. 'Elise? How are you? Did you come to see Alex?'

I looked behind her, dreading he might appear. 'No, it was

you I came to see.' The words rushed out now. Fast. Breathless. 'I have to talk to you about Alex. Have to make a—'

'Not here. Not now.' Corinne looked over her shoulder. Checking the car park.

'Where then?'

A police car pulled into the car park, and we both watched it as it reversed into a designated space near the building, but the man who got out wasn't Alex.

I exhaled silently, trying to steady my nerves. 'He's your friend, I get that, but I have to tell someone. I don't know what else to do.'

Corinne's eyes flicked briefly up to mine. I couldn't read her face.

'Get in the car. We can talk there.'

Taking my arm, she hurried me back to her car. She opened the passenger door, and I slid in, though it was difficult with you in the sling. Corinne smiled. 'She's lovely. You're very lucky.'

'Yes,' I said, because it was true, I was lucky. 'She's very good.'

The car was clean with a fresh lemon smell to it, unlike mine that was filled with the detritus of a family: packets of baby wipes in the footwell, spare muslins and your change bag on the back seat, an empty crisp packet shoved into the cup holder. But I wouldn't change it. Not for anything.

'What did you want to tell me, Elise?' Even though she wasn't driving, Corinne placed her hands either side of the steering wheel. She didn't look at me. 'I'm not sure what this is about, but I'm glad you felt you could trust me.'

I held you tighter. 'It's difficult. Hard to know where to start.'

'I know, but you've done the right thing in coming to me. Nothing good ever comes of keeping things to yourself. There's no hurry. Take your time.'

Drawing a deep breath into my lungs, I began. It was hard,

but I told her everything. The words tumbling from me, fuelled by pain, by fear, by anger. Words I'd held back for so long I could no longer stop them. And as I spoke, I looked down, as if from a height, on the woman who I knew was me yet seemed so distant. So alien.

The story spewed from me, filling the car with its vileness, and when I looked across at Corinne, it was no longer her I saw but Alex. His guilt cemented by the coldness, the thrill, in which he'd meted out punishment for something I'd never done. It was a face I'd once loved but not now. Not since he'd made me lose my identity. The part that made me who I was.

I stopped abruptly. Corinne's face coming back into focus. 'And now you know it all.'

There was no more to say. I'd told her everything and was exhausted. Stripped of all emotion. Closing my eyes, I breathed out until my lungs were empty. Expelling the last of Alex from me, the space left behind filling with a strange lightness. A euphoria.

I hugged you to me. Proud of myself. Relieved at having done what I'd come to do.

Corinne didn't speak, and I opened my eyes, terrified of what I might see. Scared that she hadn't believed me.

The dashboard of her car was smart, modern, reminding me of an aircraft. The time displayed in large neon yellow digits. I watched the minutes tick by; each one making me more nervous. Eventually, I could take the silence no longer.

'Is there anything I can do? Anything *you* can do?'

Corinne took her hands from the steering wheel, placed them in her lap.

'Thank you for telling me, Elise,' she said eventually, her head turning, her eyes finally meeting mine. Eyes that were unreadable. 'As I said before, you did the right thing.'

'So what should I do now?' I waited for more. For some direction.

Corinne ran a hand across her head, smoothing her hair and repositioning one of the clips in her bun. 'It's a difficult situation, but my advice for now is to go home. Try and work things out with Alex.'

'Work things out?' Had I heard her correctly?

'Yes.' Corinne's voice was tight. 'I think that's the best course of action for now. I shouldn't really be doing this, but I'm going to give you some advice. If you make a formal complaint against Alex, you will regret it. Think about yourself and your little one. It will be your word against his, Elise, and the odds will be stacked against you.'

I was wracked with confusion. Doubt. I'd spilt my heart out to her. Told her all the vile things he'd said and done to me, yet here she was telling me to go home. Sort things out.

I pressed my palm against my forehead to stop the dizziness that had come over me.

Corinne wasn't going to help me. And now she might tell Alex.

I was in more danger than ever.

EIGHTEEN

ELISE

Now

It's been a beautiful evening. The sun sinking beneath the horizon sending fingers of gold across the sea to the west. Painting the sky in hues of tangerine and pink. I'm sitting, feet curled under me, on one of the cushioned garden chairs on the wide balcony outside the first floor living area, a glass of gin and tonic in front of me on the rattan and glass coffee table. Kitty in my arms.

Sean has gone to Newcastle and won't be back for a day or two. Megan is in her bedroom doing her homework, or so she says. These days, I never know what she's doing, and if I go into her room without knocking first, she'll blow up at me.

Below me, the swimming pool ripples in the slight breeze that evening has brought with it, its surface striped with shadows from the long, narrow leaves of the potted palms that surround it. From up here, the blue and green of my sun patio looks like a lush oasis against the wide expanse of stony beach beyond the ornamental wall. I take a sip of my gin and tell myself I'm lucky, so lucky, to be living here. That thousands would give their right arm to be where I am now, an open book resting on my stomach, my gin shivering in its glass every time the breeze reaches me.

Yet, I can't relax. Despite the beautiful sky and the sun and the gin, I'm unable to give myself up to it... not with the spectre of Alex hanging over my head. For the first time in years, I can feel the old tension begin to tighten a band across my forehead. Feel it twist my stomach into a knot that makes it hard to eat.

As the sun dips lower, I shiver. The tightness in my chest stopping me from breathing freely. The balcony is losing its sunlight, the roof of the empty building next door casting its shade over my legs, and even though I push my chair back, it won't be long before the strip of sun that's left will disappear and I'll have to move back inside.

Kitty's awake. She looks up at me with wide trusting eyes, and the weight of responsibility for this precious being is suddenly overwhelming. I think of the newspaper article hidden under the tray of paints in the drawer of my art table. The photo of baby Megan next to the one of Alex with his accusing eyes.

When the tug of guilt becomes too strong, I remind myself of one important fact. I had to do it. He'd given me no choice. The Alex I knew back then was capable of terrible things. Once he took his uniform from his locker and put it on, he was a force to be reckoned with. Respected. Liked by his team. Me? I was nothing. Someone of interest only because I was Alex's girl-friend... the mother of his child.

If I hadn't lifted Megan from her cot and run with her to a place where he wouldn't find us, I don't know what he might have done. My fingers stray to my wrist, rubbing at the bone. It's why I'd known I could never tell him the truth. Not ever.

Yet, someone knows where I live. I'd thought it was Alex, but now I'm not so sure. What's happened recently isn't his style. The man I knew back then wouldn't threaten, he'd simply carry out whatever punishment he thought fit. Take Megan or Kitty. Hurt me. Teach me a lesson.

But if not Alex, then who? And what are they planning to do? Was the article a warning or is someone trying to make me feel uneasy so I'm vulnerable? Corinne, maybe?

The not knowing is eating away at me. The question I can't answer making me look over my shoulder whenever I go out. Move my easel away from my studio window in case someone's out there looking in.

Those eyes I'd felt on me on our night out – I'd thought I'd imagined them, but what if I hadn't?

There are still one or two people strolling along the board-walk, enjoying the soft evening air, the darkening sea. But once darkness falls properly, the only lights will come from the wind turbines – red fireflies on the distant horizon. Or from a tanker making its way into harbour. No one will come to the beach then, for there's nothing to do or see. No light to guide them along the boardwalk.

It's the position of the house that made Sean choose it. Why he pushed to buy the old bungalow, despite the costly improvements he'd need to make. He'd loved how the busy beach and boardwalk became totally private once night fell. As though, with the rising of the moon, the row of houses and their owners, could reclaim the beach for themselves.

I wait until the sea and the sky have darkened, merging into one, then step back inside, Kitty in my arms. She reaches up and bats at my face and a memory comes rushing back of Megan doing the same thing. Echoes of the past.

The memory dislodges another. Megan in her bouncy chair, her cheeks wet with tears. Wanting, with every fibre of my being, to go to her. Knowing I'd have to get past Alex first as his body blocked the gap between the kitchen island and the floor where I was lying. Knowing he wouldn't let me. The anguish I felt then is with me again as I remember how he'd picked my baby up. Pressed his cheek to hers.

Daddy loves you, darling. Mummy's nothing.

Kitty squirms in my arms, wide awake now. She missed her afternoon nap and it's going to be difficult getting her down this evening. Deciding not to try, at least until Megan and I have eaten, I slide her into her bouncy chair and tap one of the coloured elephants that hang from the padded bar, seeing how her eyes follow its movement. Watch her uncoordinated fists wave in their direction making the seat rock.

Knowing she'll be fine for the moment, I switch on the over-head lights, recessed spot bulbs in the ceiling, then open the fridge door and look inside, wondering what Megan and I can have.

Megan's in a *no red meat* phase at the moment, so I pull out a pack of salmon and turn the cooker on. Without Sean here, the vast living area feels empty. Too quiet. I wish Megan would come out of her room, even if it's only to sit with a bored expression, her eyes glued to her phone. But I won't call her; she'll come out if she wants to.

Instead, I bend to Kitty. Crouch in front of her chair and grasp one small foot in each hand.

'How's my precious baby?'

Kitty gurgles and blows bubbles. She looks pleased with herself and does it again. She's learning to experiment, and a raspberry is something to add to her repertoire.

'Cheeky monkey.'

I press a kiss to the jerseyed sole of each foot, then straighten, my eyes drawn to the window, now just a wide expanse of black behind which the sea will be writhing and breathing like a living thing. Although I can't see it, I know from looking at the tide times earlier that it will be edging nearer. Seeking out the gaps in the boulders that make up the groyne.

Agitating the shingle before peeling away again. Moving closer. Ever closer.

Tonight, there is no moon. No stars. Just a dense blackness against which my living room is reflected. Even though we've lived here a while, my instinct is still to reach for the edges of the curtains. To draw them together and shut out the world. But I don't because there aren't any. Sean hadn't wanted anything that would interrupt the view. Hadn't wanted the stark edges of the windows softened by cotton, silk, or voile. Even the suggestion of blinds had caused a pained expression to settle on his face.

'It's all about this,' he'd said, sweeping his hand in an arc to encompass the beach and sea. 'You must get that, El.'

'But what about at night when the lights are on,' I'd countered.

'What about it?' He'd looked confused. 'That's the whole point of it, babe. The whole beauty. No one goes to this part of the beach at night. No one walks along the boardwalk. There are no lights... nowhere to go.'

Reluctantly, I'd given in. No curtains. No blinds. Only a sheet of toughened glass separating us from the world outside. Making us at one with it.

I've never been entirely comfortable with it, but, tonight, as I place the salmon on the tinfoil covered tray and slide it into the oven, I feel as though I'm no longer myself but an actor on a stage. Acutely aware that anyone with a mind to stand outside on the boardwalk would see the kitchen and living room lit up as though it were a stage set. Me the lead character. Megan, conspicuous by her absence, like an actor in the wings missing their entrance.

'El enters stage left, a baby in her arms,' I say under my breath as I pick Kitty out of her chair and carry her, with one of her bottles, out of the kitchen area. But although the words are designed to lighten my mood, they do the opposite. And, as I cross the room, I'm aware of how I'm walking. How I'm *being*.

Anxiety mushrooms and I tell myself not to be so stupid. Having windows opening onto the beach never bothered me before, so why should it now? No one's out there to see us. No one.

Yet, as I tip the bottle to Kitty's lips and watch her swallow the warm milk, her eyes glued to mine as though she never wants to let me out of her sight, a shudder passes through me.

What if Alex really *is* out there watching me?

Standing up quickly, I hurry to the switch on the wall and twist it until the lights above my head dim then go out. It's how I'm standing when my phone pings a message in my pocket. Feeling my way back to the settee, I sit, Kitty in the crook of my arm and look at it, relieved to see Sean's name light up on the screen.

Only just got to the hotel. Bloody traffic. Everything okay there?

I want to tell Sean the truth. That I'm not okay. That I'm scared and wish he was here. But I don't.

Instead, I stare at the reflection of my living room in the darkened glass and see a woman and a baby. See us as Alex would before I turned the lights out. If he were out there.

Yes, I'm fine. I lie. *Have yourself a nightcap and get a good night's sleep. You don't need to worry about me.*

But he did need to worry. Very much.

NINETEEN
MEGAN

Now

Mothers should be worried about their daughters, not the other way round. It's what Megan thinks as she pushes open her bedroom door to find the house in darkness. Not a lamp lit. Not a flicker of a TV.

'Mum?'

She steps into the wide area with the metal-armed leather settees she's always found uncomfortable, the light from her bedroom spilling onto the polished wooden floor. A slice of it picking out the twin bookcases that jut, like ribs, into the space between where she stands and the vast living room and kitchen at the front of the house. Why couldn't her mum and Sean have designed something with walls, for God's sake? Like everyone else's houses.

'Mum?' she calls again, louder now. 'Are you there?'

Why is the place so dark? Surely her mum can't have gone out. Not without telling her. Not when she has a baby to care for. For the last hour, she's been lying on her bed thinking about the newspaper article she'd found in her mum's studio.

Thinking about her dad – a man who, in the space of a few minutes, had changed from a faceless, nameless idea to something altogether different. A real live person with a name... a job. Alex. As she'd stared at the ceiling, she'd said his name out loud as though trying it out. Seeing how it fit with her own. Not some person her mum had had meaningless sex with after too many drinks, but a police sergeant from Birmingham. She's still trying to get her head around it.

Megan can smell something. It's coming from the kitchen, the comforting aroma of salmon and herby potatoes, and it eases her mind. Just a bit. If her mum has put on the dinner, then everything must be fine.

But why aren't the lights on? What's she playing at?

The light from her room is just enough to see by. Not bothering to turn on another, Megan walks on socked feet to the living area, stopping when she gets there, her hand on the edge of the tall bookcase.

In front of her, the vast area of glass, which makes up the two sliding patio doors, takes her attention. With no light on, the sea is visible, stretching away from her, the ridges of the waves tipped silver by a moon that has just come out from behind the clouds. It's beautiful, otherworldly, making her feel small and insignificant. Making her feel lonely.

A noise makes her start. A small squeak. A snuffle. It sounds like Kitty.

Feeling her way to the wall by the open-plan kitchen, Megan presses the switch and the room lights up.

'No! Turn it off.'

The voice comes from the settee. Her mother's voice.

She's sitting, knees drawn up, in the corner of the white leather settee, Kitty in her arms. In the sudden harsh light, her pupils have constricted to pinpoints, making her look like someone else. Megan wants to feel angry, shout at her mum for scaring her, but she doesn't. There's something about her face that is unsettling – the paleness of her skin in the moonlight. The way her eyes flit from the window to the baby and back again.

'Mum, stop acting weird. Has something happened?' Megan looks around her, but everything seems normal. 'Why were you sitting in the dark?'

Her mum blinks, as though Megan's voice has brought her back from a dark place. Slowly, she shakes her head. Forces a smile.

'No, no. Nothing's happened.' She doesn't meet Megan's eye, but looks beyond her, as though searching for something. Is it a lie she's looking for? 'Kitty wouldn't settle, kept crying, so I thought I'd turn out the lights. See if that helped.'

'I never heard her cry. She's good at night... You always say that.'

Her mum shrugs. 'You wouldn't have heard with that music of yours.'

But Megan hadn't been playing her music or doing her homework. Instead, she'd been lying in the dark trying to decide on the best way of breaking it to her mum that she knew everything. That there was no point in her lying any more as the evidence was hidden beneath the tray of paints in her studio.

'Let me take her.' Megan lifts Kitty into her arms, feeling her mum's resistance. Her reluctance to let her go. She wonders at it as she wipes a raspberry dribble from the baby's mouth with a muslin cloth and runs her finger down her smooth cheek. There's no sign that Kitty's been crying: her skin isn't blotchy or damp with tears. Hardly a baby who was so upset her mum had needed to turn out the light to soothe her.

But she says nothing. Instead, she sits down next to her. She needs to get this off her chest. Needs her mum to understand that she's serious about wanting to find Alex. Get to know him.

'There's something I want to talk to you about, Mum.'

'Yes?'

Her mum moves up, pats the cushion beside her, and Megan knows it's because she's happy that, for the first time in a long while, her daughter wants to talk to her. She knows she misses it. Sometimes *she* misses it too... how they used to be when they were at Earthbound.

'Don't get mad or anything.' Megan flicks her eyes to her mum's. 'But I've been thinking.'

'Oh?' Her mum smiles, but there's still a tension in her neck and shoulders she hasn't managed to shake off. A nervousness in the way she glances at the darkened windows, as though waiting for something to happen. Something unpleasant. 'What is it, Megs?'

Megan feels the warmth of her mum's fingers around her own, the first physical contact they've had in a long time. Knows her mum wants to hug her but is holding back for fear of frightening her away.

Megan hurries on before she loses her confidence. 'It's about my dad.'

Her mum's face remains neutral. 'He messaged half an hour or so ago. He'd just arrived at the hotel and wanted to let us know. I'm sorry, Megs, I should have knocked on your door to tell you.'

Megan looks away. This is going to be more difficult than she'd anticipated.

'I didn't mean Sean, Mum.' She looks away, no longer wanting to see her mum's face as she says it. Sensing what's to come. 'I meant my real dad.'

Their reflections are caught inside the cold metal frames of the patio doors. The sea behind the glass no longer visible now the room is brightly lit.

Her mum's face is pale. 'What about him?'

'I want you to tell me the truth.'

'Please, not this again, Megan. I've told you a million times he was a one-night stand. I got pregnant and knew he wouldn't be able to handle it. He meant nothing to me, and he should mean nothing to you. I don't even remember his name.'

'I don't believe you. Show me my birth certificate. I have a right to know, Mum.'

She'd imagined her mum would shout, argue as she always did, but instead she remains silent. A single tear runs down her cheek, and she doesn't bother to wipe it away.

'Please, don't do this.' It's all she says.

At the sight of that single tear, Megan's filled with a strange sadness, her throat constricting so tightly she can barely swallow. She'd been going to tell her mum about the newspaper article... everything she'd found out about her dad. And then, even though she knew her mum would fight back, she'd been planning on telling her she was going to try and find him.

But now the moment's here, something stops her. That single tear. That simple heartfelt plea, *please, don't do this*, even though her mum couldn't have known what she'd been about to say. She can't do this to her. Not while she's like this.

Megan gets up. Hands Kitty back to her. 'I'll check the dinner's not burning.'

As she bends to the oven and takes out the tray of salmon, she makes a decision. She's going to have to find her dad without her mum's blessing. Reach out to him and see if he responds.

So what if her mum doesn't know?

Maybe it's better this way.

TWENTY

ELISE

Then

I took you out of your sling and placed you in your car seat. And as your arms waved and your face puckered, head turning one way then the next in the vain hope of finding milk, I remembered you were due a feed. Normally, I would have brought a bottle with me, but, today, I'd forgotten. I'd been too preoccupied. Too bound up in my own worries to think of anything as practical as that. Wanting to get to the police station before my fear got the better of me.

You were crying now, and as I buckled you into your seat, I saw the damp crescents on your jersey leggings, each side of your nappy. Not only were you hungry but you needed changing. Guilt pressed in. I'd allowed myself to forget your needs. How could I have let that happen when you were the only thing that bound me to sanity?

I reached across to the glove compartment and flipped it open, finding the spare nappy and wipes I kept in there for emergencies. Although it was food you wanted, I took you out of your car seat again, laid you on the driver's seat and pulled off

your leggings, dropping them into the footwell on the passenger
side. As I unpeeled the tab from your nappy, I tried to stem the
panic that had taken hold of me since I left the police station.
Trying, and failing, to block out the words that were in my head.
Alex's words. Ones I'd heard many, many times in various
guises since I'd known him.

*There was no point in her testifying as no one would believe
her.*

The case collapsed as there were no witnesses.

She was wasting her time.

Words I know now were used to put doubt in my head. So
that, if and when the time came, I wouldn't have the confidence
to come forward and tell someone about the things he'd done to
me. That I'd be afraid I wouldn't be believed.

Except I *had* come forward. I'd told Corinne.

It was now her words that I heard. *It will be your word
against his, Elise, and the odds will be stacked against you.*

My hands were shaking as I bundled the wet nappy and
leggings into a nappy sack. I was trying to tie it when some sixth
sense made me look up. Another police car was entering the car
park.

I waited, one hand resting on your stomach to keep you
from wriggling off the seat. Terrified of who would get out of
that car. Hoping against hope it wouldn't be Alex. And when it
was, I wasn't even surprised – for why else would every hair on
my body have raised at the sight of that patrol car? Why else
would my tensed muscles have screamed out to me to flee?

I'd thought he'd be gone all morning, that the talk at the
school would have taken longer than it had, but that had been
just a guess. I hadn't actually asked Alex how long he'd be.

And now he was here. And so was I.

I stood beside the car, not daring to move in case he saw me.
Heart pounding. But I was in luck. Without looking around
him, he strode towards the main entrance. I could see from his

expression that he wasn't happy, and I wondered why. Was it because he was frustrated at having given a talk to a hall full of kids who couldn't be arsed to listen to what he had to say? Was he wishing, that instead of bashing his head against a brick wall, he'd been out on patrol with his colleagues? Wondering why he'd ever taken the promotion, with its management and mentoring, which took him away from the real policing that he loved. That he craved.

He opened the door and as he disappeared inside the building, I was flooded with sweet relief. But it was only fleeting. I needed to get out of the place. Lifting you under your arms, I strapped you back into your car seat, my fingers shaking as I tried to snap the buckle in place. Every few seconds, I'd look over my shoulder to check Alex hadn't come out again.

But, as I started the car, a wave of panic engulfed me. What if Corinne decided to tell him? But she wouldn't, surely. There were procedures that had to be followed, consequences, presumably, if they weren't. It would be criminal to tell a victim's abuser of their accusations. Even if the abuser was a police officer. *Especially* if he was.

I put the car into reverse, and as I backed out of the parking space, a movement at one of the windows made me turn and look. It was one of the interview rooms I'd passed as I'd walked down the corridor and the person standing at the glass was Alex. As I watched, another figure joined him.

I waited. My foot on the brake. Unable to leave until I knew.

The figure moved closer. Navy jumper. Slim figure. Fair hair pulled into a neat bun. And now I wished I *hadn't* seen. That, instead, I'd driven away when I'd had the chance.

I watched in misery as Corinne laughed at something Alex said, then reached up to twist the blind closed. The betrayal was a knife in my gut and my hand pressed to it as though to heal the wound. As the gap between the slats narrowed, leaving me to guess what was happening behind them, there was only one thought in my head.

Alex was right. I was wasting my time.

If this was ever to end, I had only one option. To go home, get our things and leave Alex for good.

My mind turned to the leaflet I'd picked up at the police station. I put on the handbrake and fished it out. The picture on it was a hand holding a telephone – a number to call underneath. I stared at the words written alongside. It was as though they were speaking to me alone. ARE YOU SCARED OF YOUR PARTNER?

Of course I was scared. It was obvious in the way the edges of the leaflet shivered as I thought about what Alex would say if he ever knew what I was reading. In the thump of my heart when I thought of what he'd do if he knew what I was planning.

But I had to try. If not for myself, then for *you*, Megan.

TWENTY-ONE

ELISE

Then

It was only once I got home that reality set in. Alex would never let me go. Never. I stood in the doorway of the flat taking everything in. The highchair in the kitchen, the box of toys, your favourite board book lying open on the floor beside it. The elephant-printed change mat stuffed between the settee and the wall.

Even if I had the courage to do it, what on earth would I take and where would I go?

I was filled with an all-consuming panic. There was too much to think about. I could go to Mum's, but he'd follow me. Take me back. But it wasn't just that. I'd tried, once, to tell her what Alex was like and her answer had made me question everything: my childhood, my father, the marriage I'd always thought was sound. *Relationships are a dance, Elise, and you'd do well to learn the steps.* It made me suspect that during the years she'd been married to my dad, things hadn't been as perfect as they'd appeared to my young eyes. That she'd been sugar-coating the truth to make it taste better.

I thought of all the years she'd taken me to church on a Sunday – the seat cold beneath my skirt as she'd disappeared inside the curtained box to make her confession. How she'd always encouraged me to turn the other cheek if I'd had an argument at school. I'd thought nothing could be as bad as people not believing me if I told them what had happened, but my mum's acceptance of Alex's behaviour would be worse. So much worse.

I needed time to think about what I was going to do. How I could get away from Alex without making things worse for me or for you, Megan. Because, if there was one thing I was sure of, above all else, it was that he'd never give you up. Not because of what you meant to him... but because of what you meant to *me*. You and I had only ever been pawns in a game he'd never let us win. Not while there was still breath in his body.

A wave of helplessness crashed over me. How had things come to this? How had they got so bad? It was only your cry that stopped me from sinking to my knees. I'd placed your car seat on the floor beside me and I looked down at you, my love for you making me stronger. For your sake, I had to keep it together.

The movement of the car had settled you, but now we were home, your hunger had come to the fore again. I was your mother and you needed me. This wasn't the time to be weak. To fall apart.

Trying not to think of anything else, I went into the kitchen to warm your bottle, the simple action helping to calm me. But, as I lifted you out of your seat and took you to the settee, settling you on my lap and tipping the bottle to your mouth, I caught sight of the table leg with its pale circle.

Suddenly, everything from that evening came flooding back. Alex's anger. His strength and belief in himself. It might not be today, or tomorrow... or even next month, but he would do it again. I knew he would. The next time I answered him back or looked at him a certain way. When an interview with a suspect hadn't gone the way he'd intended or because he was simply bored.

I watched your rosebud mouth pull at the teat, your eyes on mine. Wondering if Corinne had told him yet. What she'd said if she had. How could I have been so stupid to have thought we had a connection? Just because she hadn't been as crass as the others at that dinner party. Had paid me a little attention.

Lucky you... for being the chosen one.

How could I have been so naive?

There was still a lot of milk left in your bottle and I willed you to drink faster. I felt vulnerable sitting there, the clock in the kitchen ticking down minutes I didn't have. I should have been deciding what to do... where to go. Using the time you were feeding to clear my head and formulate a proper plan, but my head was filled with white noise and I couldn't think straight. My panic throwing too many questions at me. Ones to which I had no answer.

All I knew was I had to leave him. Soon. Today, if possible.

At the bottom of my bag by my feet was the leaflet I'd grabbed from the police station. With my free hand, I dug it out and looked at it again. ARE YOU SCARED OF YOUR PARTNER? All I had to do was call the number. They'd know a place I could take you... somewhere he wouldn't find us. I had to believe it.

But before I could do anything more, the front door slammed. Alex was home early. I stiffened. Shoved the leaflet between the cushions of the settee before he could see.

He was standing in the doorway, legs apart, feet planted, looking at us both. I forced myself not to look away, terrified he'd hear the giveaway thump of my heart against my ribcage.

Something about him looked different, and it took me a moment to realise what it was. He was wearing his police uniform, something he never did, preferring to leave his fleece and work shirt, even his boots, in his locker. Stuffing them into a bag if he needed to bring them home to wash. *Safer that way*, he'd said. *Less chance of trouble.*

Yet, here he was, his black epaulettes with the three chevron stripes denoting his rank of sergeant contrasting with the crisp whiteness of his shirt. His boots polished. His peaked cap with its braiding pulled low on his head. Something had made him come home in a hurry. Me.

'What are you doing?' It was more than a question; it was an accusation.

I looked down at Megan, forcing my voice to stay steady. 'I was feeding the baby.'

'Feeding the baby,' he repeated.

'Yes.'

His eyes remained on mine too long, and I shifted in my seat. Did he know? Could he guess what I'd been about to do? But how could he?

Alex's expression was closed to me. I had no idea what he was thinking.

'Would you like me to make you a coffee?' I said in desperation.

'Why the fuck would I want coffee? Is that really why you think I'm here?'

And with those words I knew that Corinne had told him everything. It was why he'd come home in the middle of the day when his shift wasn't due to finish for another few hours. I waited. Hands sweating. My heart beating into the silence. Even you were quiet, Megan, as though you could sense something was wrong.

He said nothing more but crossed the room, his heavy boots leaving faint imprints on the carpet. He stopped in front of me.

'They all know what you're like, you know... down at the

station.' He looked down at me, the peak of his cap shadowing his eyes. 'That having the baby put a terrible strain on your mental health. How the demands of being a mother have affected your judgement. Made you...' He stopped and smiled to himself. A smile of someone who had all the power. All the control. 'Made you imagine things. Create scenarios in your head that aren't true.'

The breath left my body. Would he really have done such an awful thing? But of course he would. All this time, he'd been setting me up to fail in any attempt I might make to tell someone the truth. Any complaint I made turned against me – poor Alex, having to live with a woman who was struggling. Who was delusional.

And, if it went further, he would know who to call. What to say. How to twist the evidence to make it look like it was me who was in the wrong, not him.

'I feel sorry for her having a mother like you.' The muscles of his face were tight, his words sorrowful. Directed at the most tender part of me. 'One who lies. One who'd rather whine and complain than support her partner.'

Without warning, Alex grabbed me by the upper arm. Pulled me towards him so I was half standing and put his lips close to my ear so there was no danger of me missing what he was going to say next.

'I don't ever want to hear that you've been up at the station again. Spreading your vicious lies.' Below his police cap, a vein pulsed in his temple. 'If you do, no one's going to believe you. Understand?'

His fingers were digging into my arm.

'Yes. Yes, I understand.'

'Good. I'm glad we're on the same page.' He let go of my arm, and I sank back down, cradling your head. He sat too and with gentle fingers tucked a strand of hair behind my ear.

Traced the curve of my cheek. 'Glad we've sorted out that misunderstanding.'

I closed my eyes. Turned my head away, imagining a life without him in it. Tomorrow I would ring that number.

Tomorrow I'd be safe.

TWENTY-TWO

MEGAN

Now

The strap of Megan's school bag is digging into her shoulder, and she stops to adjust it, letting some of the other kids pass her. In no hurry to get home.

Today had been terrible. She hadn't been able to concentrate in any of her classes and had lost count of how many times she'd been told off for not listening. The problem was, it had been impossible to keep her mind on her work and even in the lessons she liked, it had wandered – trying to find a solution to her problem. When, or even whether, she should tell her mum. And, if she did, how much she should own up to. Was telling her she'd found the newspaper article enough? Or should she admit that the previous night she'd reached out to her dad, found him on Facebook and sent him a friend request?

She carries on walking, remembering her excitement at seeing his face on her phone. It hadn't been hard to trace him. She knew it was possible he still lived in Birmingham, and when she'd searched for his name, Alex Garman, it had thankfully brought up fewer results than she'd feared.

Her father had been recognisable straight away by the epaulettes on the shoulders of his white shirt – an unusual choice of clothing, she couldn't help thinking, considering it was his personal profile. He must be proud of his job. His uniform.

Megan looks down at the stupid uniform *she* has to wear. She's always hated it: the black jumper with the school logo that makes all the girls look as though they have no shape. The wide box pleats of the skirt that refuse to straighten after she's undone the button and rolled the waist over twice to shorten it. At Earthbound, there had been no rules. No uniforms. Lessons had been casual: taking place, with some of the other kids, at the Formica table of a caravan, around a fire on the grass in front of their modest homes or on a walk with Amity or one of the other adults. She preferred it like that.

Ahead of Megan is her road, the fronts of the houses nothing to write home about, the modern, open space inside and the vast windows overlooking the sea not obvious from this side. Only the cars parked in front of the double garages hinting at the wealth of the owners.

Before the row of houses starts, there is a stretch of pebbled wasteland leading down to the beach and the boardwalk. Megan crosses the road and crunches over the stones. When she reaches the interpretation board with its pictures of red-beaked oystercatchers and white-tailed bumblebees, she leans against it and slides off her shoe. Feels around the cuff of her sock to find the spiky thing that's been pricking her ankle since she left school.

She rests her hand on the weathered frame of the board, and puts her shoe back on, her eyes skimming the backs of the houses until they find hers, sunlight glinting off its huge windows. The bulldozed house next to it looking like a missing tooth in a mouth full of white concrete and steel. She's not keen to go home while her mum is in her weird mood, but she has no choice. As she walks, she takes care not to step on the cracks that separate each board – a game she used to play when she was younger. Anything to waste time.

It wouldn't be so bad if Sean was home, but he's had to stay another day, maybe two. If he was here, he'd know what to do, what to say to snap her mum out of the odd mood she's in. With him here, her mum would be less nervy. Less jumpy. Settling to her painting, or whatever it is she does while Sean's at work and she's at school. Not spending her time forever looking out of the window. Not waking Kitty from a nap before she's ready, to hold her close to her chest, her hand on her sister's curly head, muttering words Megan can't hear.

After Kitty had been born, her mum had taken a while to adjust to motherhood again. Jumping at the slightest noise. Not wanting to leave the house or care for the baby. Post-partum depression the doctor had called it. It had been several weeks before the medication she'd been given had taken effect and, until then, it had felt like both she and Sean had been walking on eggshells. Unsure how to be around her. Their offers of help rebuffed. When, at last, her mum had emerged from the dark fog that had wrapped itself around her, they had both been relieved.

Please don't let it be happening again.

Megan steps off the boardwalk and sits on the stones beside a clump of pink mallow. She takes her phone out of her school bag and clicks onto Facebook. Searches in her notifications to see if her dad has accepted her friend request. He hasn't and her mood sinks lower. Why hasn't he? The article she'd found had been written a year after her mum had left him. He missed her – why say it if he didn't mean it? Surely that means he misses her still. Would want to meet her.

Her father's face stares back at her from his profile picture: he's older than in the article, but there's something in the dark eyes that strikes her as it had then. A determination in them. A confidence. For an old guy, he's still good-looking. His hair shorter. A little greyer. He looks at home in his uniform. Stares out from the screen as though he's daring anyone to question him.

His profile is set so that only friends can see his posts and it frustrates her. She wants to know what he's doing. How he lives and what his hobbies are. Whether he ever talks about the past and the baby who was taken from him. For those were the words he'd used in the article – *taken from him* – as though she was a possession.

Pushing the thought away, she clicks off Facebook and opens Instagram instead. Waits for her page to open before scrolling through the photos she's taken. Photos of the beach. Of the sea as flat as a millpond, the row of wind turbines looking like sentries. Another of the sun setting over the beach huts near the town.

Thinking she hears the sound of her back gate opening, Megan quickly clicks off the app, opening it again when she sees she's mistaken. That it was only the wind rattling the latch. Her mum would kill her if she knew she was on Instagram. Had made her promise she would never waste her time on social media. When she'd asked her why, her reply had been that Megan would just have to trust her and the subject had ended with a big fat full stop. She hadn't cared when she was younger, hadn't been bothered with all that stuff, but it's different now she's older. Everyone is on social media and why should she be any different.

Megan flicks through another few photographs before clicking off her phone. She leans back on her elbows and closes her eyes. Inhales the air through her nose. It smells of the sea... of stones warmed by the late afternoon sunshine. Her stomach rumbles, and she wonders what's for dinner. Yesterday, she'd had to make do with leftover chicken and some salad she'd found in the fridge. Her mum had said she wasn't hungry.

Very slowly, Megan counts to ten, and when she gets there,

she pushes herself to her feet. Hoisting her school bag onto her shoulder, she walks across the stones to the boardwalk, waiting for a mother with a pushchair to pass by before crossing over it and heading for the gate in their wall.

As she lets herself onto the patio, closing the gate behind her, she looks up. Through the fronds of the palm, she sees her mum as she has many times before. Standing in her studio, her brush to the painting in front of her. Kitty in a bouncy chair beside her.

Megan studies her, wondering what it is that causes her mother to press the front of her forearm to her forehead. What she's painted on that flat white surface. More sea, she presumes. More boring sky. It's hard to see clearly, as the sunlight's shining on the glass, but, as Megan watches, her mum stands back from the canvas, covering her face with the palms of both hands. As though unable to stand the sight of what's in front of her.

Megan turns away, not wanting to see. Apart from that time after Kitty was born, she'd always thought of her mum as strong. Now the vulnerability she's shown recently scares her... leaves her wondering where that leaves *her*. What's clear is she can never tell her mum what she's done. Not unless she wants to make things worse.

Alex will have to remain her secret.

Her mum drops her hands, and Megan steps back into the shadows of the oleander, not wanting to be seen. As she waits for her mum to move away from the sliding doors, she sees that the fat buds in the leaves that hide her from view have produced their first flower. It's something her mum would celebrate, seeing as how, every year in November, she and Sean have to drag it, in its giant pot, into the sunroom so the winter frosts don't get it. She wonders whether she's seen it, but, from the look of her mum now, it's clearly the last thing on her mind.

Megan snaps the pink flower head from its stalk and tosses it into the swimming pool, watching as it drifts into the centre on the breeze, its petals turning transparent. Taking her phone out of her pocket, she brings it to life, then kneels beside the water. Then she opens her camera and takes a photo of the bloom. Adds a few hashtags: #shorehambeach #swimmingpool #homesweethome before posting it to Instagram.

Waiting for the likes to come in.

TWENTY-THREE

ELISE

Now

Since the article was pushed through my letterbox, since Sean went to Newcastle, I haven't been able to paint. There are two commissions for watercolours waiting to be started, and I need more seascapes for the exhibition at the Ropetackle Centre. Yet, each time I've entered my studio, lifted the paper I stretched the night before onto my tabletop easel, and tried to start, something has stopped me. An invisible hand staying my brush.

I hoped that today would be different, but it's happened again.

In front of me are the photographs I've taken over the last few weeks. The sea in all its moods: in some, flecks of sunlight gild the surface of the water, in others the sea is so dark, the waves so huge, you feel you could drown in them. I select the one I think my client would like best and push the others to the side. The photograph should be easy to replicate, but as I paint a wash over the surface of the paper, and add more colour, letting it bleed into it, as I layer the blue hues, manipulate the darkness and saturation of the pigment with more water, the result is flat. No life in it. The techniques I've used successfully for years letting me down for the first time.

I step back and cover my face. What's wrong with me?

But I know what it is. Instead of the cool blue calmness I need to create this seascape, there's a red-hot anger inside of me. Because everything has been in vain. All the things I've done, all I've fought for in the last fifteen years, could come crashing down like a house of cards.

It's not just anger, though, it's fear.

At night when I lie in my bed, a bed that feels so huge without Sean in it, it takes me an age to fall asleep. And when, eventually, in the small hours, I manage to drift off, exhaustion dragging me under, the nightmares I used to have return. Bringing it all back. If only I could rid myself of the thought that Alex is out there somewhere, biding his time.

Yesterday, on the phone, I'd told Sean I wanted to move. That I thought the house was too big. Too empty. I could stop in at the estate agents. Ask them to send through some properties – a small village in the country, maybe. One with a church and a pub and neighbours rather than houses that were unoccupied like the ones next to ours. Desperate for him to agree. I didn't tell him the real reason was the wide expanse of glass windows that were open to anyone who cared to look. But Sean had just laughed. Said we'd never find a place as fabulous as this. And how could he windsurf in the country?

Lifting the board with the painting off the easel, I stare at what I've done. The colours are all wrong. Everything's wrong. Alex has ruined this for me too. I'll never be rid of him... never. Whatever I do.

With a swift movement, I rip the watercolour from the board and shove it into the wastepaper bin. Unused canvases of all sizes are leaning against the wall, and I pick one up and prop it on the easel. I reach for the tin of acrylic paints I love so much, and with angry, shaking fingers that make the task diffi-

cult, prise open the lid. I grab the reds. The purples. The black.
Then, turning my back to the sea, I squeeze globs of colour onto
the palette and with no thought, no care, begin to paint. Wildly.
Madly. All the hatred pushing from the very core of me into my
fingertips. Guiding my brush. Creating my picture. My memory
of Alex.

There's a bang and my hand stills. I'm back in my studio,
dragged from my feverish painting and into the present, as
though from a deep sleep. A dream I didn't know I was having.
Reality comes crashing in. Megan's home from school. For those
few frenzied minutes, I'd forgotten about her.

I stare at the painting, knowing she can't see it. Mustn't.
She's already far too interested in her past. Too keen to know
her father. The door to my studio is closed, but in the building's
vast open-plan first floor, you can hear every footstep on the
wooden floor. Every open and shut of a door.

I turn from the easel, my back blocking the painting I've
done from anyone who might decide to come into my studio.
Hold my breath.

The footsteps stop outside the door, and I wait. Frozen. I've
always had secrets from my daughter, but now, more than ever
before, I have to keep them. No good will come from her
knowing the truth. Knowing what a terrible father she'd had.

Anger floods me again, as it always does when I think
of him.

He didn't deserve you. *Doesn't* deserve you. It's what I tell
myself every day. What I *have* to tell myself.

Sean is worth a thousand of him. A million. How I wish he
wasn't over three hundred miles away but here with us now –
leaving clothes on the bedroom floor, the toilet seat up, an
empty tea caddy when he's used the last bag. None of this I care
about because for the last eight years he's made me feel safe.
Made me feel I can't be such a bad person if he loves me that
much. Just one more night without him. Just one.

The footsteps move on. Megan's going to her bedroom. I close my eyes and let out a breath. Thank God.

Leaving the painting, I go to the table where my paints are and pull open the drawer beneath. Inside is the old wooden box, filled with half-used tubes of oil paint, where I've hidden the newspaper article. Lifting the wooden tray containing the top layer of paints, I put it aside, then take out the torn page.

There's a blast of music from Megan's room and my eyes flick to the door then back to the eyes that stare out at me from the photograph. You made me do it, Alex. You gave me no choice. I trace a finger over the baby's face, feeling again that tug of love. I shouldn't keep it in case Megan finds it, but something stops me getting rid of it. Something I can't explain.

Stuffing the page back into the box, I shove the tray of paints back on top, but before I slam the drawer closed, my fingers close over the Stanley knife I keep in there. The metal handle is cold against my palm as I take it back to the easel where my painting is drying. I stare at the canvas, all the hurt, all the fear, all the agony rushing back.

Before I know what I'm doing, I draw back my hand and lunge at the painting, dragging the blade down Alex's face. Through his eyes. His nose. His mouth. The blade scarring him.

Again.

And again.

And again.

Wishing I'd never met him. Wishing he were dead.

TWENTY-FOUR

ELISE

Then

'This is where you and your baby will sleep, Elise.'

The woman, who had told me her name was Louise, stepped back so I could go through.

I felt numb. My body functioning without my brain being a part of the decision-making. Limbs moving on autopilot. I was still in shock. Still stunned that I'd gone through with it: filled just one small rucksack and left the flat while Alex was at work. As I'd driven here, the car's temperature gauge slowly dropping, I'd almost turned back – knowing it wouldn't be long before he discovered what I'd done. Terrified he'd find me, even though the woman on the end of the phone had told me he wouldn't look for me here. First, he'd try my mum's. Phoebe's. Other people I'd left behind from a past I could barely remember.

I had you in the sling now, bound to me tightly, and as I pressed my lips to your head, hoping the smell of you would calm me, I took in the room. It was medium-sized, with a sink at one end and a single bed under a window that looked out over a

small courtyard filled with children's play equipment that had
seen better days.

'You'll be safe here.' Louise touched a hand to my arm. 'You
and your baby... you need to know that.'

'Thank you.'

How I wanted to believe her.

I stared at the magnolia walls. They looked newly painted,
the patterned carpet freshly hoovered. Sunlight shone through a
window framed by cheerful curtains – bright sunflowers against
a dark background. Someone had made an effort to make the
room feel homely, but the front of the building had told another
story. It was plain, modern, built of red brick and standing in an
unremarkable road of similar buildings. Blank windows, blink-
ered by blinds, looked out onto a busy road and a CCTV
camera, that I wouldn't have noticed had it not been pointed out
to me, stared down at a solid-looking door. One that, once
inside, could be securely locked. There had been no sign to indi-
cate what the place was. Nothing to single it out from the other
drab two-storey buildings on the street.

'Megan can sleep here.' Louise indicated the cot beside the
bed. It wasn't new but looked clean and sturdy. A cellulose
blanket was neatly folded on the end bars. 'The mattress is new
and all the linen's fresh. It's going to be cold tonight, so I've put
a spare blanket in the wardrobe for you in case you need it.'

'Thank you,' I said again, as though all other words had
been left behind in Alex's flat.

'I'll leave you to settle in then. The bathroom's just along
the corridor if you need it. There's a communal sitting room and
kitchen at the end, but you have a kettle and a small fridge for
milk next to the bed. Just like a hotel really.' Louise gave a bark
of laughter at her own joke, then, seeing my expression,
stopped, her hand over her mouth. 'I'm sorry, love, that was in
bad taste. Ignore me. I always did have a big gob.'

She had kind brown eyes and skin the colour of burnt

caramel. Ropes of thick black hair hung down her back and large silver hoops swung from her earlobes. What I wanted, more than anything, was for her to take me in her large, soft arms and let me weep. But I stayed where I was. If I gave in to weakness now, I'd never pull myself back.

Louise pointed to a box beside the bed.

'There are nappies, toiletries and other bits and bobs you might need in there. Things for the kiddie.' She folded the key fob into my hand. 'We can apply for housing benefit to cover the housing cost, but we'll need to charge you five pound fifty a week to cover utilities. Also, I'm afraid we'll need a weekly deposit of five pounds that we'll return to you when you hand back your key at the end of your stay. Is that okay?'

I felt myself tearing up. Overwhelmed, yet scared to show any emotion in case it took me over and refused to let go. Other people came to places like this. Not people like me. Yet, even as I thought it, I knew it was ridiculous. Abuse didn't recognise class or colour or age. It could happen to anyone.

'If that's a problem, please tell me now and I can see what I can do.'

'I'm sorry.' I blinked away the tears. 'No, that's fine... really.'

But she'd seen. Knew there was something else bothering me.

'Was there anything you wanted to ask me? It's what I'm here for, after all.'

I looked up at her through wet eyes, hardly daring to put my fear into words in case it made it happen. 'What if he comes here? Alex... my partner.'

'He won't. And even if he did, there's nothing he could do about it. Try not to worry, love. You're safe here.' She picked up a baby's bib from the box beside her and studied it, smiling at the yellow chick that was embroidered on it. 'I'll be your key worker for as long as you're here and you can ask me anything. I'll meet with you once a week to make sure you're getting the support you need, but you can come to me any time.' Dropping the bib back into the basket, Louise walked over to the kettle and flicked it on. 'Now, you look done in. Make yourself a drink, and if you're hungry, there are some sandwiches in that paper bag on the table beside the bed. I know you probably don't feel like it, but eating something will help... keeps the sugar levels up. When you're ready, come and find me.'

'How will I know where you are?'

Her laugh was deep and throaty. 'Believe me, I'm so bloody loud, you won't be able to miss me... ask anyone. And remember, lovey, all the women here in the refuge know what you're going through. Okay, their experiences might be a bit different to yours, but they've all been through something similar. They wouldn't be here otherwise. They'll understand how you're feeling. Don't be afraid to talk to them and promise me you'll remember one thing.'

'What?'

'That none of this is your fault. Whatever has brought you here, you've done nothing wrong.'

She left the room, shutting the door behind her. The sun, which had been shining when I'd arrived, had gone in and now the room looked gloomy. I slumped down on the bed and tipped my head back. There was a damp patch on the ceiling, the shape of Australia, and when I lowered my gaze, it was impossible not to see the stain on the carpet by the sink. The cracked tile behind the tap.

With Louise gone, my emptiness returned. What on earth had I done? Would I ever survive this? More importantly, would Alex ever let me?

But I had to be strong. I had to remind myself I was safe here. It was what the woman on the phone had told me. What Louise had told me too.

My stomach rumbled, not surprising seeing as I hadn't eaten anything since the night before. Reaching across to the paper bag on the table, I felt inside and drew out the packet of sandwiches. They were cheese and tomato, the juice from the tomato seeping through the white bread, and when I picked one up, it bent in my fingers. But I was too hungry, too grateful, to care.

When I'd finished, I unbound you from the sling and offered you the bottle I'd brought with me. Glad when you took it from me and drank it thirstily, your eyes on mine. It wouldn't be long before I'd need to start you on solids, but I'd cross that bridge when I came to it.

When the bottle was empty, I sat, my eyes on the door. I couldn't stay in here for ever. Lifting you onto my shoulder, I opened the door and looked out. The floor outside my room was laminate, scuffed here and there with the tyre marks of the pushchairs and folded strollers that were parked outside a few of the doors. Now I was outside my room, the sounds of the refuge were more obvious: mothers chatting, a child's cry, laughter. All coming from the open door at the end of the corridor.

I walked towards the sound, a moth to a light. I didn't want to be alone any more. I needed to be with people. Needed to know that I could do this. Carry it through. When I got to the door, I hesitated. Looked in.

The room reminded me of the common room in my university hall of residence. At one end there was a large rectangular table, at the other a worn settee and a scattering of mismatched chairs. A woman of around my age, fair hair tied into a high ponytail, lay along the length of the settee, a toddler on her lap. An older woman, with a chic dark bob and perfectly applied makeup, had the chair opposite. On one of the long walls, a large widescreen TV flashed images, the sound turned down. Some film involving a car chase. Two teenage boys of around thirteen or fourteen lay on the floor on their fronts, chins cupped in their hands, their eyes glued to the subtitles.

Not knowing what else to do, I coughed. All eyes turned to me, including the boys.

'Fuck, you made me jump.' The blonde girl's hand was pressed to her heart. 'Excuse my French.'

'Sorry.'

'You don't need to apologise. It's just we're all a bit jumpy here. Come in. That's a pretty baby you've got there.'

'Thank you.'

'Take a pew.' The girl made room for me on the settee. 'Haven't seen you before. When did you arrive?'

'This morning.' Already time was playing tricks on me. Making me feel as though it was days ago I left Alex, not just a few hours.

'I'm Lara, as in *Tomb Raider*, and this is Jack.' She ruffled his hair, then wagged a finger at the older boys. 'The two big ones are Tanya's.'

The dark-haired woman smiled. It made her face beautiful, but there was a sadness behind her eyes. 'They're twins. Peas in a pod. Should be at school but... you know.'

I didn't, but I could guess. Somewhere, outside this place, was a husband or partner who could wait for them outside the school gates. Take her boys from her at any time. I didn't blame her for wanting to keep them with her where they were safe.

'Don't look so worried. They'll help you here. See you right.' Lara offered me one of the Twix bars from the packet she was holding, but I shook my head.

'Thanks, but I've just eaten.'

'Please yourself.' She took a bite, a flake of chocolate dropping onto her T-shirt. 'People get the wrong impression of places like this, think they're like some kind of institution, but they're not. We can come and go as we please here, just as long as we aren't stupid about it. The only rule is we have to be in by nine thirty so they know we're safe and can lock up. You get used to it, don't you, Tan? And they help you with stuff you don't know – legal stuff. My support worker is helping me prepare for my child contact battle.' She looked down at Jack. 'I'm not good with forms. Haven't a bloody clue about the language I'll need to fight him in the court.'

My fingers balled into fists. Court. It was something I hadn't thought of – that Alex might go down a legal route to get custody of you. Payback for taking you from him.

'I'm sorry.'

'No need. Wish I'd never put the bastard's name on the birth certificate now. Gives him automatic parental responsibility. It's going to be a long fight.'

My heart sank. I'd somehow presumed that because we weren't married, Alex wouldn't have the same rights as he would if we'd tied the knot. How naïve I'd been.

'Look, I know it's scary, but you've done the right thing, running from the bastard.' Lara picked the flake of chocolate off her T-shirt and licked her fingers. 'Yeah, I know what you're thinking – that I don't know anything about you, but you wouldn't be here if he wasn't one. My advice is to take each day as it comes. Listen to what your support worker says and plan a new life for yourself... one without him in it. One where you're not forever looking over your shoulder. Everything's going to be all right now you're here.' She looked at the dark-haired woman for her agreement. 'Ain't that right, Tan?'

Tanya nodded. Repeated what everyone else had said. 'It is. You and your baby are safe here.'

If only I'd known how wrong they were.

TWENTY-FIVE

ELISE

Then

There was shouting. The sound of a door banging. I sat up in bed, my heart hammering, for a moment unsure where I was.

The room wasn't dark, the thin curtains unable to trap the moonlight. Slowly, as I made out the shape of the sink attached to the far wall, the box containing baby toys that must once have belonged to another child, your wooden cot next to my bed, I remembered where I was. And with that knowledge, the memories came flooding back.

I lowered my hand to the side of the bed, feeling the rough material of the rucksack I'd stuffed with enough of our clothes to get by for a few days, the outside pocket harbouring the envelope I'd filled with my important documents: our birth certificates, my driving licence and national insurance number, some cash I'd taken from the small amount of savings I had in the only account that was in my sole name. A separate carrier bag for your nappies, bottles and formula was pushed under the bed to make space.

More raised voices. A woman's now, coming from the corridor. *For God's sake give it a rest. Some of us are trying to sleep.*

Checking the shouting hadn't wakened you, I slipped my feet out of the covers and crept to the door, pressing my ear against it. More banging, More shouting. What was happening?

I unlocked my door, pressed on the handle and pushed it open, just enough to peer out. I wasn't the only one. Others were doing the same. Two women I'd not seen before, hair tousled from bed, one with a baby on her shoulder, were standing side by side, whispering. Another, further down, was zipping a hoodie over her pyjamas as though about to investigate.

I stepped into the corridor.

'Do you know what's going on?'

The woman with the baby shook her head. 'Not really. But I know the police are here.'

She pointed to a window further down the corridor, which looked out onto the road. A roller blind was covering it, but, even so, it was still possible to see flashing blue lights.

Police.

It felt as though my heart had stopped.

'What do they want?'

The woman shrugged. 'How the hell should I know?'

Our bedrooms were in a purpose-built wing to the right of the main building. I'd thought that the shouting was coming from inside, but now I realised it wasn't. I hurried to the window and lifted the side of the blind, just enough to be able to see. Further along, in the main part of the building, a woman was leaning out of another window, her ample bust resting on the window frame. Her dark hair wild. Her face angry.

'You have no right to be here. Come back when you have a warrant.'

I recognised the voice. Louise.

Pulling back the blind further, I pressed my face against the cold corridor wall, hoping I'd see who was hammering at the front door. But the lights from the patrol car were blinding. All I could see was a figure in a dark uniform.

His voice came through the glass. Through the bricks and mortar. Through my body to my very soul. Chilling me. Terrifying me.

I didn't need to see him to know who he was.

'I don't need a warrant to see my kid. Open this fucking door before I break it down.'

I dropped the blind. Flattened myself against the wall, my palms pressed to my face. Not caring that the other women were staring at me. The only focus of my attention, the insistent voice in my head.

You have to leave.

You're not safe here.

Despite what I'd been told, I'd always known he'd find us, and he had. He was a policeman. That was what he did. Find people. Hunt them down.

I felt a hand on my arm. It made me jump.

'Are you okay?'

It was Tanya, the woman with the dark hair and the teenage boys. An oversized cardigan covered her pyjamas. Her feet were bare.

'No, not really.' It was an understatement. I was unable to move from where I was standing. Rooted to the spot by my rising panic.

The voice came again. Alex's voice.

'Shut the fuck up. I'm the police. I make the rules not you.'

Louise replied, something I couldn't hear, a last thud on the door and then there was silence. I waited, my eyes screwed tight. Counted to ten, over and over. Not daring to believe he'd gone. When, at last, I forced my eyes to open again, the lights were no longer flashing through the material of the blind.

Tanya looked out. 'It's all right. He's gone.'

She didn't ask me anything more. In here, everyone had their own story. The policeman hammering on the door was mine, and she knew better than to pry. Had no need. All the answers were written in the pallor of my skin. The tremble of my hand as I pushed my hair from my face.

The other women had gone back into their rooms, but Tanya hadn't moved from the window.

'You're afraid he'll come back.' It was a statement not a question.

I nodded. My eyes still fixed on the blind.

I didn't know when. Later tonight? Tomorrow morning? It made no difference. Alex had made a mistake coming here in the heat of the moment, but once he'd had time to cool down, once his head was clear, he'd think of a legitimate reason to return... to demand Louise let him in. And maybe, this time, she would have no choice but to comply.

Tanya stood looking at me, her face a mixture of emotions: pity, concern, understanding. Eventually, she drew in a deep breath.

'Wait here.'

Leaving me in the corridor, she went back into her room. A few minutes later, she reappeared, a piece of paper in her hand.

'Take this,' she said, pressing it into my palm. 'Do you have cash?'

'Some.'

'That's good. I'd have lent you some, but...' she looked back into the room '... the boys. You know. This is the number of a taxi. You may find it useful in the future. How did you get here?'

'I drove.'

'You shouldn't have. Number plates can be checked. Your partner's a policeman. He might well have people looking out for it.'

'I left while he was at work and got here before he would

have finished. In any case, Louise told me to park it around the back where it can't be seen from the road. I did think about taking a cab, but it would have been too dangerous. Alex knows most of the taxi drivers in the city. Checking their bookings would have been the first thing he'd have done once he'd discovered I'd left with Megan.' I was close to tears again. 'I thought I'd be safe here... that he wouldn't find me. That's what they told me.'

Tanya looked at me with sympathy. 'Where's your phone?'

'In my room.'

'Get it for me.'

'Why do you want it?'

'Please, just get it. Quickly now. Number plates aren't the only thing that can be traced.'

'Okay.'

With a growing dread, I went back to my room. Checking first to see that you were still asleep, as you'd taken longer to settle, I fished my phone from my bag and ran back into the corridor.

Tanya was waiting for me. 'Let's have a look. Unlock it first.'

I did as she asked and waited as she trawled through my apps. She frowned. 'Just as I thought.'

'What is it? What have you found?'

She tapped the screen with her nail. 'Look, it's here. A tracker app. They're easy to put on. My husband did it with my phone.'

She handed the phone back to me. 'Get rid of this and only use your car if you have to. If you decide to use a cab, the number I gave you is for my brother. He's a taxi driver. Works the smaller towns and doesn't often come into the city, so it's unlikely your guy would know him. If you do ever need him, tell him you're a friend of mine and that he isn't to let on to anyone where he's taken you or even that he's taken you anywhere at all. Dave will understand. He's seen it all before.'

Her face closed for a moment and her fingertips rose to touch the soft skin below her eye, remembering. And, in this gesture, I understood. Our stories might not be so different, after all.

'And this?' I asked. There was something else written on the scrap of paper. A name.

Earthbound.

Tanya looked at me from under her shiny dark fringe. Her face deadly serious.

'It's where you can go,' she said. 'If there's nowhere else.'

'I don't know what you mean?'

Before she could answer, the door to the room behind Tanya opened wider. 'Mum? What are you doing?'

Tanya turned, distracted. One of her boys was standing there scratching at his arm.

'Sorry, love. Wait there.'

She stepped back into her room, and I heard the murmur of voices. A second or two later, she came out again. Put her hand on my shoulder and looked down the corridor to make sure no one was there.

'Earthbound is a special place. It's where people go...' the pressure of her fingers on my shoulder became firmer '... if they want to become invisible. It's what you want, isn't it?'

I nodded. It was what I wanted more than anything.

'I'll leave you to think about it.' She gave a small smile. 'Good luck, Elise. Whatever you decide.'

I had to leave this place, that much was clear. I had no choice. Alex *would* come back. And, when he did, he would make sure everyone knew what a bad mother I was. How unstable. Not fit to have access to you, let alone custody. And, whatever anyone said, I couldn't trust a system that Alex was a part of. If I had to fight him for you, I'd stand no chance.

Tanya had gone back into her room, closing the door behind her, and I did the same. Trying not to wake you, I lifted you from your cot and wrapped you in the sling, tying the ends around my waist. When you were secure, I hoisted my heavy rucksack onto my back and hurried down the corridor. The plastic bag containing your bottles and formula banging against my legs as my shaking fingers struggled with the locks on the door.

The night was cold as I stepped into it. Looking over my shoulder to make sure I was alone, I hurried to the car. I opened the passenger door, leant in and strapped you into your car seat, then I went round to the other side and got in.

It was only as I was securing my seat belt that a thought occurred to me. One that made my blood run cold. I'd locked the door when I'd left the car earlier, I knew I had, but the car had been open when I put you in your seat.

When I felt the weight of his hand on my shoulder, I didn't jump. I'd already worked it out and fear had made me numb.

Alex's eyes locked with mine in the rear-view mirror and he smiled. 'Going somewhere, baby?'

TWENTY-SIX
ELISE

Then

There's no point in dwelling on what happened next. What Alex said in the car. What he did after he shoved me through the front door of the flat.

All I know is that from that moment on, I lost all hope. This would be my life now... Alex would make sure of that. The refuge had been my one and only chance to get away from the power he wielded over me, but he'd found me. He would *always* find me. It's what he'd told me time and time again, and now I believed it totally. He didn't care about me. He didn't even care about you, Megan. All he cared about was maintaining the control he had over us. That and his reputation.

How dare I challenge the first.

How dare I threaten the second.

Every day he checked my phone: my messages, the calls I'd made – not that there were many as I had no friends. Was estranged now from my mother. Even a call to the dentist warranted an explanation. A trip to the park with you questioned. I was a disgrace and could no longer be trusted. It's what he told me every morning when I woke up. Every night when I went to bed.

Alex had segued from partner to gaoler in one simple move, and there was nothing I could do about it. All I could do was be the best mother to you that I could. Make sure you knew you were loved. Treasured. It was my job to keep you safe because I'd seen the look of irritation in his eyes when you cried. Seen how the muscles of his cheek worked when you were hungry or tired and needed to let me know. Taking my attention from him. Becoming my first priority. Shifting him down the pecking order.

It had been two weeks since I'd tried to leave, and the days had taken on a familiar pattern. If Alex was on an early shift, I'd listen to him as he showered and dressed, only letting out my breath once I'd heard the door click shut. If he was on a late, I'd lie in the darkness hoping he'd believe I was asleep. Praying he'd had a good day, that nothing had happened to make him drag me from my bed. Clip the cold metal around my wrist and tighten it. In between those times I carried on. Cleaned and cooked and looked after you. My mind numb. All actions automatic and functional.

I was just ironing one of Alex's shirts, when the door buzzer made my head jerk up. The only people who came to our door were delivery drivers and as far as I knew we weren't expecting anything.

It buzzed again and I put the iron down, checked you were all right in your seat, then I went to open the door. Whoever had pressed the buzzer had got through the front door that led to the communal entrance hall. Was it one of Alex's colleagues? Was this a trick of some sort? I'd come to mistrust everything. Everybody.

The girl who stood on the landing was slight in build. Older than me by a few years with a narrow fine-boned face. She wore no makeup, and her dark hair was pulled back in a ponytail. She wore jeans and a leather jacket despite it being winter, but it wasn't her clothes that my eyes fixed on; it was the baby in her arms.

I glanced behind me to make sure you were okay, then back at the girl. 'Yes?'

She placed a hand on her baby's head. 'I'm Kristen and this is Chloe. I'm sorry, but I don't know *your* name.'

I folded my arms, unsure of where this was going. 'I'm Elise.'

'Alex's girlfriend.'

I nodded, hating the word. Knowing I was many other things to him. 'Yes.'

'Can I come in?'

I painted a bright, artificial smile on my face. 'I'm afraid I'm really busy.'

'It won't take long.' When she smiled, her face was transformed. The hard edges softening. Letting me see how pretty she could be.

'I'm not sure. I'm very—'

'Busy. Yes, you said.' She glanced around the landing. Her smile just a memory. 'Does he have any surveillance? Any cameras?'

'Alex?' My fingers tightened around the door handle. 'No. Not that I know of. What's this about?'

'Not here. Get your baby and meet me at the bus stop across the road. I have things to say, and you need to hear them.'

'I don't know you. I don't know anything about you.'

She looked at me sadly. 'I know. But I want to remedy that. Please, Elise. You need to trust me. I don't mean you any harm. Quite the opposite.'

'All right. Stay there.' I went back into the living room, grabbed my coat from the back of the chair and put it on. Then I got your sling, picked you up from under the arc of swaying animals and wrapped you in it before remembering you hadn't had your milk. Grabbing the bottle from the worktop in the kitchen, I pushed it into the pocket of my coat, then went out to the landing, closing the door behind me.

We didn't speak as we took the stairs down to the entrance hall, but I couldn't help myself from stealing glances at the young woman who walked beside me. Taking in the short tartan skirt, the thick woollen tights and the black leather Dr Martens. The leather jacket that would do little to keep out the cold wind that hit us as we stepped outside.

'Are you warm enough?'

'Believe me.' She gave a half-hearted shrug and pulled up the collar of her jacket. 'I'm used to it. If you need to put food on the table, you'll be prepared to stand outside in all types of weather.'

Unsure of what she meant by that, I hastened my pace so we could get to the bus shelter quicker. The metal seat was cold beneath my legs as I sat down. It would be colder through Kristen's tights.

'Anyway,' she continued. 'It's got to be better than my flat at the moment. The heater's playing up and I need to get the landlord to take a look at it.'

The baby in the woman's arms, Chloe I think she'd said her name was, had started to cry, her face puckering. Kristen bounced her on her knee. Kissed her cheek. 'She's tired, that's all. I'll take her home for a nap after.'

'How old is she?'

'She'll be six months next week. Yours?'

I looked down at you, ran my lips over your hair. 'Five and a bit.'

Kristen looked at you, then away. Concentrating on the cars that moved past us on the road. There was a certain tension in the way she held her body, one I recognised in my own, and it made me curious.

We were the only ones in the shelter, and I guessed a bus

must have turned up just before we arrived. It gave the space between the glass-walls the feel of a confessional.

'What did you come here for? What do you want?'

Kristen didn't reply. Her eyes were fixed on the road outside, making me wonder whether she'd changed her mind. Thought better of whatever it was she'd come to say.

A strong gust of wind thumped against the side of the shelter, making the windows rattle.

'What do you want?' I repeated.

She dragged her eyes away. 'I don't want anything. I just came to warn you... about *him*.'

In that moment, everything around me dissolved, leaving me aware of nothing but my lungs, my ribcage... the simple act of breathing. The desire to leave her here and flee the conversation before she had the chance to say any more was strong, but something stopped me. A sixth sense that told me I'd be better off knowing.

'You mean Alex?'

'Who else would I mean? Of course Alex. Your baby's father.' She ran a finger down her baby's cheek. 'Chloe's too.'

The world stood still, and I gripped at the edge of the cold metal seat to stop myself from falling. Scared I was going to be sick.

'You're lying.'

She looked genuinely surprised. 'Why would I do that?'

'I don't know. Money, jealousy, revenge? There are a thousand reasons.' I was grasping at anything. 'You tell *me*.'

'One of the girls told me he had another woman. I didn't believe it at first, but then why would I? He was so lovely to me. So different from the other men. Considerate. Thoughtful. He said he wanted to save me. Give me a better life. Gave me extra money so I'd be able to rent a better flat. When I fell pregnant with Chloe, I thought all my prayers had been answered.'

I stayed silent. The picture she painted of him was familiar.

This was the Alex I'd fallen in love with. The Alex I no longer knew. As she was speaking, I was piecing bits together. *One of the girls. Different from the other men. Extra money.* I'd started to suspect, but now I knew.

I felt bitterly cold. 'He was visiting with you while he was living with me. He got you pregnant. How could he when...?' I stopped, not sure what I was trying to say. When he'd told me he loved me and only me? When he'd promised me the earth? When he'd said I was the only woman he'd ever want to have children with? Because now I knew he'd never meant any of those things. They were simply what he knew I wanted to hear.

Kristen's cold hand covered mine. 'With Alex it's all an illusion. He chooses his time carefully... his women too. Preys on the vulnerable. He knew I was living alone, struggling to pay my rent... that my mum had thrown me out when I was nineteen and too much for her to handle.'

'How did he know that?'

'He's a police officer. It's not difficult to find these things out. It feeds his ego to be needed, but it also means the women he chooses will be less likely to do anything about it when he shows his true colours. Being in the police gives him respectability. People trust him. Believe him. Listen to me, you need to get away from Alex... as far away as possible. Before he does something that can't be undone.'

'I've tried.' Couldn't she understand?

'Then try harder. I've seen some of the other girls I used to work with. Seen the look in their eyes after he's been with them. A dead look. Not wanting to talk about it when I've asked them. They were scared of him, Elise, really scared, and by the time I made the break, I was scared of him too.'

'Yet, you had his baby?'

'Yes. And that's the difference between us... He doesn't know about Chloe. I left him before I'd begun to show. Seen by then what he was like. How it would be. When he found out I'd told one of the girls about us, he was livid. Told me if I ever said anything to anyone again, he'd cut my tongue out.' She shivered. 'There was a part of me that believed he'd do it too. It's then I knew that those promises he'd made... they meant nothing.'

'Yet, you managed to leave him. How did you do it?' I had to know. Maybe I could do the same.

'As far as Alex was concerned, it was just me, remember. By then I'd found out about you and took a chance that he'd be glad to be shot of me. It would make it easier for him to play happy families, play the doting father.' She gave a wry smile. 'And there were plenty of other girls he could pick up on Soho Road to take my place when the need for something different became too much for him.'

I closed my eyes a second, trying to blot out the picture. 'What I don't understand is why you've come to me now?'

'I'm not sure myself.' She reached across and stroked your hair. 'Maybe it's because these two little ones have a bond. Maybe it's because I feel guilty for not having done something earlier. Something's brewing with Alex. I still see one or two of the girls when I think it's safe to do so, and they're all talking about it. How he's got more...' she searched for the right word '... extreme. Not that the girls involved have said anything, but it's impossible not to see his calling card.' She rubbed at her wrist and shivered. 'I was lucky to get out when I did.'

An elderly lady with a tartan shopping trolley had come into the shelter. She took a seat at the end of the metal bench, and when she smiled at us, I saw the two of us through her eyes. A pair of young mothers waiting for the bus to take them to a baby group or a soft play area. Using the time before the bus's arrival to catch up.

The pain invisible.

The fear too.

A bus pulled up and the elderly lady stood. She smiled at us. 'Is this your one?'

I shook my head. 'No, mine's gone. I missed it.'

She wheeled her trolley to the bus, and I watched as a young man helped her lift it in. It was only as the bus pulled away, I realised how true those words were. The refuge had been my one and only chance.

With a feeling of panic, I reached out to Kristen, clutched at the sleeve of her jacket. 'Will you come again?'

'If you want me to.'

'I do.' I stood up. 'I need to go before Alex gets back.'

Kristen nodded, understanding. 'Take care.'

I hurried across the road, praying that he wouldn't have come home early again, that he wouldn't surprise me as he had before. The tightness around my chest, which I'd come to accept as the norm, loosened a little as I let myself into the flat and saw it was empty. There was a lightness in my step as I put you in your chair and went to fill the kettle.

It was because there was someone out there who knew what I was going through.

Someone who made me feel that I was not quite so alone.

TWENTY-SEVEN

MEGAN

Megan Now

'No phones in class.'

Megan looks up, forgetting for a moment where she is. Her history teacher, Mr Lawrence, is standing by her table, his arm outstretched. The palm of his hand flat.

'I'll have that now, if you don't mind.'

'I'm sorry.' The phone is on her lap. How he saw it she doesn't know. Quickly she blanks the screen. 'I won't look at it again.'

'You won't because it will be in my drawer. From the minute you came in you've spent more time looking at your lap than at your book. Don't think I haven't noticed you have one assignment missing too.'

Megan feels the heat climb up her neck. The rest of her class are looking at her. A couple of the boys are sniggering behind their hands. She's never got on with Mr Lawrence. He has a way of looking at her that makes her feel small. Unimportant.

Mr Lawrence moves closer, his shadow falling across her.

He taps his fingers into his palm. Once. Twice. 'Come on. Phone.'

'Please don't take it.' She presses her mobile against the top of her leg. Knows her voice is embarrassingly pleading. 'It's just today. I promise I won't look at it again.'

'Phone.' His growing impatience is clear from his tone. 'Now.'

'I said I don't want to.' Megan locks eyes with him. She tells herself she mustn't cry. 'I'm waiting for something important.'

This morning, when she'd clicked onto Facebook, the notification on her phone had jumped out at her, making her heart beat faster. Her dad had accepted her friend request!

At first, she'd been stunned. Unsure what to do. She'd checked the door in case her mum should come in and ruin everything – even though she always knocked first – then, in a panic of anticipation, had sent him a message. Nothing elaborate, just a simple *Hi Dad. Thanks for accepting my friend request.* She'd hoped he'd reply before she left for school. Was disappointed when he hadn't.

As she'd walked to school, her eyes had been fixed to the phone's screen. Willing him to reply. Terrified of what he might say if he did. She'd hardly been aware of anything – not the roads she'd crossed nor the people she'd almost walked into. As the building had come into sight, her feet had slowed. She'd hoped he'd reply before it was time to go in, but as she'd crossed the playground, the screen remained stubbornly blank, and she'd had no choice but to follow the others into class.

Each lesson, she'd check to see her teacher wasn't looking before bending to her bag and taking her mobile out. Imagining she'd heard the ping of a message back. Shoulders slumping when she saw it had been nothing but her imagination.

Even though she knew little about his life, she'd tried to persuade herself that Alex had been caught up with work. Too busy catching criminals to get back to her. He'd do it when he was ready.

Anything rather than think he wasn't interested.

Mr Lawrence folds his arms. 'What's so important it can't wait until the end of school?'

His eyes bore into her, making her feel trapped, and she's painfully aware they have an audience.

'It's none of your business.' The words come out before she can stop them. Shocking her.

Naomi, the girl sitting beside her gives a sharp intake of breath. No one speaks to Mr Lawrence like that. No one. Ignoring the voice in her head that is telling her she shouldn't, Megan looks up at him again even though she's scared of what she might see.

Mr Lawrence's face has changed. Darkened.

'I think you'd better leave the class.' There's a chill to his voice. 'I'll be speaking to your mother at the end of the day to let her know what's going on.'

Megan fights back the tears. Drops her phone into her school bag. 'You do that.'

Pushing back her chair, she picks up her bag and leaves the classroom. Scared of what her mum will say. Scared of the lies she'll have to tell her.

They've been silent for the drive home, but once they've parked in their driveway, her mum turns to her.

'Want to tell me what's going on, Megan?'

Megan stares straight ahead. 'Nothing's going on.'

'It's hardly nothing when I get a phone call from the school telling me my daughter has been sent out of her history lesson for being rude to her teacher. I thought I'd misheard when they said it might be better if I came to collect you.' Her mum's fingers tighten on the steering wheel. 'What in the world's come over you? You've never been in trouble before. In fact, at the last parents' evening the teachers were falling over themselves to say how well you were doing. How impressed they were with the effort you were putting in. To put it bluntly, I was embarrassed walking through that door.'

Megan pushes her chin inside her coat. 'He's an idiot. He tried to take my phone and he had no right.'

'He has every right. You're at school to study. It's as simple as that. What gets me is it's so out of character, Megs. Is something wrong? If there is, you know you can tell me.'

Without answering, Megan unbuckles her seat belt. If only her mum knew the truth... that she's the last person she'd be able to tell. She opens the car door and gets out. Then, without looking back, she lets herself into the house and runs up the stairs. Slamming the bedroom door behind her. Hoping against hope her mum won't follow her.

Megan drops her school bag onto the floor. It's only two o'clock and she has no idea what to do with the rest of her day. Throwing herself onto the bed, she folds her arms over her eyes. Why doesn't her dad want to speak to her? What has she done to deserve this silence?

Her phone is on the bed next to her, and when it pings, Megan is too shocked to move. She wants to look, but how will she face the disappointment if it isn't who she hopes it will be? If it isn't *him*.

But if she doesn't look, she reasons, she'll never know.

She pushes herself up and scoots back so she's resting against the headboard. Reaches out her hand and drags her mobile across the covers, waking up the screen and flicking through her apps. When she sees the unread message on Messenger, she forces herself to click on it.

The face of Alex Garman stares back at her from his profile picture. Beside it is his message. *Great you got in touch! I see you call yourself Megan now. Let me know when you get this.*

Megan glances at the door then back at the phone. Quickly, she types a reply.

Hi Dad. I'm here.

She sees he's typing. Waits, with racing heart, for his reply. When it comes, her face breaks into a smile.

I've missed you.

The happiness she feels is because these three small words change everything. They prove that what he'd said in the newspaper article all those years ago was true. But it also confirms what she's come to suspect. That her mum has been lying to her.

She pulls a pillow behind her back and settles more comfortably. Thinks for a moment before writing back.

If her dad is to come back into her life, her mum can't know. She'll have to be careful. Very careful indeed.

TWENTY-EIGHT

ELISE

Now

I'm in the kitchen making soup for supper when Megan comes out of her room. She looks different. Happier – although I can't imagine what could have happened in the hour or so since she flounced into her room to change her mood.

'That smells delicious.'

She comes up to me and puts her arm around me, something she hasn't done in a long time, and it instantly makes me suspicious.

'It's just carrot and coriander. Nothing special.'

Megan drops her arm and hovers. When I glance over at her, I see a telltale flush on her neck above her school T-shirt.

'You're in a good mood.'

She shoots me a look. The old Megan back. 'Can't I be?'

'I don't know. You tell me. I'm just surprised, that's all, after what happened earlier at school.'

I sense Megan bristle. 'Why did you have to bring that up again?'

'Because it's important, Megs.' I look back at the pan, give it a stir. I don't want to fight with her. 'I just need to know it won't happen again.'

'It won't.'

I look at her, only just managing to hide my surprise. 'That's good then. Want to watch a film later? Something Sean would hate if he was here?'

'Why not.' Megan gives me a rare smile and I feel stupidly grateful that we're back on good terms.

Taking a teaspoon from the worktop, I scoop out some soup and taste it. Add some more seasoning. 'Great. I'll call you when this is ready.'

I think she'll go back to her room, but she remains where she is. 'Mum?'

'Yes?'

She leans against the island, one foot resting on the chrome bar of the stool that's beside her. 'If I was to go out one evening after school, would that be okay?'

I turn and look at her. 'To one of your friends'? That should be okay if you let me know when. If it's when Sean's back, I could come and collect you later.'

'You don't have to do that.'

'I do if it's going to be dark. I'm not keen on you walking home alone. When were you thinking of anyway?'

Megan looks away. I think I see a flush on her cheeks, but it might be just the heat from the kitchen.

'I don't know yet.'

She looks on edge. Chews at the skin of her fingernail. Something's going on that she's not telling me.

Suddenly, it all becomes clear. 'It's a boy, isn't it?'

'What?'

'You heard me, Megan. Only a boy would make you glue your eyes to your phone so much that you get thrown out of class.' My skin grows cold imagining some spotty youth with my precious daughter. Pawing her. Persuading her. Making her believe she's said yes when what she's really said is no. 'You know how I feel about it. You're only fifteen and too young to be bothering with boys. Believe me, there'll be plenty of time for that when you're older. More mature and able to think about the consequences—'

I stop. Megan's staring at me as if she doesn't know me. Doesn't like what she sees.

'Because that's what I am, isn't it, Mum? Just a consequence of your actions.'

'That's not what I meant.' I reach for her, wanting to make amends, but she moves out of my reach.

'Leave me alone.'

I hate how she sounds. Miss the days when I'd hold out my arms and she'd run into them as though she belonged there. I'm scared that I might have pushed her further from me.

'Can't you get it into your head that I don't *need* to tell you everything, Mum. I'm my own person not a bloody extension of you.'

I'm shocked at the venom in her words. The harshness.

I stand, hands loose at my sides, wondering, as I've done so many times recently, what I've done wrong. What I've done to make her hate me. Can it really be just the simple difference in our natures... our temperaments? That's what Sean says, but what does he know?

'There's no need to be rude, Megan. You know I only ask you these things because I care about you.'

She shoots me a look. 'Then don't. And for your information, it's not a boy.'

I turn off the hob. Balance the wooden spoon across the top of the pan. 'You wouldn't lie to me, would you, Megs?'

'What? The way *you* lie to *me*, Mum?'

I freeze. Wondering what she means by that. There's no way she could know about Alex or our lives before Earthbound. I've never told her about all that, and she'd have no memory of it. No one knows the whole of it. I chew my lip knowing that's not true. Someone knows, but I don't want to go there.

'I've never lied to you, Megan.' I'm not proud that I've covered one untruth with another. Not proud at all. But what alternative do I have? 'So if it's not a boy, where were you thinking of going?'

Megan gives me a withering look. 'What part of *don't ask* don't you understand, Mum?'

She takes her phone from her pocket and scrolls through, holding it away from me so I can't see. I feel myself tense.

'You know I don't want you on social media. I hope that's not what you're doing? Especially after the trouble at school.'

I grab her hand, hating myself even as I'm doing it. Try to take the phone from her. But she wrenches it away, her eyes blazing.

'It's not all about *you*, Mum. Just because you have some stupid obsession about it, doesn't mean I have. What's your problem anyway? It's not as though I have anything to talk to anyone about, is it. It's not as though you actually allow me to *do* anything that would be interesting to share anyway. Jesus, I wish Sean was back.'

My eyes travel to my own phone, and I go over the conversation I had with him earlier. Things aren't going well. He'll need to stay up in Newcastle for the rest of the week at least. *At this rate, I'll need a trip to M&S for a new shirt and some undies,* he'd joked.

'Well, he isn't back,' I tell her, not wanting her to hear from my voice how scared I feel at the prospect of more nights without him in this house – its huge sliding doors and windows an open invitation to anyone standing on the boardwalk to look in. 'He'll be stuck there for another few days. So until he's home, it's just you and me and I'd be grateful if you'd at least try to be civil.'

Through the baby monitor I can hear Kitty. She went down

for her nap late and it's going to be a problem getting her to sleep tonight.

Megan glares at me. 'It's not me who runs this house like a bloody prison. Who wants to know who I see and what I do. Who won't even tell me about my dad.'

'Jesus, not that again.' I lean my forearms on the worktop, fighting my irritation. 'You have a good life, a lovely home, a kind and loving stepfather. What you are is ungrateful, Megan. Selfish and ungrateful.'

I see how my daughter's face pales. Wonder if I've gone too far. Wonder, too, how my worry about her when she walked in the door from school has changed so quickly to this... this horrible ugly thing.

She turns on me. Lips thinned. Eyes narrowed. 'You're right about Sean. He *is* kind. *And* funny. But there's something I've always wondered about him?' She points a finger at me. 'How he puts up with *you*?'

Shoving her phone in her pocket, she pushes past me. She climbs the spiral stairs and, a minute or two later, appears on the screen of the baby monitor, Kitty in her arms. As she buries her head in the baby's neck, I know she's forgotten I can see her.

Megan rocks her sister, her hand pressed to her curly head, getting comfort from her, and I get a glimpse of the Megan she is... not the one she wants me to see. Instead of the spiky teenager who's quick to anger, she's just a child herself. One who, as she holds Kitty to her as though she might lose her, seems lost. And oh so very lonely.

It makes me sad, but worse than that, it makes my guilt for keeping her from her father, all the greater. More all-consuming.

I will always have to keep them apart, and I hate that I can't tell her why.

TWENTY-NINE

ELISE

Then

Kristen was my lifeline. The person who got me through the next few weeks. We met again a few days later and she told me more about her life. How having Chloe was the wake-up call she needed to sort herself out and how she could just get by on benefits and the money she'd managed to squirrel away. When Chloe was older, she'd get herself a proper job. Care work, maybe, or she'd heard they were always looking for shelf stackers at the Asda down the road.

I admired her for breaking free of Alex. Envied her the luxury of loving her baby without having to live in fear at the same time. Never having to keep Chloe quiet if he was tired. Never having to race to clear all her things away before he came home for fear of him losing his temper over a soft toy that had been stuffed down the side of the settee or a dummy left on the coffee table. Always watching. Always looking for an excuse.

If she saw the bruises, she never said anything. There was no need to. Nothing she didn't understand. Nothing she could say that would help. We'd choose the places we met carefully, different places where we wouldn't be recognised. Where there would be no one to report back to Alex. The park or a coffee shop on the other side of the city. Somewhere that was on a bus route.

And when I went out to meet her, I'd leave my phone at home, knowing he could track me if I took it with me. Enjoying how it felt to have tricked him... until one ill-fated day, I didn't.

That afternoon, when I unclipped the car seat from the pushchair frame, carried you upstairs and into our flat, Alex was waiting, leaning against the dining room table, my phone in his hand.

'Where have you been?'

I stood there, your car seat swaying in my hand and desperately searched my mind for an answer. 'It's a nice afternoon. I took Megan for a walk.'

Alex looked at the phone. 'Do you usually leave your phone at home?'

I was still jittery from the shock of seeing him there. Back home before his shift had ended. Thank God I'd deleted all Kristen's messages.

'I didn't know I'd left it.' I put the car seat down, praying he'd believe me. 'It wasn't until I got to the park that I realised.'

'Really.' His face was neutral. 'Is that right?'

'You don't need to make a big thing of it, Alex. I wasn't out for long. It's not as though anything was likely to happen.'

He was in front of me in just a few steps, his fingers pressing into the sides of my chin.

'So you know all about that, do you? You know all the users and the dealers, the ex-cons and the fucking lowlife who have wormed their way out of getting the justice they deserve. The ones who don't forget and would give their right arm to hurt something of mine.'

My heart was beating too hard. My insides knitting tight. His fingers were pressing harder, making it difficult to speak.

'I'm sorry, Alex. I left my phone here by mistake. I do usually have it with me. I'll make sure I check before I go out next time.'

He dropped his hand, and I rubbed my chin thinking it would be the end of it, but I should have known. With Alex, there never was an end. The next day, I woke late to find him up a ladder in the living room, a drill in his hand. Fixing something to the wall. I wasn't surprised when I saw the unblinking eye of the security camera. I was only surprised that he hadn't done it sooner.

I met up with Kristen two days later, long enough for the numbness to have set in, but not long enough for the red welt around my wrist to have faded. We were sitting in a quiet area of our local park away from the cafe where most of the mothers with young children collected to chat. I had brought my phone with me as I didn't trust Alex not to appear at the flat as he had before. Couldn't risk him finding it.

Today, Kristen was unusually quiet. Chloe was in her pushchair, and she pushed her back and forward, her eyes on the treeline in front of us.

'It can't go on,' she said, eventually, lifting my wrist. '*This* can't go on.'

I pulled my hand away, tugged at the sleeve of my coat to cover it. 'There's nothing I can do. Alex has everyone in his pocket.'

Kristen looked pained. 'You don't know that.'

'I do.'

'Your mum. Couldn't you—'

'No.' I didn't say any more. Not wanting to think how she'd taken his side when I'd tried to speak to her of my concerns in the early days. How she'd excused him. I could never forgive her for that.

Over on the pond, a moorhen gave its high sharp squawk,

giving a feeling of normality to the day. Yet, nothing was normal. Hadn't been since the day I met Alex.

'You have to leave him, Elise.' Kristen put a hand on my arm. 'You *have* to.'

I felt weary. 'I told you before, he'd never let me leave with Megan, and there's no way I'd ever go without her. I tried, Kristen, I really tried, but he's too clever for me.'

We sat in silence for a while, then Kristen got up, bent over your pushchair and pushed the cover back to see you better. 'You say it's only Megan he's bothered about. That he wouldn't care if you left on your own.'

I nodded. 'I think so.'

'Then what if you did just that.'

'I told you I could never leave her.'

Kristen reaches down and lifts you from the pram. It looks empty without you in it.

'What if he thought she was dead?'

My heart stops. 'What do you mean?'

Her forehead creases in thought. 'What if your baby went missing and he believed she'd never come back?' She walks towards me, you in her arms. 'A grieving mother. Parents unable to comfort each other. Unable to live together. No one would think it strange if after a week or so, three at the most, you decided you could no longer be together. People would understand. The police would understand. You'd collect Megan, then get as far away from that bastard as you could. Start a new life without Alex.'

I stared at her. 'That's impossible. Where would Megan go? Where would she be?'

Kristen smiled. 'She'd be with me. We'd have to plan it all carefully, make it look like a real baby snatch, but I have all Chloe's baby equipment and a travel cot. I'd look after Megan and message you to let you know she was all right. A few weeks might seem like forever, but you have to see it would be worth it to get away from him. To be safe.'

She handed you to me, and I wrapped you in my arms. The whole scheme sounded mad. Deluded.

'We couldn't use my phone. He checks it.'

'We'll get cheap pay-as-you-go ones. Without a contract. Ditch them once this is all over.'

I couldn't believe I was even discussing it. 'It would never work, Kristen. How could it?'

Her expression changed, became solemn, serious. And, to this day, I've never forgotten her words.

'It will work because it has to.' She lifted my wrist and ran a finger over the angry welt. 'It will work because the alternative is unthinkable.'

THIRTY

ELISE

Then

A week had gone by since that day and now Alex was at the flat
waiting for me. As I fumbled the key into the lock, the door flew
open, almost taking my arm off. Grabbing the sleeve of my coat,
he pulled me inside.

'What the fuck is going on, Elise? What do you mean the
baby's gone?'

I thought of the phone message I left him. Garbled.
Panicked. My words swallowed up by my fear.

Alex gave my shoulders a shake. 'Answer me goddammit.
What's happened?'

The tears that slid down my face and into the collar of my
coat were real. The gravity of what I'd done, what I was doing
still, hitting me with force. The woolly edges of the plan Kristen
and I had devised and honed, only now sharpening into something real. Something that was actually happening.

'The baby, our baby.' I choked on the words, missing her
already. 'Someone's taken her.'

Alex took a step back from me. Linking his hands behind

his head, he stared at me in disbelief. 'Is this some kind of sick joke?'

'Of course not. Why would I joke about something like this? I don't know where she is, Alex.' I bent at the waist, my hands covering my face. 'Oh God, I don't know where she is.'

His face paled and he swallowed. 'Tell me everything.'

His voice had changed. His posture too. The edges of him hardening, tightening. Legs planted. Shoulders braced. He was no longer Alex my partner, the owner of this flat, Megan's father, but Alex the police officer. As I looked at the thin line of his lips, the muscle working in his jaw, I wondered what the hell I'd been thinking. How I'd imagined we'd get away with this.

I hadn't moved from the door. Couldn't remember what it was I was supposed to say. To do. My mind blank. Frozen.

'For God's sake, Elise.' Alex's voice broke through my torpor. Sharp. Commanding. 'Talk to me.'

Somehow, I made my legs move. I pulled out a chair from beneath the dining table and sank onto it, focussing my eyes on the pale line around the table leg. Reminding myself of what he'd done to me, what he would do again if this didn't work.

'I went to the playground, the one by the housing estate.' I choked back a sob. 'I sat on the bench and—'

'Why?' Alex's eyes were boring into me. Through me. 'Why did you go to the playground? She's a baby. It's not as though she could go on anything.'

'I... I just did. I needed some air. I like it there.' Frustration was building at his line of questioning. He was Megan's father, but, from the tone of his voice, his control, you'd think I was talking about someone else's child. Not his. 'We need to call the police, Alex. Tell them what happened.'

'Tell *me* what happened.' He didn't need to say the words for me to know what he meant. I *am* the police. Even now, with his baby missing, it was important for him to remind me of it.

'What time was this?' He was standing in front of me. 'What *time?*'

'I don't know exactly. The sun was going down.' It was like my mind had closed. My memory of what just happened shut off from me. Locked into the past. Unable to break into the present. 'It must be half an hour ago. No more.'

I stood. Grabbed his arm, eyes wide. As though it had really happened. As though my baby really had been taken from me. 'We need to go back there. We need to look for her.'

He looked at my hand, peeled my fingers from his shirt. 'It's not how we do things.'

'What do you mean? Your fucking baby is missing, Alex. What more do you need to know? You should be out there looking. You're not just a police officer, you're her father. What's wrong with you?'

The sharp slap on the side of my face whipped my head back. I pressed my hand to the place and stared at him in shock, fresh tears starting in my eyes. Kristen and I hadn't planned for this – the part of him we couldn't control, the unpredictability. Had only thought through the skeleton of the plan, not the rancid flesh Alex could bring to the bones of it.

Alex had moved away. He was pacing the room, his back to me, his mobile to his ear. I heard the words *daughter, playground, priority.* Turning to me, his words became clearer.

'Yes, it was my partner Elise.' He stopped walking. Looked at me accusingly. 'She was the one who was looking after her. Was *supposed* to be. Ten minutes? Right, mate. Ta.'

I was standing at the window, palms pressed against the cold glass, staring out at the darkening sky. Trying to picture you. My crazed mind desperate to create a tableau that would ease the agony of separation. I could almost hear your coo of delight as Kristen handed you your bottle, the heels of your Babygro pressing against the soft padding of Chloe's car seat. Beside you, on her playmat, Chloe's chubby hands would bat away the swaying animals and a song would be playing on the radio, something happy. In my head, I made Kristen sing along to it. Filling the time until I came back. Waiting for me to return so that Megan and I could start our new lives.

My heart constricted. It hadn't worked. Already I was missing your smell, the softness of your skin, the baby fingers that grabbed at my hair, making me wince and laugh at the same time.

I collapsed in on myself, my arms on the windowsill, my forehead pressing down on them. How could I do this? How would I survive each day without seeing you?

By being strong, Kristen's voice was in my head. *For this to work, you have to stay strong.*

She was right. It was the only way. I'd tried all the others.

I turned to Alex, my voice broken by sobs. 'Please find her, Alex. Please find our baby. I don't know where she is.'

Yet, even as I was saying it, I was wondering what he would do to me, to us, if he ever found out the opposite was true.

Worse still, was the thought that had suddenly come to me – one that made goosebumps rise on my arms – that the only person who stood between my baby and Alex, the person I'd put my whole trust in, was Kristen.

A woman I'd only recently met.

A woman I hardly knew.

THIRTY-ONE

ELISE

Then

The police arrived before I'd had a proper chance to collect myself. Their patrol car parked on the yellow line outside the block of flats, the flashing blue lights eliciting stares from the passers-by on their way home from work or an early session at the pub.

'They're here.' I dropped the curtain. Wrapped my arms around my body to stop the shaking. 'They'll find her, Alex. Please tell me they will.'

He was sitting on the settee, elbows on his knees, his fingers pressed to his temples. He raised his eyes to me. 'Where's her pushchair?'

'What?'

'Her pushchair. Are you stupid? Where is it?'

My brain was fogged. I couldn't think properly. Pushing through the damp murk in my head, I retraced my steps... steps planned with Kristen. Each one coming back to me in slow motion as though time had stood still. First, there'd been the slow walk from where I'd been standing, phone to my ear, back to your pushchair. Then the feel of my coat tightening uncomfortably around my middle as I'd bent to push back the concertinaed hood and peer in. Finally, my fingers acknowledging the emptiness of the space inside as I'd run my hand over the diamond quilting.

I remembered how I'd let out a cry. Turned around in a circle in that empty playground as though you might appear by magic. As though that simple act would bring you back. Even though I knew where you were. Knew you would soon be safe in Kristen's flat. Safe from Alex. A charade played out in a playground that had emptied long before. No eyes to see what had happened or what I was doing now. An act that had to be carried out just in case. Just in case.

'I left it there.'

His face was set hard. 'You're telling me the pushchair is still there? In the playground? Vital evidence to be tampered with?'

'I wasn't thinking.' I left the window, knowing that soon the police would be ringing the entry buzzer, waiting to be let in before climbing the stairs to our flat. Alex's mates from the station. There would be more questions. Difficult questions. Ones Kristen and I had gone over. Rehearsed.

'I phoned you and ran straight here. I didn't know what else to do.'

Alex hit his forehead with the heel of his hand. 'Whatever made me think you'd be able to look after her? Look at you... You can barely look after yourself.'

I looked down at my green jumper and jeans, wondering what he was seeing. What I was missing. Could he be right? Was I not fit to be a mother? But I knew I was. This was just another example of what Alex did, belittled the people he should care about. Make them doubt themselves. Make *me* doubt myself. I had to remember that it *was* possible to break free of him; Kristen had shown me that. This plan, *our* plan, was my chance to do the same. Alex didn't care about me, and once he'd accepted Megan was gone, he'd never bother to come after me if I left him. Why would he when he could move on to the next person? I thought of Corinne. How I'd seen them laughing together the day I'd gone to the police station. Maybe he already had.

The entry buzzer reverberated in the room. Alex released the door that led from the street into the entrance hall downstairs and it wasn't long before there was a sharp ring on the bell. Alex threw open the door. Two officers stood in the hallway, one male, one female, neither of whom I recognised.

Alex stood back. 'Come in. You took your time.'

'I'm sorry, Sarge. We came as quickly as we could.'

They stepped inside and, without thinking, I grabbed the arm of the nearest officer, a constable of around thirty with a thin pale face and watchful eyes. 'Please. We need to go to the park and look for her. She'll be cold. Frightened.'

Alex stepped forward. Put an arm around my shoulders. The perfect partner, the perfect father to my child. 'Come on, El. These guys need to do their job. Nothing's to be gained by panicking. They've seen this a hundred times and there are ways of doing these things.'

I shrugged his arm away. 'I don't care about the others, Alex. I care about *our* child. The one we should be looking for.'

'Of course. We understand.' The female officer indicated the settee with her hand. Her smile was kind, reassuring, yet I couldn't help wondering if she was another one of Alex's conquests. 'Please, Elise, it would be better if we all sat down. We need to find out exactly what happened. The more information we have, the quicker we can act on it and the better our chances of finding your baby.'

'She was taken from the playground two streets away. What more do you need to know than that? We should be finding her. Asking people if they've seen her.'

'It's hard, I know.' She put a guiding arm around my shoulder, led me to the settee and waited for me to sit. 'But it really is the best way.'

Alex didn't sit and I knew it was because remaining standing was his way of keeping control. Of stopping himself from being seen as a victim too. Something he wasn't used to.

'Elise has given me a lot of the information already.' He turned to the young male constable. Tapped his notepad. 'You might like to take it down.'

'Of course.' He pulled the lid of his pen off with his teeth and placed it on the arm of the settee. 'Please start.'

Alex drew himself up. 'The baby's name is Anne. She's five months old. Brown hair. Blue eyes.'

The officer's pen scribbled across the page. 'Any distinguishing features?'

Alex frowned. 'For God's sake, why is that important?'

'No,' I chipped in, not sure why Alex felt the need to antagonise him. 'None. She was wearing a blue padded snowsuit with yellow ducks on.' My voice quavered as I pictured it. 'Blue mittens and a white hat.'

'That's very useful. Thank you.'

Alex was staring at me, and I knew that look. It was the one he used when he thought I'd overstepped the mark. The one that said, *shut up and let me deal with things*. But I couldn't. If I cowed to him now, stayed quiet, it would look as though I didn't care that my baby was missing. Worse still, they might not believe me.

The image of you in your snowsuit, your blue mittens reaching up to me whenever I bent to take you out of your pushchair was too much. Even though I knew you were safe, I was so caught up in my own story that my mind was beginning to believe it.

It was because I missed you so much, Megan.

Already.

'Elise?'

I looked up. How long had the female officer been saying my name? It could have been seconds. Minutes. Time had lost all meaning.

'I asked if there was anyone else in the park when you entered it?'

A siren wailed in the street, and I looked towards the window. Was it a patrol car going to the playground and, if it was, what would they find? I turned back, knowing I shouldn't let it distract me.

'A couple of kids, about ten or eleven, were on the swings. It was getting dark, cold too, most had gone home.'

'Cold,' the woman repeated. She looked down at her hands. Twisted the engagement ring on her finger. 'Was there a reason you took your baby to the playground at that time?'

It was a question I hadn't thought of. I felt my stomach clench. Fought through the brain fog for an answer. 'Megan hadn't had a nap all day... was fractious. I thought that if I took her out in her pushchair, it might help her to settle.'

'And is it usual for her not to sleep?'

'Yes. She's never been a good sleeper.'

I looked at Alex who nodded his affirmation. 'We think she might be teething.'

I thought of your red cheeks, the constantly wet chin and soaked bibs. I hated the look and feel of them when I held you to me, but now that seemed trivial. I'd have suffered a year of baby dribble against my cheek if I could have had you back in my arms.

The pale-faced officer looked from me to Alex. 'Do you have the pushchair?'

'It's still down there.' Alex's eyes were on mine as he said it, loaded with meaning. 'Hopefully, no one's taken it. We need to get a patrol down there sharp.'

'I'm on to it.' The officer walked out of the room onto the

landing. Through the part-open door I heard the crackle of a radio. The officer's voice giving orders.

A wave of desperation washed over me. I just wanted this to be over. For the days and nights to pass until at last I could leave this flat. Leave Alex once and for all and get as far away from him as possible. Start a new life with *you*, Megan. The baby he'd think was missing. Presume was dead.

I stand, agitated. 'Can we go now? Can we look for her?'

The female police officer smiled kindly at me. 'Yes, a patrol will be at the playground very soon. With luck the pushchair will still be there, and we can start a search. Make enquiries.' She looked at Alex. 'Any idea what the situation is regarding CCTV in the area of the playground, Sarge?'

Alex frowned. 'Nothing at the park itself, parents round here have been lobbying for one for as long as I can remember. Nearest is outside the kebab shop by the viaduct. You've organised the dogs?'

She looked over at the pale officer who nodded his affirmation. 'On their way.'

Dogs. Fear gripped me. I hadn't thought about dogs.

'You'll find her, won't you?' Tears were streaming down my face. I was caught between fiction and reality, unsure what was real and what wasn't. Panic was stopping me from thinking straight. My baby had been taken. Someone had her. For the first time since she was born, Megan was no longer real to me. She had become a name to be picked over, questioned about. The reality of her reduced to a page of notes in the officer's pad.

I had to pull myself together or I'd go mad. 'Please,' I said. 'Please do what you can.'

'We'll do everything in our power, Elise. Be reassured on that.'

An image pressed into my mind. Corinne sitting in her car, her hands either side of the steering wheel. Her neat hair smoothed back into a bun, her face a mask as she'd listened to my story. Then, later, the image of her through the window of the police station laughing at something Alex had said.

I looked up at the ceiling, blinking. Wondering at the irony of the officer's words. Trying to comprehend how it was possible for the police to do everything in their power to find a missing child, yet do nothing to save a broken woman.

But my thoughts hadn't stayed on Corinne for long, they'd moved on to something more worrying. I'd made a mistake before... what if I'd done it again?

Put my trust in the wrong woman. In Kristen.

THIRTY-TWO

ELISE

Now

Something wakes me and I sit up too quickly, lightheaded in the darkness. It's hot in the bedroom and my throat is dry. Last night I'd kept the patio doors that lead out onto our second-floor balcony shut and locked and the room is too stuffy.

Kitty's still asleep, starfished on her back in her cot, arms raised above her head. Her face just a white shape in the darkness.

The noise comes again. A scrape, metal on stone. It's coming from outside. I sit motionless in the darkness, my ears straining, but now there's nothing but silence. Only the sound of my own heart beating in my ears.

My forehead feels damp, and I crook my arm to wipe my brow. The thin camisole I wear in bed is stuck to my chest. Jesus, this room is hot. Airless. No wonder I'm imagining things.

Being careful not to wake the baby, I get out of bed and go over to the panel of sliding doors. Taking hold of the gauzy muslin drapes, I pull them aside and look out, but there's nothing to see – the night is so dark it's engulfed everything. The huge expanse of wall-to-ceiling glass of our bedroom on the top floor is not as wide as on the first floor below, but still, as I stand there and run my fingers down the metal frame to find the lock, I feel oddly small. Vulnerable.

Sweat beads on my lip. Finding the lock, I flick the metal lever, then pull, the glass doors sliding soundlessly on their runners. The night air hits me as soon as I step out onto the wide balcony, bringing with it the briny smell of the sea. It's colder than I'd expected it to be out here and I shiver, but at least it's clearing my head. It must be nearing high tide as, beyond the patio and the boardwalk, I can hear the sea heaving and stirring like a black beast, the lips of the waves sucking at the stones before retreating. Maybe if I stand here long enough, the sound of it, and the cool night air, will soothe me enough that I'll be able to sleep again.

I'm just going back inside when I hear something else. A scrape. Not loud but enough to make my heart quicken. It came from the patio below, but when I step forward, lean my arms on the metal rail and look down, there's nothing to see. Just dark clumps where the palms and the yuccas are.

If someone was down there, the security light would have come on, but the patio is in darkness. A gust of wind flaps my pyjama bottoms against my legs, and I hear something else, a squeak. A clang. It comes again as another gust of wind blows in from the sea.

My heart clenches. I know that sound. It's the gate that leads from the boardwalk onto the patio. Swinging when the wind catches it. The latch not quite catching before it opens again. Usually, I lock the gate before I go up to bed, but I can't remember now if last night I did. I'd been worried about Megan. Distracted. But I'm not going to go down now; it will have to wait until the morning.

Stepping back inside, I slide the doors closed, shutting out the relentless wash of the sea. The squeak and clunk of the gate. After checking Kitty, I get back into bed, but as I lie there, the air becomes oppressive again.

I can't sleep. Something is bothering me, but I'm not sure what. Turning onto my side, I face the window and suddenly it comes to me... the thing that's keeping me awake. It couldn't have been the gate that woke me as, with the double-glazed doors shut, I can no longer hear it. It was something else. Something louder.

I know I should go down and see, but my fear is stopping me. If something or someone is outside, I'd rather not know. But even as I think this, I'm aware of how cowardly that sounds. It's not just me in the house, it's Megan and Kitty too. I'm their mother; it's my job to protect them.

But what if it's Alex who's out there? What if, even now, he's trying to get in?

Dread threatens to calcify me, but I have to do something. Reaching to the bedside table, I feel for the remote. It controls all the lights both inside and out, including the security ones on the back wall and the sunken spotlights in the pool.

Although it's the last thing I want to do, I get out of bed again and pad on bare feet to the window. Sliding it open again, I press the button for the security light. Nothing happens. The patio below is still in darkness. I press it again, then once more to be sure. Maybe the bulb's blown. Security is Sean's department. I'm not even sure where the spare bulbs are kept.

Not liking the darkness and what might be lurking below me, I find the button that controls the sunken lights to the swimming pool and press it. Immediately, the patio comes alive with light and shadow. Through the serrated leaves of the palm, the water of the pool glows turquoise, darker in the middle, lighter around the edges where the lights are embedded in the tiles.

But wait, there's something else. Something in the pool. A dark shape in the water. I lean over the rail, trying to see, but the palm fronds limit my view. Whatever it is, it's floating. I move along to the far end of the balcony where the plants below make way for the swing chair where we usually leave our towels. Through the gap in the leaves, I get a better view of the water and as the dark shape moves into my vision, I stifle a scream.

It's a person who drifts in and out of view, partially obscured by the leaves of the plants. They're floating on their front, long dark hair spread around them, the strands moving as if alive.

Is it Megan?

I cry out, but her name, forced through the narrow passage of my constricted throat, comes out soundless.

I tell my limbs to move. Scream at them to do so and find myself back in the house, taking the spiral stairs two at a time, to the floor below. Almost missing the final step in my haste.

The house has never seemed bigger. So much area to cover. I have to get to my daughter. I have to save her. When I reach the sliding doors in the living area, the lock slips under my shaking fingers. I can't move it.

Come on. Come on.

At last, it releases, and, with two hands, I haul the window open. Run out onto the wide veranda, pushing aside the garden chair as I pass it, a loose piece of rattan scratching my leg through my thin pyjama bottoms. The metal rail of the outside spiral staircase, which will lead me down to the patio, is cold beneath my fingers as I grip it, but I'm hardly aware.

When I reach the bottom, I stumble blindly in the direction of the pool, panic overtaking me. Instead of taking the path around the edge of the plants, I take the shortest route, thrusting through the palm fronds. Arms folded across my eyes.

'Megan!' I've found my voice at last.

The body floats, arms and legs spread, face obscured by the water. And I watch it. Too shocked to move. To think. Aware of only one thing.

I'm too late. I know she's dead.

But it's not Megan...

THIRTY-THREE

MEGAN

Now

Megan hadn't been able to sleep. Not surprising after the fight she'd had with her mum. Or when the inside of her closed eyelids had been imprinted with the image of her dad in his police uniform, her head bursting with the new message he'd written. One she'd never be able to tell her mum about, *I'd love to meet you, Megan.* And the reply she'd written. *I'd like that too, Dad.*

The smile on the emoji he'd sent when he'd read it had mirrored the one on her own face as she'd left her bedroom to find her mum. The idea had been to sound her out, get her mum to agree to her going out one evening after school, but it hadn't worked out like she'd hoped. In fact, it had only made her suspicious. More overly protective, if that was even possible.

Megan gets out of bed. Pads out onto the landing. Past the wide-open area with its settees and tubular armed chairs overlooked by her mum's huge acrylic seascape – only the white crests of the waves visible in the darkness. Past the skeletal bookshelves. Her hand outstretched to avoid the large, spiralled ammonite sculpture on its plinth, the tall narrow spikes of the giant houseplants in their seagrass containers that are hard to see.

She likes it in the house at night when the only light is the moon shining through the wall of glass, but, tonight, as she moves closer, Megan sees it's not the moon that's brought the outside of their house to life. It's something else – bathing the palms, the ornamental bamboo, the seating area, in a blue light. Making it almost magical.

The pool lights.

But why are they on?

A gust of cold air makes Megan shiver. One of the large windows is open. The wind agitating the leaves of the weeping fig in its large white pot. Her mum must have gone outside, but why?

There's a movement below, and Megan steps out onto the veranda. Leans on the rail and strains to see. A deep moan fills the night air, like an animal in pain, and only then does Megan see a hunched shape by one of the rattan sunloungers. Her mum. She's sitting on the cold, flat paving slabs beside the pool's edge. Her knees drawn up. Rocking forward and back. Fingers drawing through her hair as though she'd like to tear it from her scalp. It's as though Megan's watching someone else and it's terrifying. Something must have happened, but she has no idea what. A cold dread creeps its way up her body. Might it be the baby? Might something have happened to Kitty? But if it has, it doesn't explain why her mum's out here.

The metal steps are cold beneath her bare feet as she runs down the staircase.

'Mum? Are you all right? Are you ill?'

She stops in front of her, reaches out a tentative hand and places it on her shoulder.

Her mum's head jerks up. Her eyes widening as though seeing a ghost.

'Megan?'

'What is it, Mum? What's happened? Shall I call Sean?'

Her mum doesn't answer but turns her head to the pool. Megan's eyes follow hers. Sees what she's seeing.

A body in the water. Face down.

Megan stares, disbelieving. It's a woman, her denim shorts contrasting with the white of her legs, the water darkening the material of her blue T-shirt to ink. As Megan watches, the iridescent pool water moves her hair. Medusa-like.

'Jesus!' The word is expelled from her. There's a body in their pool. Whoever it is might still be alive and she has to get her out. Megan drops to her knees, then lays flat along the edge of the pool. She reaches out across the water and stretches a desperate arm across to her. The bones of her fingers pulling away from their sockets as she reaches. Megan closes her eyes with relief as her fingertips make contact with the woman's hair. She agitates the water to get hold of a strand, her fingers closing around it. Pulling.

The body bucks. Legs thrashing. Megan lets go, the flat of her hand pressing to her chest. Her heart thudding with the shock. 'What the hell?'

Slowly, the woman's legs sink in the water, finding purchase on the pool's floor. She stands, looking at them, waist-deep, her fingers exploring the side of her head.

'Why the hell did you do that?'

Megan can't speak. Can't breathe. Her mum is standing now, and she feels the pressure of her arms as they wrap around her, pulling her tight. Normally, she'd pull away, but this is far from normal and, after seeing her mum so traumatised, she's afraid of how she might react if she does.

'Why are you here?' Her mum's voice is shaky. 'What are you doing in our pool?'

Megan stares at the woman, watches as she pulls her wet

hair from her face and holds it behind her head, squeezing the water out.

'I didn't want to wake you. It's warm tonight, so I thought I'd take a dip and then knock on your door in the morning. The sunbed looked pretty comfortable.' She rubs the side of her head again and looks at Megan. 'Did you have to pull my hair?'

'I thought you'd drowned or something.'

Her mum drops her hands from her shoulders. When she speaks, her voice is shaky. 'You were so still. I called out to you, but you didn't move.'

'I'm sorry, I was floating. Remember I told you I've always loved the water.' It's said matter-of-factly, as though what she's done is normal. As though it explains everything.

Megan's shock turns to anger. 'You must have heard Mum? She called to you. You really freaked her out.' She knows the woman but can't place her. It's a face from the past, and she wracks her brains to remember.

The woman shakes her dark head like a dog, presses the heel of her hand to her ear and agitates it. 'My ears were under the water. I didn't hear anything.'

Lowering her hand, she wades through the water to the crescent of wide stone steps and gets out of the pool, water dripping from her hair, her clothes, her chin. Pooling on the paving slabs beneath her bare feet.

She frowns. 'Have you got a towel or something?'

Megan watches as her mum, her face ashen, walks over to the wooden bench by the fence where they keep the towels. Lifts the seat and pulls one out.

She throws it to her, and they watch as she dries her hair. Dabs at her arms and shoulders.

'You don't remember me, do you, Megan?' She sits on one of the sunloungers and stretches her legs out in front of her. Studies the water droplets that run down her shins. 'But then you were only seven. I remember *you,* though. Such a lovely little girl. You've grown up to be a beauty too.'

Megan frowns. Looks harder. Recognises something in the blue eyes with their short lashes, the slight downturn of her mouth.

Despite her earlier shock, her lips curve into a smile. 'It's you.'

She turns to her mum. In the blue glow from the pool, she looks sickly. Shaken. Megan watches as she wraps her arms around herself as though they're a shield.

Her voice has an edge to it. 'What do you want?'

THIRTY-FOUR

ELISE

Then

How could a day stretch for so long? That's what I asked myself as I lay, fully clothed, on my bed in the flat, unable to settle to anything. My eyes trained on the bars of your cot as though I might miss something. Some miracle that would see you sleeping there. Alex had wanted to move the cot into the room we were to use as a nursery, saying no good would come of the constant reminder, but I *wanted* to be reminded. Every. Single. Day.

Could it only have been the day before yesterday that I held you for the last time? Kissed your cold cheek and adjusted your hat as you lay in your pushchair in the playground, before turning away. Knowing what was to come.

I looked at the door, glad that Alex wasn't there, yet hating the silence he left behind him. He'd gone out earlier, saying he'd go mad if he had to spend any more time staring at the four walls or drinking the endless cups of coffee DC Ellen Shipman, the family liaison officer who'd been assigned to us, made. It wouldn't help us get our daughter back.

At the thought of you, tears slipped from the corners of my eyes, seeping into the pillowcase. Why hadn't I realised it would be this hard?

Leaning over the bed and reaching under the mattress, I brought out the cheap pay-as-you-go phone Kristen had bought. Clicking onto her name, I read the messages I'd read a thousand times already, hoping they would comfort me,

Megan is fine. She had me up in the night a couple of times, but I sang to her and gave her warm milk.

I don't want you to worry. Soon you will be together again and can start a new life.

It's hard work juggling two babies, but it's worth it if it means you can leave the bastard.

Reassuring words that answered my frantic questions. Letting me know that, yes, she had remembered Megan liked to be sung to when she was put in the cot at night. No, she hadn't forgotten that she liked her milk warmed. Yes, I could trust her. Yes, she was fine, fine, fine.

Except *I* wasn't.

The navy arm of Alex's spare uniform micro-fleece was caught in the door of the wardrobe, and I couldn't take my eyes off it, my emotional reaction to it no less strong than if the man were actually standing there. The same reaction I had when I took his blue trousers out of the wash or spotted the epaulettes he'd left on the side of the bed.

I felt nausea rise. Got off the bed and shoved the sleeve back inside the wardrobe, holding the door shut as though it might escape and harm me. I hadn't known it was possible to hate a physical thing in this way, but I did. Even when Alex wasn't here, the flat was full of constant reminders of him.

A few roads away, the playground where I'd taken Megan had been closed, the gate and fence sealed with blue police tape. On the day of her disappearance, Megan's pushchair had been found where I'd left it by the little roundabout with its yellow seats and blue handrails. It had been taken away for analysis, part of the investigation that had involved house-to-house enquiries and a trawl through CCTV footage from the local area. So far, though, there had been nothing: they'd found no one who had seen what happened and no one from their door-to-door enquiries knew anything about it. Even the sparse CCTV coverage in the area had thrown up no helpful images.

Guilt nudged at my misery, reminding me of the trouble I'd caused. The wasted manpower, time and effort. But I couldn't allow myself to think like that. To buckle. It was a small price to pay for my safety and for yours.

The buzz of the entrance door brought me back to the here and now. It would be Ellen, back from the corner shop with a carton of milk and the digestive biscuits I'd asked for but knew I'd never be able to stomach. I'd just wanted a bit of time to myself.

She'd arrived at our house soon after the other officers had left on that first day, introducing herself and telling us she would be there to give us support and updates on any developments when and if they arose. This morning, she'd arrived soon after eight. Melting into the background. Giving me space when I needed it, and those endless, bloody cups of tea and coffee.

I let her in. Stood back to let her go through to the living room. She asked how I was, then went into the kitchen to put the milk away in the fridge.

'A detective inspector will be coming over to speak to you sometime this morning, Elise.' She closed the fridge door. Gave a smile designed to reassure. 'She'll be the one leading the investigation from here on in.'

She said more, something about photographs of the baby, but although I tried to listen to what she was saying, I couldn't concentrate. All I could think about was you in Kristen's flat. What you were doing. Whether your nappy rash had reappeared. Whether you were aching for me as much as I was aching for you.

I took a shuddering breath, and Ellen set the kettle she was filling on the worktop and hurried over. Took my hands in hers. 'It's going to be okay.'

I pulled my hands away. How could she know that? How could anyone know how this would end? Because this charade, this terrible endless charade I was playing, had grown so much bigger than I'd ever imagined. It was only now I realised what a fool I'd been to believe it could work. I was no actress... it was the pain of missing you, the blunt pain in my sternum that never let up that lent me my tears, my heartache. Made me look like the mother of a missing child. Because, in a way, I was.

But soon they'd see through those tears. See through *me*.

I wanted to scream, *Alex drove me to it. He would have killed me if I hadn't done something. No one believed me. You didn't believe me.* But of course I couldn't, and it was wrong to tar this pleasant warm-hearted officer with the hazel eyes and the nice smile with the same brush as the others. Before this, she'd never met me. Maybe never heard of me. Not everyone was like Alex and his friends. I had to believe that.

'I just want Megan back,' I said, for even though the storyline DC Shipman was following ran a parallel path to my own, I meant it.

'I know, love. I know.' There was nothing else she could say that she hadn't said before and we both knew it. 'What time will Alex be back?'

'I'm not sure. He's finding this... difficult.'

A look crossed her face, fleeting but there long enough for

me to read it. What kind of father would leave his grieving partner alone at night so soon after their baby had gone missing?

'He says seeing me like this makes him worse. He likes to walk. Says it helps.' How easy it was for me to fall into the old habit of making excuses for him.

'Yes.' Ellen nodded as she said it, but it didn't sound as though she agreed. 'Look, Elise, I can stay the night if you want. It wouldn't take long to make up the bed in the spare room.'

'Please, you don't need to. I'll be fine on my own and I have your number if I need it.'

'Okay.' That uncertainty again. 'But you must let me know at any time if you change your mind. It's what I'm here for... to help you through this difficult time.'

Her kindness threatened to overwhelm me. 'I will. I promise.'

'Good, then let me fix us some supper. Will an omelette do? Could you manage that?'

'I don't know. I think so.'

'Then I'll get started. You need to eat to help your body cope with all that's happened.'

'I know.'

I watched Ellen at the kitchen counter whisking eggs into a bowl. Her presence was comforting, but later, after she'd gone, I would be alone. Waiting for Alex to come home. Knowing that when he switched on the bedroom light in the early hours of the morning, not caring that it would wake me, his face would be dark. His narrow eyes full of blame for what had happened. Leaving me in no doubt of his feelings. Ones he was unable to act upon when so much attention was on us.

But it would come. It always did.

And it was only the thought of you that kept me going. Stopped me from grabbing Ellen's arm as she was leaving and telling her I'd changed my mind. That she couldn't leave me alone with a man whose mind was so twisted.

Because I couldn't risk her not believing me... the danger it would put me in if she didn't.

Not again.

THIRTY-FIVE

ELISE

Then

It had been twelve hours since Kristen's last message. One that told me you'd taken your morning bottle and everything was fine. It was the longest she'd left between messages, and my nerves were frayed.

The minutes ticked by. Outside, the sky darkened and the flat, that I had once found so spacious, now felt like a prison. The walls closing in on me.

I'd taken to pacing, counting the number of steps between the kitchen island and the door that led onto the landing. *Seventy-five. Seventy-six.* Without a bottle of milk, without the car seat, without *you*, my arms felt empty. Useless. As though they no longer had a purpose.

It had been days since I'd reported you missing, and in that time your father had hardly been at the flat. Despite my protest, he'd told Ellen we would no longer be needing her, hating to have someone else in the house. Nosing. Meddling. I'd liked her, and she was at least company, but there was no arguing against Alex. Yesterday, he'd tried to go back to work, but they hadn't let him. Told him he should be on compassionate leave. It was only this morning he'd told me – yesterday he'd come home in the early hours and had fallen into bed, stinking of drink. I didn't ask where he'd been. Didn't want to know.

Anyway, he wasn't my priority, *you* were. You would be missing me. Wondering why it wasn't my arms that held you. My lips that whispered to you. My heart that beat against yours when you woke in the night and needed comfort.

I missed you so much it was a physical pain around my heart. I'd never been away from you before, except for a few short hours when Alex was still trying to show what a doting father he was. Had never had a day when I hadn't been able to kiss you, or smell you, or tell you I loved you.

My body and mind were reacting as though you really *had* been taken. As though I might never see you again, and I didn't know how to stop it. I needed to see you. Make sure you were all right. Except I couldn't. It was what we had decided, and if I went to Kristen's flat, I could jeopardise everything.

Every few minutes, I took the burner phone from my pocket. Stared at the old messages telling me I wasn't to worry. Yet, how could I not? Only three days, yet my heart felt like it had been ripped out of my chest. I walked back to the kitchen, tapping the phone in my palm as though the action might bring it to life – make a message from Kristen appear. We'd agreed to keep the messages to a minimum, knowing it might be difficult for one or other of us to reply, but this radio silence was making me uneasy. How long would it take for her to tell me you were okay? She'd had all day. I looked at my watch. It had been twenty-four hours since her last message.

Without thinking, my feet had taken me into the bedroom. Led me to your cot. I bent over. Placed my hand on the yellow sheet, then picked up your cellular blanket and pressed it to my nose. Smelling you. Drawing you in. Even though you'd never formed a particular attachment to the blanket, might you settle better with it? Should I have left it with you?

My eyes filled with tears. Why hadn't Kristen messaged? Why *hadn't* she?

The room was dark, my reflection in the window blackened by the night. My fingers tightened around the soft fabric of the blanket, bunching it. Dreading the long hours to come, for the evenings were so much harder to endure than the days. The nights worse.

The doctor who had seen me on the first day, had prescribed something to help me sleep, but I hadn't wanted to take it. I was too scared of losing control. Too scared of what Alex might do if the sleeping tablets worked too well. For that is how I had become: ever watchful, my senses on high alert even when I managed to sleep. The merest squeak of the bed when Alex turned over, after he'd got home, or the patter of rain on the window, wakening me from a restless sleep crowded with unwanted dreams. Dreams of *you*, Megan. Where you cried for me. Lifted arms to me. Looked right through me because I was dead to you.

I couldn't take any more. Took out my phone and jabbed at the buttons. *Is everything okay?*

I waited, desperate for Kristen to answer. Just one word would do: fine, okay, good, yes. Anything that would reassure me. Anything except this blank screen. But there was nothing. I brought the phone to life, saw that it was seven twenty. Somewhere, streets away, a siren wailed, making me squeeze my eyes shut. My nerves were frayed, panic starting to take hold. I knew I had to stay calm, our plan depended on it. But as the pulsing sound grew fainter, the image it left behind remained strong. Alex standing outside the refuge after I'd tried to leave before. Thumping on the door. Demanding to be let in.

What if he had found you? Discovered our plan? Was at

this very moment battering down the door of your flat and snatching you from Kristen's arms?

Even though I knew it couldn't be happening, that Alex had no reason to suspect I'd ever met Kristen or even knew of her existence, the panic that had been building pushed aside any rational thought. Despite what we'd agreed, I had to go to you. See you. Even if it was just for one minute. One second. If I could have that one thing this evening, I could endure the many others that would come after.

With the blanket gripped tightly in my hand, I found my coat and scarf and ran down the stairs to the street. With a quick look around me to make sure no one was watching, I put on my coat, then turned left, into the road where my car was parked and got in. Kristen's flat was only a twenty-minute drive away, what harm could it do just to check? Your blanket was on the passenger seat. It need only be a brief visit, a chance to give it to her.

By the time I'd reached the outskirts of the city where Kristen lived, my heart was catapulting against the walls of my chest, my thoughts all over the place. I slammed on the brakes, seeing, just in time, the sign with the horizontal, red line that told me the road I was about to turn into was one way. I needed to concentrate. Mustn't do anything to attract attention to myself. To my car.

Not wanting to park too near Kristen's road, I found a space a few streets away and got out. The main roads would more likely than not have CCTV cameras, so I avoided them, keeping instead to the quieter residential streets. As I walked, I kept my head down, the fur hood of my coat partially hiding my face. Hoping it was enough.

The street was empty, and I was grateful for that; it would make this easier. Not wanting to give myself the opportunity to back out, even though I knew what I was doing was foolhardy, I opened the gate and ducked into the tiny, overgrown space that served as a front garden. I looked at my watch: nine thirty. Was it too late to be visiting? Would Kristen, tired from juggling two children, already be in bed?

With a quick look behind me, I pressed the bell with Kristen's name on it, thankful that her ground floor flat didn't have a shared entrance hall. Not hearing anything, I pressed the bell again. Was it even working? I waited, rocking from foot to foot, desperate for the door to open. Desperate to see your face. To see you reach out to me. Even though I knew that when I left again, the parting would be just as painful second time around.

With that thought, the desolation I'd felt as I'd sat in the park, my back to the pushchair, hit me again. For, as I'd pretended to call someone on my phone, I'd known that Kristen would be pushing back the hood and lifting you from the covers. Known I wouldn't see you for a time that was longer than my heart could take. Known I had no choice.

A fresh wave of missing rushed at me, and I rapped on the door with my knuckles. Why wasn't Kristen answering? On my right was a large bay window – the living room I guessed. A light shone through the crack in the curtains; Kristen must still be up. I walked back to the front door, bent to the letterbox and lifted the flap. With my cheek pressed to the cold metal, I looked through.

The hallway was narrow, leading to a dark kitchen at the back of the house. There were two doors on the right, both of them shut. Through the nearest, the one that opened to the living room, I could hear a man's voice talking. His voice raised.

I froze, every fibre in my body telling me to turn and run. It was Alex; it had to be. But then the voice stopped. Music replaced it – the theme tune of a programme I couldn't place. I wanted to laugh. Cry. The voice hadn't been Alex at all, simply the television. The spectre of him conjured up by imagination, nothing more.

Alex didn't know where Kristen lived. Never *had* done. There was nothing to worry about.

I rang the bell again. Once, twice, three times, even though it was clearly not working, then banged once more. Harder this time. Desperate for Kristen to hear it through the closed door. Over the sound of the TV. Nothing.

I looked around the sad little front garden. Kristen had told me she kept a spare key in the gap created by loose mortar under the windowsill. Had said I could use it in an emergency – though neither of us had wanted to imagine what that might be. I stepped off the path onto the small patch of grass under the window. Ran my fingers under the cold, painted wood until they made contact with the key's plastic cover and pulled it out. Then, making sure no one was coming down the road, I slipped the key into the lock and let myself in.

The first thing I saw as I stepped inside the flat was a baby carrier. It was propped up against the wall on top of a pile of Kristen's shoes and, although it was Chloe's, just the sight of it made me all the more desperate to see you.

'Kristen?' I called. Not knowing how she'd feel about me being here. 'It's only me.'

I turned the handle and let myself into the living room, unsure of what sort of reception I'd get. We'd agreed I wouldn't come here unless I had no choice, and I knew that missing you could never be classed as an emergency. But surely she'd understand. She was a mother, after all.

The room was small and chaotic, baby paraphernalia taking up every available space between the settee and the television where a police drama was playing. In the corner by the window was a low canvas baby seat, a frame of plastic, coloured animals clipped to its metal legs. On the floor by the television a packet of baby wipes and a pile of nappies lay next to a change mat. The room was overly warm, even though an airer, its rungs draped with baby clothes, was opened out in front of the heater, blocking most of it from view.

I stepped into the room and saw Kristen. She was fast asleep on the settee under a soft pink-and-yellow checked throw, her head resting on a cushion that had seen better days. Chloe was in her arms and Kristen's head was turned to her, her lips grazing the soft down of her head as though she'd just kissed it.

Despite my earlier anxiety, I felt a smile form on my lips.

'Kristen,' I said again, but as soon as I'd said it, I wished I hadn't. It would be unkind to wake them.

I was just wondering what to do, whether I should leave or go and find you, when the baby monitor on the table next to the settee sprung into life. Filling the room with your cry. On the monitor's screen, I could see you clearly, lying on your back in Chloe's travel cot. You'd kicked your cover off, but your cry was half-hearted now, your eyes still closed.

The sight of you filled my heart – every space in it that had been empty since I last saw you. I'd thought that seeing you would make the difference. Enable me to leave the house again. Leave you here and return to the flat. But, instead, it had the opposite effect. I couldn't leave you here. How could I have ever thought I could? It would be weeks, months possibly, before the word *missing* would take on another meaning to the police... something more permanent. Weeks or months before Alex accepted you were unlikely ever to be found and I could safely leave him.

I couldn't do it. *I couldn't.*

Kissing my finger, I held it up to the screen. Even though you couldn't see it, it was my silent promise to you. A promise that told you I'd do everything in my power to keep you safe from Alex... even if this wasn't the way.

In a few minutes, I would leave and take you with me.

I backed out of the living room and closed the door, but

even as I walked to the bedroom, I was starting to doubt the logic of my actions. For where could we go? I couldn't return to Alex's flat, and I certainly couldn't go back to the refuge. I remembered the blue lights of the police car that had flickered between the slats of the blinds. Alex's fist on the door and the earnest look on Tanya's face as she'd folded the small piece of paper into my hand. I'd pushed it into the back of my purse and hadn't looked at it since that night.

I'd reached the bedroom door, but I didn't go in. Instead, I stopped outside, took the piece of paper from my purse and unfolded it. There, scribbled in Biro, was the name of Tanya's brother, his taxi just a call away. But it wasn't his name I was thinking of as I gripped the paper in my fingers. It was the word beneath it.

Earthbound.

What had Tanya said? *Earthbound is a special place. It's where people go if they want to become invisible.* It's what I needed to do and even though I knew nothing about the place, hadn't thought to ask her more, anything was better than leaving you here. At least this way we would be together.

Your cry came again. I knew I should wake Kristen and tell her what I was planning to do, but if I did that, she'd only try to persuade me to reconsider. Tell me what an idiot I was being and how it would never work. And I didn't want that.

This piece of paper could be our lifeline, Megan. Mine and yours.

It was time to leave. It was time to disappear.

THIRTY-SIX

ELISE

Now

'Why are you here, Amity?'

The woman smiles. 'No one calls me Amity any more... but I don't mind if you want to.' Her eyes slide across to Megan. 'It's only a name, after all.'

'You could have messaged... phoned. Why sneak around the back of the house in the middle of the night? You could have been anyone.' My voice fades to a whisper. 'Anyone.'

Megan is staring wide-eyed at me. 'Why are you being like this, Mum? It's amazing she's here. I thought the two of you were best friends at Earthbound. Aren't you glad to see her?'

'Not now, Megan.' I sit heavily on one of the sunbeds. 'How did you find out where we lived?'

'It wasn't hard.' Amity looks at Megan, and I see the answer written in the guilty look on my daughter's face.

Of course, I think, remembering all those times I'd seen her tapping away at her phone. All the occasions she'd blanked the screen of her computer when I'd come into her room.

'I told you, Megan.' My anger battles with my worry. 'I told you no social media.'

'Don't blame her.' Amity drops the wet towel onto the sunlounger next to me. Wipes a strand of wet hair from her face. 'It's surprising how easy it is to track someone down when you put a mind to it.' She smiles at Megan. 'Your Instagram pictures are really good. Every time I looked at them, I could imagine being here. Living here. And your house...' She looks up at the expanse of glass set in the concrete and wood. 'Bloody hell! It's like something out of a magazine.'

'Oh, Megan.' My heart drops further. 'Don't tell me you shared photos of our home. Not after everything I've said about online security.'

Megan folds her arms defensively. The pool lights cast a strange blue glow on her skin. 'Not all of it. Just parts. I didn't think that counted.'

'Believe me, it counts. I want you to promise me you'll take off any photos that would show where we live. It's important, Megan. Promise me that one thing.'

She shrugs. 'Okay, but I can leave the other stuff?'

I think for a moment. I don't want to fight with my daughter and, as Sean would tell me, what's done is done. At least if Megan removes the photos, we can make sure something like this won't happen again.

I turn to Amity. 'You still haven't said why you're here. What you want from me.'

She smiles. 'I just wanted to look up an old friend. Is there any harm in that?'

I take my phone from my pocket. Look at the time. 'Swimming in someone's pool at gone three in the morning with no invitation, scaring the life out of them, isn't exactly normal behaviour.'

Amity narrows her eyes. 'And disappearing without a word is? I thought you were my friend. I was the one who welcomed you with open arms. Helped you settle in and looked after Megan when you were teaching the older kids in the commune.'

'I'm sorry. I had my reasons.'

'You could have told me them. Didn't you owe me that?'

Megan stands in front of me, her arms folded. 'You've never told me why we left Earthbound, Mum. I liked it there. I had friends. It was fun.'

'You were a child, Megan.' I don't mean to snap, but I can't help it. 'You're looking at the place through rose-tinted glasses. Yes, we were a community, but it was hard work for me making ends meet. Keeping you safe.'

'Safe from what?'

I glance at Amity. 'It doesn't matter.'

'So you haven't told her then?'

The corner of her mouth twists; she looks pleased by this. And then I realise why she's here. Those words, that confession over our tea in the caravan all those years ago. If Megan doesn't know about that, then she holds something over me.

'What, Mum? Stop talking about me as though I'm not here.'

'It's nothing, Megs. Go back to bed and we'll talk about this in the morning.'

Realising I mean it, that I'm not going to say any more on the matter, she huffs and walks away, her feet clanging on the metal steps as she climbs back up to the living area.

Amity watches her, then turns back to me. 'All right if I stay the night?'

Beyond the boundary wall, I can hear the sea rolling up the shore, retreating with a rattle of stones – not soothing but distracting. I take in Amity's bedraggled hair, no longer twisted into tight cornrows, the wet clothes she's wearing. Realise I can't just send her back out onto the street. I don't trust Amity, don't trust her motives for being here, but where would she go at this time of night?

'I'll make up the spare bed and get you something dry to wear. We'll talk tomorrow. Right now, I'm too tired to think. This has been a shock, Amity, you coming here like this out of the blue.'

Amity looks at me steadily. 'Of course. Nobody likes surprises.'

I don't like how she says it. Know she's talking about more than just her unexpected appearance on my patio. I clasp the fingers of one hand tightly with the other, wishing Sean was here to make things feel normal again.

Yet, as the wind rustles the long leaves of the palms, blows ripples across the ghostly blue surface of the pool, I get the distinct feeling nothing will ever be normal again.

Because Amity's here and she knows the unthinkable.

THIRTY-SEVEN

ELISE

Then

Sometimes, when you've told someone the truth, you get a strange sick feeling in your gut. The syrupy sweetness of overtelling sticking to your insides, making it hard to know what to do.

Because what *can* you do? It's your body reacting to your oversharing. Telling you you've been weak. But this is just your body. Worse is to come. For, next, your brain kicks in. Trawling through all you've said, all you've offloaded. Hitting you with its conclusion.

You've been an idiot.

A fool.

For some, it takes a while to reach this state of clarity. For me, it was almost instant.

But I'm getting ahead of myself. For before I made that terrible mistake, I'd lived a life at Earthbound that suited me. I wouldn't say I was happy, for how could I possibly be happy after everything, but I was content. Recognising, as Tanya's brother, Dave, drove me through the gates of the large derelict house and stopped in front of the sprawling mass of tents and caravans, that Earthbound might just be the place to save me.

Maybe things would have been different had Amity not been the first person to welcome us. Stepping from her faded orange campervan, and walking towards us with outstretched arms, her tanned face breaking into a smile.

'New blood! Welcome!'

Her dark hair was twisted into cornrows interspersed with jewel-coloured beads, and when the rows of jangling bangles slid down her arm as she reached up to embrace me, I couldn't help thinking she looked, and acted, like no one I'd encountered before in my previous life. For that's how I would start to think of it, before and after Alex.

Even her name had been seductive.

'It means loyalty.' Amity stood back from me and gestured to the people milling around their makeshift homes. 'Many people here change their names... it helps them to distance themselves from whatever has made them want to change their lives. You don't have to, though. It's up to you.'

I'd liked the idea; it felt like a fresh start.

'I'll call myself Hope,' I said.

It was a name that made the future feel a little brighter. For back then I was numb, as though a heavy darkness was forever pressing down on me. Reducing me to nothing more than flesh and bone. Too scared to feel or think too much for fear I might never come out from under it. The only thing keeping me going the baby in my arms.

As Amity had shown me around, introducing me to people whose names it would take an age to remember, she'd explained how Earthbound worked. It was a collective. Everything we did was for the good of the others in the community as well as ourselves.

'The main thing you need to know is that the people who

decide to stay here are asked to look to the future, not back at the past. Our stories are ours and ours alone.'

She'd shown me the caravan I would live in, one recently vacated by a couple who had moved on, and, in the blink of an eye, that first day slipped into the second. The weeks turning to months and the months to years.

As I say, it suited me at the commune, and, when I look back, I'm surprised how quickly I settled. I had my own space, however small, and no one bothered me unless I wanted them to. Over time, Amity became more than just my welcomer. She became my friend, and I started to thaw a little. It had been years since I'd had a true friend and I missed it: the closeness, someone who understood me and was ready to share a joke or be a shoulder to cry on if I needed it... not that I needed it often.

It was something I'd been deprived of when Alex had forced a wedge between me and Phoebe all those years ago. Alex. Over time, I'd started to think of him less, fear him less, but it wasn't Alex I needed to look out for, it was myself. For once I'd realised he wasn't coming for me, I grew careless. Earthbound might have been the thing that saved me from him, but it also gave me a false sense of security.

One night, with the curtains of the caravan drawn tight against the winter sky, I did the unthinkable. I told Amity everything.

'You know you can tell me, Hope.'

It had come out of the blue, the words uttered between sips of hot camomile tea.

I lifted my cup to my lips. Took a sip. 'Tell you what?'

'About before. Your other life.' She shifted on the padded bench seat. 'Your past is like an aura around you. I feel it. I sometimes think this idea of never talking about the lives we had before coming here is bad for us.'

I was surprised at her U-turn. 'Really?'

'I've been thinking it more and more recently. I lived by the sea,' she said. 'No one knows that, only you. I used to swim every day. I miss it. Yet, why do I feel I shouldn't talk about it?'

I put my cup down on the vinyl surface of the table. My *other life,* as she called it, was a burden I carried with me always. The horror of it tamped down by the monotony of my days here. The person I'd become supressing the one I was before. Making me believe she'd never existed. Thinking that it was only by concealing the truth of the *before* that I could carry on living. Existing.

'You can trust me.' Her fingers reached out and linked with mine. 'You know that, don't you? If you think you're ready. If it would help.'

I closed my eyes – wrestling with myself. In that moment, I wanted to tell her. About Alex. About everything that came after. But I knew it was dangerous. That, despite our close bond, I couldn't know for sure she could be trusted with it.

The gentle, reassuring, pressure of Amity's fingers made new tears form, squeeze between my tightly closed lids and trickle down my neck. I missed my old friend Phoebe, and the knowledge that, once, in a time that felt so long ago now, I could have told her anything. My heart clenched. Well, maybe not everything. Some things were too raw. Too terrible. She might not have understood. But Amity...

I swallowed. Couldn't look at her. I wanted to tell her more than anything. Needed to.

'When I was just twenty, I met a man called Alex.' My voice was so quiet, Amity had to lean forward to hear. 'He was a police officer and I thought I loved him, but I don't think a woman really knows what love is until they have a child.' I stopped speaking, thinking of the rush of love I'd had for my baby. The love I still had.

The pressure of Amity's fingers increased. 'You're doing great.'

My breath shuddered out of me. I didn't know whether I

should even be telling her this, but each word, each sentence, was a release. Cathartic. 'He was nice to me at first but then... then...' My face contorted as I remembered. 'He changed. Did some terrible things. I was so scared of him, Amity. So frightened of what he'd do next. And nobody believed me. Nobody. He made sure of that.'

Outside the little caravan window, the sun was sinking behind the trees. A neighbour, Lani, and I shared the home-schooling of our kids. This afternoon it was Lani's turn, and Megan would be back from her caravan soon. I closed the curtain. Wanting to carry on with my story yet scared.

'Go on,' Amity encouraged. 'You'll feel better for it. You know you will.'

I pressed my palms against my face. Against the horror.

'He'd handcuff me to the dining room table.' I gave a shudder. 'Did things that I never want to talk about. I wished he was dead. *Still* wish he was dead. And even when I forced myself to leave him, managed finally to get away, he still found me.'

There was a noise outside, but it was only the wind rolling one of the bins. Amity sat back. 'Jesus.'

I turned wet eyes to her. 'How could I have loved a man like that?' How could I still? For even now, however much I despised him, feared him, my traitorous heart still lurched at the thought of him.

'There's more, isn't there? You've gone this far, you might as well tell me the rest. I'll never tell a soul.' She crossed her chest with her forefinger. 'God's honour.'

So I told her. I told her everything in all its gory detail. Knowing that if she ended up despising me for it, she couldn't hate me as much as I hated myself. It was like a dam had burst. Letting through the festering water of words that were rotting me from the inside out.

Yes, I told her everything.

About me. Alex. Megan. Until there was nothing left to tell. Nothing.

And now I wonder if she'd recognised something in me. Some weakness – the same thing Alex had seen.

Because there is one person I'm more afraid of than Alex.

And that's Amity.

THIRTY-EIGHT

MEGAN

Now

'Amity? Are you awake?'

The older woman groans. Rolls over and pulls the duvet over her head.

'Amity?' she says again.

Reluctantly, Amity shoves the duvet back down. Peers at Megan over the top of it. 'Morning, Megan.' Her voice is still thick with sleep.

Megan sits on the edge of the spare bed, hoping she won't mind. 'I just wanted you to know that I'm really happy you came.'

With effort, Amity pushes herself onto her elbow, rubs the sleep from her eyes. 'That's nice.'

'It's true.'

And it is. When she'd put those photographs on Instagram: photos of the beach from their living room window, their palm-fringed swimming pool and the wildflowers that bloomed between the stones and the boardwalk, she hadn't imagined it would lead to this. Amity here in their house. In their spare bedroom. Reminding her of when she was at Earthbound. The lonely years since she and her mum had left the commune, banished in one night.

She wraps the tie of her dressing gown around her first finger, watching the tip redden. 'You know I hate living in this house. In this boring town. Sometimes, I wish I was back in the commune. It was like living in one big crazy family, and I don't know why we had to leave.'

Amity pushes her hair away from her face. 'Be careful what you wish for, Megan. You might not like what you get.'

Megan smooths the cover of the duvet with her hand, looks around her at the large guest room with its built-in mirrored wardrobes and thick carpet. The tasteful furniture. The white plantation shutters. Seeing it as Amity must be seeing it.

'I guess you're thinking I'm ungrateful, but this place is sterile. I might as well be living in a show house. If I ever have a house of my own, I'm going to paint it in the brightest colours I can. I'm not kidding you, there won't be a scrap of white in the place. And as for bloody palms...' She tails off, aware of the expression on Amity's face.

'Did your mum ever tell you how I came to be living at Earthbound?'

Megan shakes her head. 'No. I was too young to understand back then, and she hasn't mentioned it since I've been older.'

Amity pushes herself further up the bed. Rests her head against the padded headboard. 'The reason she didn't tell you is because she didn't know. At Earthbound, we weren't encouraged to talk about our pasts. We were like a band of nomads who'd left our normal lives behind us and joined together. Arriving one day, leaving another. Some staying days. Some, like me and your mum, years. That anonymity... it was what made it work. But it was stifling. All those wiped-out pasts.' She smiles to herself. 'All those bottled-up secrets.'

Megan feels gooseflesh rise on her arms, but she doesn't

know why. She'd just been a kid. Surrounded by other kids like herself. Enjoying the freedom. The lack of structure. No one in your face telling you what to do. Where to be. Now she can see there was more to it.

'So why did you go there?'

Amity looks around her as though choosing the right words, and Megan thinks she's going to tell her, but instead she folds her arms across the T-shirt that she recognises as one of her mum's old ones.

'You were the lucky one. The one fate smiled upon. At fifteen, you might not see it, but you have it all. A million-pound house on the beach, a stepfather who's nice to you, a mum who...' She stops and chokes back a laugh. 'You certainly hit the jackpot. Whereas me...'

Megan waits for her to elaborate, but she doesn't. Her eyes have left hers and are now taking in the tasteful furnishings of the room. Her fingertips running over the Egyptian cotton duvet cover, feeling its quality.

'Are you going to stay with us for a bit?' Megan can't hide her eagerness. 'Now you've found us.'

'That depends.' Amity's eyes are back on hers.

'On what?'

She presses her lips together. 'On how accommodating your mother is. There are things we need to talk about.'

'What things?'

Amity blinks, then coughs as though remembering herself. 'Nothing for you to worry about. Anyway, enough about me. What about you, Megan? Tell me what I've missed in the last eight years. Got a boyfriend?'

She smiles warmly, taking Megan back to those easy days when she could be herself. The kids running in and out of each other's caravans. Talking to their parents as easily as their own. Amity had always been an easy ear to bend when she'd fallen out with someone or when her mum was having one of her sad days.

'You hesitated too long which makes me think you might.' Amity's voice is playful. Coaxing.

Megan feels herself redden, though strangely, she doesn't mind that she's asked her this. Talking to Amity about these things is different to talking about them with her mum or Sean.

'Actually, I don't. But there is someone...' She picks at a loose thread on her dressing gown, wondering if she should say what's on her mind. If she could tell her about her dad.

'Now you've got me intrigued.' Amity twists one of the silver studs in her ear. 'You can trust me with your secret, you know.'

'How do you know I have a secret?'

'I've been around enough teenagers at Earthbound. Believe me, I know.'

Megan shifts on the bed. 'If I tell you something, Amity, do you swear you won't tell my mum?'

'If you've murdered someone, then I can't promise.'

Megan laughs. 'No nothing like that, though I can't say the thought hasn't crossed my mind.' Mr Lawrence's face comes into her head. His mouth twisted into his trademark sarcastic smirk. She pinches between her eyes to get rid of the image. 'It's my dad.'

'Sean?'

She shakes her head. 'No, my real dad. Alex.'

Megan sees something cross Amity's face. 'What about him?'

'I know he wasn't a one-night stand.' She takes a breath. 'Mum lived with him until I was six months old.'

Amity sits up straighter. 'Your mum told you that?'

'You must be kidding.'

'Then how do you know?'

'It doesn't matter. I just do. Anyway...' Megan leans

forward, her eyes sparkling. 'I got in contact with him. Isn't that great?'

She waits for Amity's reaction. Is surprised when it isn't what she's expecting.

'I don't think that was a very good idea, Megan.'

Megan feels deflated. She'd been so desperate to share her news. 'Why not?'

'Because you don't know him.' Her tone is cautious. 'You've never met him.'

'And whose fault is that? All these years Mum's kept him from me. Lied to me. She treats me like a bloody kid. Makes all these stupid rules and regulations. Don't go on the paddleboard. Don't go out without letting us know where you are. Don't think for yourself. Don't breathe. You're right, I don't know him, but I want to change that and my mum's so pig-headed, she won't see it.'

The words feel disloyal, but they're true.

Amity regards her coolly. 'So what did he say in his message?'

Megan's lips curve into a smile as she remembers. 'That he misses me.'

She holds her breath, waiting for Amity to reply. Desperate for her to be happy for her.

'Have you told your mum any of this?'

'You have to be kidding! She'd go mad.'

Amity frowns. 'Maybe she has reason to.'

'What do you mean?' Megan fights to keep the frustration out of her voice. 'I thought you were on my side.'

'I am on your side, Megan. I just think you need to be cautious. Think about how your mum and stepdad would react if they knew he'd contacted you. I understand why you'd think your mum's overprotective and sympathise, but my advice is to forget about him.'

'He's my dad.'

'*Sean* is your dad. This man is a stranger. Look, Megan. You're a teenager. It's natural to want to push a few boundaries, but this thing with Alex isn't one of them. See friends your mum might not approve of, break your evening curfew, go out on the paddleboard, fight your corner – it's what I'd do at your age. But what I'm trying to say is choose your battles with your mum wisely.' She takes Megan's hand in hers. 'I know you think I'm a miserable old bag, but I know what I'm talking about. Still friends?'

Megan smiles. Even when she'd been little it had been hard to stay mad at Amity for long. Despite what she's just said, she's glad she's here. Someone to confide in. Someone who'll listen to her, even if she doesn't agree with her response.

She gets off the bed, feeling the soft carpet under her feet. Amity says she doesn't know Alex, should be wary of him, but the way her mum's been acting these past few days it's as though she doesn't know her any more, as though *she's* the stranger, not her dad. She thinks of the message Alex sent earlier and smiles.

Amity sees, gives a smile of her own. 'Penny for them?'

'It's nothing.' So what if the adults don't understand. They never do.

Alex is her father, and she'll find a way to meet him if she wants to. They can't stop her.

THIRTY-NINE

ELISE

Now

I stand outside the spare room, a mug of tea in my hand, listening to them talking. Megan and Amity. As I hear the rise and fall of their voices, a green wave of jealousy catches me by surprise. They're talking in a way Megan and I haven't in a long while. Animatedly. Their words not laced with sarcasm or derision. Sentences longer than the bare minimum. Answers to questions given freely, not punctuated by suspicion.

As I wait, wondering what to do, I catch sight of my drawn face in the large, white-framed mirror. Take in the dark circles under my eyes. The pinched line of my lips. Last night, I hadn't managed to get back to sleep. For what seemed like hours, I'd lain on my side, my eyes fixed to the window, the glass covered by nothing but the thin gauze curtains. Imagining Alex outside on the boardwalk, looking up at us. Nothing between him and me but the low wall; the metal steps of the spiral staircase; the locks on the sliding doors that, as a police officer, he'd surely be able to pick.

And, even when morning had broken, the room lightening

and Kitty's cot coming into sharper focus, my dread had remained. How much longer would he leave it? How much longer?

I move closer. Megan's talking now. I hear the words *there is someone* but can't make out the rest. I press my hand against the door, frustrated not to be able to hear more. I knew I was right. That conversation we'd had... it's some boy. From her school most likely. I wouldn't let her meet him, and now she's going to use Amity to get round me. Megan's only fifteen; she's too young to be thinking about things like this. Doesn't know what boys can be like, especially older boys. How persuasive.

I think of the boy at uni, my old housemate. On the night of the assault, I'd been several years older than Megan is now, yet still I'd wondered if it was me who had done something wrong. Whether there was more than one version of the word *no* and that maybe I had used the wrong one. Too ready to give the benefit of the doubt. Not ready to believe otherwise – that sometimes people could simply do a terrible thing and mean it.

Until I met Alex, that is... then I learnt the hard way.

He'd taken everything from me: my trust and my belief in good. He'd turned me into someone I hardly recognised, someone who could do desperate things, and I need to save Megan from people like him. But it's a task that will be increasingly difficult now Amity, the person I was once so close to, is here.

I don't know what she's playing at, but I need her gone.

My breath is caught in my chest as I wait for Amity's reply, but when it comes, I can't hear it. What will she be saying? Will she be encouraging her?

I can't let this go on.

Raising a hand, I rap my knuckles sharply on the door. A moment later, it opens, and Amity is standing there, her dark hair messy from sleep. In the stark light of morning, the eight years since I've seen her are more evident. I see it in the scattering of grey strands I missed when her hair was wet. The fine lines around her mouth and eyes.

'Morning, Hope.'

'Please don't call me that.' Her use of the name I haven't used since Earthbound is unsettling. I'd chosen it because it helped to separate me from the person I was when I was with Alex. It was a name I'd dropped once I'd left.

I lower my voice, seeing Megan through the part-open door. She's sitting on the bed that Amity slept in, frowning at having had her conversation disturbed. 'I need to speak to you in private.'

'Sure.' She smiles and the years fall away again, taking me by surprise. I've missed those years we had together, but that doesn't mean I trust her.

Megan gets off the bed. She crosses the room and stands next to Amity. 'We were talking, Mum.'

'I know, and I'm sorry to interrupt, but Amity and I have things we need to talk about too.' Not wanting to give Megan any indication of the magnitude of the problem that Amity's brought into our house, I keep my voice steady. The less she knows, the better. 'Why don't you see if Kitty's awake? She'll be wanting her milk.'

'Do I have to?'

'It's all right, Megan.' Amity's voice is placatory. 'We won't be long.'

To my relief, Megan reluctantly agrees. I wait until she's out of earshot, then go into the room and shut the door. There's a large wicker settee next to the en suite bathroom and I perch on the edge of it, feeling the wicker press into the backs of my bare knees.

Amity joins me. 'So let's talk.'

On the wall of the spare bedroom is one of my seascapes, smaller than the one on the wall outside in the living area. I stare at it, trying to think of the right words. Deciding, eventually, that there's no point in dressing them up.

'I don't know why you came here, Amity, but I think it would be best if you left.' When she doesn't answer, I turn to face her. 'Today, preferably, before my husband gets home.'

I think she's going to argue, but she just nods, arms folded across the T-shirt I lent her last night.

'Or what?'

'*Excuse* me?'

She looks at me with interest. 'What will you do if I don't leave? Call the police?'

I freeze at her use of the word. 'I'm sure that won't be necessary.'

Amity raises a knee and inspects one of her toes, scraping away at the already chipped polish with her thumbnail. It's something I remember her doing in the days we were together at Earthbound, pale pink flakes of polish settling on the worn seat in the dining area of the caravan. The one I'd convert each night to a bed. It's still hard to believe she's actually here.

'It wouldn't be the first time the police came here, would it, Elise?' She steeples her fingers and points them at me. Gives me a knowing look. 'They must think you're paranoid.'

A kernel of discomfort lodges in my stomach. 'I don't know what you mean.'

Amity tips her head and looks up at the ceiling. 'You said your baby was still asleep.'

'Yes.' I look at her suspiciously. 'Why?'

She shrugs. 'It's just that she's very quiet.' There's a heartbeat's pause. 'Are you sure she's still there?'

'Why wouldn't she be?'

'How do you know someone hasn't taken her?'

My mouth dries on whatever it was I was going to say. It's obvious now what she's talking about.

'It was you who made that call to the police. You who told

them a baby from this address had gone missing.' My anger is rising. 'Why would you do such a stupid, thoughtless thing, Amity? What on earth did you hope to gain from it?'

Amity thinks, mulls the question over, and I wait, wanting, yet not wanting, to know the answer.

'It was nothing personal,' she says eventually. 'Simply a warning. A little reminder in case you were too settled in your new charmed life to remember where you came from. Not everyone's as lucky as you, Elise. We don't all get to have a second chance... one that's better than the first.'

My hands twist in my lap, and I watch the skin slide over the bones with morbid fascination. How could she do this to me, after everything she knows? 'You clearly have no idea what you did. How bloody terrified I was that something had happened to Kitty. I want you to go now before you do any more harm.'

Amity settles back on the settee, the wicker creaking. Tucks her feet under her. Her mobile is on the bedside table, and she points to it. 'Why don't you phone the police and get them to remove me? Alex, maybe? I'm sure he'd understand. Feel free to use my mobile if you want.'

I stare at her, wide-eyed. Fight to control my breathing.

'How can you do this? Use what I told you against me? I told you because you were my friend. Because you made me feel safe... persuaded me to open up.' I give a bitter laugh. 'I suppose it was *you* who sent me that article too?'

Amity's face remains impassive. 'Article?'

'Don't play the innocent, Amity. Not after everything. You thought that if the baby nonsense didn't work, it would press the message home. Scare me. Soften me up so that when you appeared like some madwoman on my doorstep, I'd be willing to do anything.'

I look at the woman who sits in my guest room. The one who has taken the trouble to find me after all this time. She still hasn't told me why she's here.

'So what *do* you want, Amity?'

Amity gets up, walks to the seascape and traces a finger over the white crests of the waves.

'What does anyone want? I need money.'

And there it is. Not dressed up or embroidered. Just the simple bald fact. Hanging there between us.

'I can't give you any. Sean would know.'

'You'd find a way. People do.'

I think of our joint account, the savings locked away. The money from my paintings. Wrack my brains to think whether it's possible.

'How much?'

'How much is it worth for me to keep my mouth shut about what I know, you mean?'

My insides tense. 'You'd tell Alex?'

'I was thinking I could tell Megan.'

Something inside me shrinks. All those things I'd told Amity about my life before Earthbound. The terrible, terrible things that happened. The details. Megan can never know the truth. It would kill her. Kill *me* for her to know.

'Please.' I'm desperate now. 'What good would it do to tell her?'

Amity smiles. 'None at all, which is why I know you'll try your best to see things through my eyes. You have everything... a beautiful house, a happy family. Things I'll never have.'

I stare at her. I should have known that was why she was here. To blackmail me. If Alex finds out where we are, it's all over. He will make me pay – a price higher than anything I've paid before. With my life, most likely. If Amity tells Megan, the result will be the same. Either way I'll lose her.

I lower my voice. 'I want you to stay away from Megan. What were you talking about in there? She's seeing someone, isn't she? Some boy.'

Amity looks surprised, then smiles. 'Something like that.'

'Please.' I grip Amity's wrist. 'You know what I've been through. I don't want the same thing happening to her. I'll get you the money, but I want you to promise me that you won't interfere. Won't encourage her.'

Amity looks at the closed door then back at me. 'Oh, believe me, I won't.'

Her voice has changed, turned serious, and it confuses me. I have no opportunity to ask her more though as there's a bang on the door and Megan's voice floats through.

'Mum. Kitty wants her breakfast. How long are you going to be?'

Panic courses through my body as I pray she hasn't heard any of our exchange.

Amity leans in. 'So you'll get the money then?'

'I said I would.' The words are hissed. 'But what will I tell Sean?'

She runs fingers through her dark hair. 'I don't care. Make something up... It's what you've been doing most of your life anyway. I'll stay until you get things sorted.'

I can't think straight. The thought of Amity staying here, driving a wedge between me and Megan, her threat a Damocles sword suspended over my head, is appalling. But what choice do I have?

I leave the room and take Kitty from Megan's arms, then carry her through to the kitchen and put her in her highchair so I can make up her bottle. As Kitty bangs her fists on the white plastic tray, I glance out of the wide windows just as the sun comes out, sprinkling the sea with silver. Throwing patterns onto the worktop. Bathing my home in sunlight.

I give Kitty her bottle and walk to the window, a question forming. Despite everything that's happened, I feel better than I should about things. Why would that be?

As I stand, framed in the glass, the beach opening out in front of me, the answer is suddenly obvious. What I'm feeling now is relief. All this time I'd thought it was Alex who'd been behind the police hoax and the news article. It was him I'd pictured on the boardwalk as the sun went down, staring up at our window. His eyes I'd imagined looking at me through the window of the restaurant on our night out. But it had never been him. It had been Amity.

All these weeks of worry have been for nothing. Alex doesn't know anything about my life here, and never will, as long as I pay Amity off.

I press my forehead against the glass. Want to shout it out to the couple who are walking hand in hand along the boardwalk. To the woman chasing after her dog on the stones. If I could, I'd scream it to the world. Because after all the anxiety, all the stress I've been under and the sleepless nights, I can breathe again. Live again.

Alex doesn't know where we live and never has.

FORTY

MEGAN

Now

'Mum's a bit precious about her studio.' Megan closes the door behind her. 'She doesn't normally like me going in here.'

Hands on hips, Amity assesses the room. 'A couple of minutes won't hurt. I'm curious, that's all. At Earthbound your mum never did any paintings of her own, just taught others how to do it. If she finds us here, we'll say you were showing me around... which you are.'

'I suppose so.' Megan stands in the middle of the paint-spattered floor and looks around her. 'It's not that interesting. Mum usually just paints boring stuff she sees from her window. The sea, the sky, a boat if you're lucky. Everything's blue, green and white, and I sometimes wish she'd brighten things up. Add a bit of yellow or red. Give her pictures some life.' She walks over to the painting that's on the easel. It looks much like the ones in the gallery. In their house. 'Still, I suppose it must be what people want.'

'Maybe she feels she's had enough drama in her life.' Amity folds her arms. 'Doesn't need it in her pictures as well.'

Megan turns to look at her. 'Why do you say that?'

She smiles. 'No reason.'

'It seems to me Mum's had a cushy life. I was only a kid I know, but from what I remember, living at the commune was hardly taxing.'

Sunlight floods the room with light and, outside the window, the sea sparkles liquid silver. Megan watches it move, her hands thrust into the front pockets of her jeans. 'Meeting and marrying Sean after we left Earthbound was a stroke of luck. He pays for all this, you know.' She turns. Waves her hand round the room. 'While Mum swans around painting clouds.'

Amity stays silent, her lips pursed, and Megan wonders if she's said the wrong thing. She was, after all, her mum's best friend once. Those things she'd told Amity about her dad, earlier that morning – the way Amity had responded – it makes her wonder, now, if maybe she should have kept them to herself.

If only she could find a way to make her understand how important all this is to her.

Megan's eyes slide to the drawer beneath her mum's art table. Maybe there *is* a way. Going over to it, she pulls open the drawer, takes out the paint tin and lifts off the lid. She takes out the newspaper article.

'I wanted to show you this.'

'What is it?' Amity walks over to her.

'It's an article about my dad. About me. He was cut up about Mum taking me from him and disappearing. He missed me desperately. It says so here...' She knows she's gabbling, but she really wants her to understand. 'Look, you can read it for yourself.'

Amity takes the torn page from her hand, glances at it, then hands it back to her. 'Don't believe everything you read.'

'Why do you say that?'

'Because it's a bloody tabloid. Everyone knows they put a spin on things. Put it away before your mum finds out you've seen it.' Turning her back on Megan, Amity walks over to look at the paintings propped up against the wall. 'You're right, Megan. They're all seascapes. Pretty good, though. Your mum always did have talent. They must fetch a good price.'

Disappointed that the conversation has swerved so abruptly, Megan puts the article back and goes over to join her.

'They do. I don't think Mum ever expected it.'

Another set of paintings, new ones, are propped up against the opposite wall. Megan goes over to them and idly flicks through. She leans each one against her leg to get a better look at the ones behind, but as she reaches the one at the back, she stops, her hand hovering over the wooden frame. Her heart beating wildly in her chest. This painting is different from the others. Instead of the usual blue sky and green sea, this one's a portrait. Abstract – the vivid red, purple and black paint strokes screaming out from the white canvas.

But this picture will never be hung in any gallery because the face that's painted in such angry acrylics is defaced with slash marks, giving it a grotesque leer.

'What the hell?' Megan leans forward and touches the ripped canvas. Wonders at the eye that's been blinded by the violence of the knife's blade. 'Who is this?'

Amity turns to look. Moves closer. 'Guessing by the state of it, someone your mum doesn't like very much.'

'Yes, but who?' Megan pushes the flap of canvas into place with her thumb. The eyes stare back at her. Daring her to look away. And despite the abstract nature of the painting, she knows she's seen those eyes before.

'It's my dad.'

Amity stays where she is. She doesn't answer, but Megan knows she's seen those eyes before too. In the photograph in the newspaper article.

Megan turns to her. 'But why did she do it? Why ruin the picture?'

'Because she was angry with him.' Amity puts an arm around Megan. She pauses a fraction too long – as though considering the wisdom of what she's going to say next. 'I wasn't going to tell you this, but there's something I think you should know. Alex wasn't always good to your mum. He did things he never should have done. Bad things.'

'I don't believe you. He's my dad. He wouldn't do that.' Megan wants to put her hands over her ears. Block out what she's saying. Amity doesn't know what she's talking about. 'Mum put you up to this, didn't she? Told you lies about him.'

Amity looks at her sadly. Pushes the paintings back against the wall so the portrait of Alex is hidden once more. 'She told the truth, Megan. I saw it in her eyes.'

Unable to hide her frustration, Megan folds her arms. Gripping the material of her sleeves with her fingers. 'You said I didn't know him, but neither do you. And for your information, he's asked to meet me. I wasn't sure if I'd go before, but now I am. At Earthbound, when I'd fallen out with someone, you'd say there were always two sides to a story. Don't you think he should be given the chance to tell me his? I'm going to meet him whether my mum likes it or not.'

'You haven't told him where you live, have you?'

Megan pushes out her bottom lip. 'No, I'm not stupid. Mum would kill me.'

'And you got rid of those photos on Instagram like your mum asked?'

She nods, is about to say that she and her dad don't need to meet at the house, that they could find somewhere else, when the door opens.

'What are you doing in here, Megan?' Her mum's face is pale.

Megan swallows. 'Nothing. I was just showing Amity around the house.'

'Don't be hard on her.' Amity steps forward. 'It was my idea. I wanted to see your paintings.'

Megan holds her breath, waiting for her to say something about the portrait of her dad. For her to tell her mum what she's planning to do, but she doesn't. Instead, she looks around her. Points to all the finished landscapes. 'You're doing well, Elise. Reckon they'd make a bob or two at the right auction.'

Her mum's expression tightens. 'I don't think so.'

'Maybe you should find out.'

Amity brushes past her, and her mum's eyes follow her until she's out of sight.

Megan frowns. What the hell is going on with the two of them? Not liking the strange atmosphere, she steps out of the studio, but when she turns to shut the door, she freezes. Her mum's standing at the art table, her hand gripping the metal handle of the drawer beneath. The points of her knuckles white. Her face closed.

Panic floods her. Did she close the lid of the paint tin properly? Will her mum know what she's found?

A small voice in her head is telling her that maybe this is her opportunity. A chance to talk to her about the newspaper article – about the mutilated portrait of her dad. But something stops her. The certainty that her mum wouldn't tell her even if she asked.

So, instead of saying anything, Megan closes the door and leans against it. The flat of her hand pressing against the serpents twisting in the pit of her stomach.

It's a strange feeling. Brought on by the knowledge that even if her mum *did* tell her, it might not be something she'd want to hear.

FORTY-ONE

ELISE

Now

Sean pushes in the handle of his weekend case and sits on the stool at the breakfast bar.

'I'm sorry, you've lost me. You mean to tell me the Amity you've talked about so much from your years at Earthbound is here?'

I keep my back turned from him, crouch by Kitty's bouncy chair and blow raspberries at her. My relief at having my husband home is tempered by my anxiety at having Amity in the house. The knowledge we share binding us with bonds invisible, yet impossible to break.

'You okay, El?'

'Yes, I'm fine. I just don't sleep well when you're not here. I feel so exposed with the glass windows.'

'You have curtains in the bedroom.'

I think of the gauzy, translucent fabric. It's not much comfort. Even so, I give Sean a reassuring smile. I have to act normally in front of both him and Megan. What choice do I have? I know Sean loves me, but I also know he'd never be able to look at me the same way if he knew everything.

'Anyway,' Sean continues. 'You haven't really answered my question about Amity.'

'What do you want to know? She was my best friend.' I keep my voice as steady as is possible with a hammering heart and look down at Kitty, hoping her dimpled cheeks and cherub smile will calm me. 'We helped each other out when we were at Earthbound. She was kind to me when we were new there and good with Megan.'

Sean runs his fingers through his thick hair, making it stick up in an endearing way. He's tired, his thoughts implicit in the look he gives me. 'I know all that, but what you haven't told me is why she's here... after all this time? And you say she just landed on our doorstep?'

I bite the inside of my lip, struggling to think of how to make this sound normal. 'She thought she'd surprise me.'

'She certainly did that. Megs says she came down in the middle of the night to find her in our swimming pool.'

I try to make light of it. 'She always was a free spirit.'

Sean sighs. Reaches for the bottle of wine that's always open on the island and pours himself a glass. He takes a couple of large mouthfuls, then pushes the glass towards me. 'You've always had too kind a heart. Her being here has rather thrown me, though. I'd been hoping for a romantic weekend with my gorgeous wife before going back.'

I stop, the glass halfway to my lips. 'You're going back to Newcastle?'

'Don't look at me like that, love. I told you. The distributer has really fucked up and I haven't managed to sort it out. I'll need another couple of days there at least.'

I look at him accusingly. '*When* did you tell me?'

Sean sighs. 'I left you a message on your phone.'

'You did?' I pull out my phone and see the missed call notification. Listen to his voicemail. Amity arriving as she did has thrown me so much I've been oblivious to everything else. 'I'm sorry. I'll make sure I check next time. I wish you didn't have to go back.'

'I do too. I hate it as much as you do, but I promise, once this is sorted, I shouldn't have to go back up there until the exhibition next year.' He stops and looks at me, disappointment written across his features. 'Why the long face? I thought that would make you happy.'

I know I have to get a grip on myself. 'Of course it makes me happy. I don't like us being apart, that's all... I wish we never had to be.'

Yet, even as I'm saying it, I'm thinking how tenuous our life together is. How it would only take one wrong word to blow it apart.

I close my eyes and drink a mouthful of Sean's wine. Watch as he walks over to Kitty, picks up the chair with her in it and plants a kiss on each round cheek. Putting her chair down again, he goes back to his seat at the island. I get up and go over to him. Put my arm around his shoulders and press my cheek to his. Breathing him in.

'I've missed you, you know.'

Sean's arm snakes around my waist. 'I've missed you too.' He draws me onto his lap and nuzzles my neck. 'But I wasn't expecting to come home to visitors. How long is she staying?'

'Not long. She'll be gone by the time you're back.' I pray she will be. I haven't mentioned the money. How can I? I'll have to get it somehow.

Sean drains the glass and pinches the soft skin between his eyes. 'Jesus, it's been a long few days.' He nudges me gently off his lap and stands. 'Where is she anyway?'

'Megan's showing her the beach.'

'Well, it will be good to meet her in the flesh.' He pulls out the handle of his suitcase and wheels it towards the stairs. 'I'm going to grab a shower.'

I go over to the window and look out. See Amity and Megan walking back along the boardwalk. Two boys are behind them. One points at Megan and whispers something to his mate, reminding me of what I'd overheard this morning when I was outside Megan's bedroom door. How she'd confessed to liking someone. Had asked Amity for advice.

'Would you do something for me, Sean? Before you go again?'

'Of course. What?'

'Have a word with Megan about...' I breathe in, embarrassed at what I'm about to say. 'About being careful... with boys.'

Sean's face breaks into a grin. 'Tell her about the birds and the bees you mean? Don't you think she's a bit old for that? Anyway, isn't that *your* job?'

I turn back from the window. 'I just need you to explain what boys can be like, Sean. She'll take it from you.'

He gives a small shake of his head. 'She'll just tell me to mind my own business, as she has every right to do, but I'll give it a go if only to keep you off my back.'

'Thank you.'

I'm hoping that Sean's influence on Megan will be greater than Amity's. I walk over to Sean and hug him.

'What's that for?'

'For being you.'

He gives me a lingering kiss, then leans back and grins. 'As I say. Shame we've got a visitor. I was hoping we could have another night out, but I presume that's off the cards now.'

'Yes, sorry.' I force a smile. 'You'll like her, and it won't be forever.'

He doesn't need to know about the real reason Amity's here or the money I'll be transferring into her bank when I work out how to get it.

My husband doesn't need to know more than he has to.

Has never needed to.

FORTY-TWO

MEGAN

Now

Megan is knee-deep in the water, Sean's paddleboard in front of her. She'd pulled a T-shirt and shorts over her costume, but the light wind is chilly on her face and legs. She rubs at the goose-bumps that have risen on her arms, then, resting the paddle on the board's rigid surface, wades deeper.

She pushes through the water, her legs numb with cold. Puts her hand on the board, testing it. What's the worst that could happen? She could fall in. Big deal.

Gripping the sides of the board, Megan lifts her knee onto it, steadying herself until she's ready to lift the other. She stays there on all fours, the sea moving beneath her, but she knows she can't stay like that forever. Carefully, trying not to rock the board too much, she straightens until she's kneeling.

On the ridge halfway up the beach, a group of boys from her school are sitting on the stones. As she watches, one of them stretches out on his back along the length of his own paddle-board, his arms folded over his eyes. Some girls approach and a couple of the boys jostle over to make room for them, their voices carrying to her on the wind.

A small swell wobbles her, and Megan grips the sides. She's seen Sean do this a thousand times, and he makes it look so easy, but out on the water, the paddleboard seems bigger. It's unsteady beneath her knees, its rocking making her feel drunk. Her stepdad won't be happy if he finds out she's taken one of his boards without asking, but Amity's words had made her brave. What was it she'd said? *Break your evening curfew, go out on the paddleboard, fight your corner – it's what I'd do at your age.*

She'd practically given her permission.

Glad she's not being watched, she dips the paddle into the water. Tries a tentative stroke. When the board turns, she's filled with a sense of achievement.

Now she's parallel to the shore, she can see the group on the beach better. They haven't seen her yet, and she's glad. How embarrassing it would be to be caught out here, faffing in the shallows like a kid. Hopefully, by the time they look she'll have got the hang of it.

Mustering her courage, she finds her balance, then pushes the paddle into the water on the left-hand side. Twice more she does it and the board starts to come around until she's facing the horizon. Feeling more confident, she pushes her paddle into the water on the other side and the board moves forward, its nose lifting as it heads into a small wave that covers the fibreglass surface with foamy water.

With every stroke, Megan's confidence grows. She smiles to herself. 'This is wicked.'

Megan turns the nose of the board. Takes the opportunity to check the beach again. She's surprised to see Amity at the edge of the water, her hand tenting her eyes.

Watching her.

Her attention forces her to concentrate harder to keep the

board steady. While she's been deciding what to do, the board has moved further out to sea, drawn silently away from the beach by the outgoing tide. Amity raises a hand. She looks smaller now. Is she waving?

Megan lets go of the oar with one hand, tries to wave back but falls forward onto her hands and knees as a large swell rocks the board.

'Damn.'

The group on the beach must have seen. Are the boys laughing? She can't tell; they're too far away. She's going to try to stand. She's seen Sean do it many times and he makes it look easy. Megan lays the paddle horizontally across the board as she's seen Sean do and grips the sides of the board with both hands. One foot at a time, she places her feet where her knees were and grips the sides harder, stabilising herself.

The beach is even further away now. She sees how far she's drifted out, knows she should paddle back, but a stubbornness is stopping her. She needs to do this. Needs to prove to herself she can.

Slowly, unsteadily, she pushes herself up, trying to centre her core over the board. A rush of adrenaline floods through her as she manages it, but, out here, the water is no longer flat. It moves and rolls beneath her in small uncrested waves. Unbalancing her. With a small cry, she drops the paddle, bends, and grabs the sides of the board. Too late, she sees the paddle slide into the water. In horror, she watches it slip beneath the surface, and it's only then she pictures the blue buoyancy vest hanging on the hook in the garage. The one she didn't think she'd need.

Her heart's beating too fast. This is no longer fun. She can swim but not that well and certainly not as far as the beach. Instinct makes her lie flat on her stomach. She's cold now, the water washing over her with each small wave.

She doesn't hear Amity's frantic shout. Doesn't see her strip off her jumper and run into the water. All she's aware of is how alone she is out here. That and the way the fibreglass surface of the board amplifies the pounding of her heart.

FORTY-THREE

ELISE

Now

'What were you thinking? How many times have I told you not to go out there?' I jam my hands into my pockets, scared of what they might do if they are free.

Megan shoots me a look. 'What's the problem, Mum? I'm all right, aren't I?'

'That's not the point. Think about what *could* have happened. You've never been on a paddleboard before. Jesus, Megan, you've heard Sean preaching about offshore winds enough times. He's experienced, but even *he* checks the tides carefully before he goes out.' I look at my husband for support. 'Tell her Sean.'

Sean leans his back against the kitchen island. Folds his arms. 'I don't think there's anything I can say that she hasn't already found out herself this afternoon.'

Megan is sitting on the settee, wrapped in one of the throws we keep on the back of the chair for winter days, her head bent to her phone. Is she even listening? Walking over to her, I snatch the phone from her hands. 'This is important, Megan. You could have drowned.'

Megan looks up in shock. 'Give it back, Mum.'

'Not until I know you're taking this seriously.' I glance at the phone in my hands. There's a message on there, but the screen goes blank before I can see who it's from. I wave the phone at her. 'What's this?'

'It's none of your business.' Megan jumps up, the throw dropping to the floor. Tries to take the phone back, but I'm too quick.

'Is it from the boy you were so keen to meet up with? Was it his idea that you go out on the paddleboard? Answer me, Megan.'

Sean shakes his head at me. 'Stop shouting, Elise. You'll wake the baby.'

I glance at the monitor, feeling guilty. It took Sean longer than normal to get Kitty down for her nap. Babies are sensitive to atmosphere, and this proves it. The last thing we need is for her to wake.

'Sorry.' I lower my voice. 'But I'd be grateful if you could tell me, Megs.'

'It was my idea.'

We both turn to look at Amity and anger flares. What a surprise – it was obvious something like this would happen. Her coming here has upset the equilibrium of our lives, and it makes me want to scream. Since leaving Earthbound I'd been so careful. So vigilant. My whole life reduced to keeping Megan safe. Now this.

But I can't show it because, until I can get the money, I have to keep Amity on my side. I can't risk her saying anything.

'We're your parents, Megan. You knew how we felt. You could have said no.'

Megan sits down again, picks up the throw from the ground and drapes it over her shoulders. Her voice is sullen. 'I wanted to go out on it. I do have a mind of my own, you know, but oh no, you have to treat me like a kid. Perhaps you should be thanking your friend for saving me.'

I feel wrong-footed. 'Yes, thank God she was there.'

'It *was* actually.' She looks at Sean for support. 'Tell Mum to give me my phone back.'

'Give it back to her, El. She's entitled to some privacy.'

I feel a flash of irritation that he's taken her side. 'Not where her safety is concerned. That boy who's messaging her was probably one of the group of kids on the beach. Encouraging her to show off.'

Sean frowns. 'You don't know that.' Without saying anything more, he pushes himself away from the island, comes over to us and takes the phone from my hand. He gives it back to Megan. His action speaks louder than words, and I feel shame at what I did. But it's like I no longer know how to act around my family... how to be. Over the last few weeks my world has pitched and turned, leaving me directionless like a boat on a stormy sea.

I want to say something to Sean, but I don't. He is my anchor. Without him, there is nothing to moor me. Keep me tethered to reality. Outside the window, the sky is darkening, merging with the sea. The four of us now reflected in the glass. I hate being like this, but when I'd arrived home to find Megan soaked to the skin, her face white, her teeth chattering, I'd been overwhelmed with fear. Terrified of what had happened to my child.

Knowing it's dangerous to say any more, I leave the matter of blame for a moment and return to what's important.

'How long has he been messaging you?' I demand.

Megan pales. Her eyes looking up at me from under the strip of wet hair that's fallen across her face. Wary. 'Who?'

'You know who. The boy on your phone.'

Sean shoots me a warning look. 'Leave it, El.'

But I can't leave it. I have to know. 'How old is he, Megan? Don't you remember what Sean said to you about—'

'For God's sake, Mum!' Pushing the throw off her shoulders, Megan thumps the drink I made her onto the table and pushes past me. A few minutes later, I hear the slam of her bedroom door.

Sean shakes his head. 'You handled that well.'

'Please, Sean, just don't.' My voice cracks and my eyes grow glassy with tears.

'I'm sorry, that wasn't helpful, was it.' Sean's arm is around my shoulders, and I don't resist as he leads me to the settee Megan has just vacated. He looks over his shoulder at Amity, who's watching us with interest. 'Would you mind giving us a bit of time to sort this out, Amity? I'm sure you understand.'

'Sure. I'll go and see if Megan's okay.'

Our eyes lock, but she doesn't say anything more, just slips off the stool and heads out of the living area. As I hear her knock on Megan's door, I can't rid myself of the resentment. It should be me comforting Megan, not her.

'Leave them.' It's as though Sean's read my mind. 'It will probably do Megs good to talk to someone outside of the family.'

It's only now the tears come. 'What if something worse had happened? What if I'd lost her?'

'What if *we'd* lost her? Come on, El. Don't shut me out.' He pulls my head to his shoulder, strokes my hair. 'I know you don't want to hear it, but it's like I've always said... to be safe on the water you need to understand it. How can Megan do that if you don't give her any freedom? I could have taken her out on the paddleboard years ago. Shown her how to do it safely. How to check the tides and the wind. She's not a child.'

I lift my head from his shoulder. 'She *is* a child, Sean. She's only fifteen.'

'She will be sixteen soon. You have to give the kid some freedom.' He angles his body so that he can look at me properly.

'What's up, Elise? You've not been yourself for a while. Is it something I've done? Said?'

I'm shocked that he can think that. Sean is my rock. My world.

'No, of course it isn't.'

'What is it then?'

I wipe away the tears with the heel of my hand. 'I don't know. I'm just on edge. Unsettled.'

'Are you still worried that Alex sent that newspaper article that freaked you out?'

'Not any more. I made a mistake. I don't think he sent it, after all.'

'Really? Why not?'

'Just something Amity said.'

Sean twists a strand of my hair around his finger. 'I don't think I like her much. Does that bother you?'

'No. For a long time we were close, but life can change you. It changed her.' I stop, scared I've said too much. 'I want to help her, though. Just until she sorts herself out.'

Sean smiles. 'You have a big heart. It's one of the reasons I love you. What is it then? What's bothering you?'

'He might not have sent that article, but I suppose Amity arriving here out of the blue has made me realise how easy it is to find someone if you have a mind to. Especially if you're a police officer.'

I freeze. I've never told Sean this.

He moves back. His smile slipping. 'Alex is a police officer?'

'Yes. It's no big deal, Sean. It's just made things a little difficult for me in the past.'

'How difficult? I think you should tell me. There's more to this, isn't there? You're scared of him. I hear it in your voice whenever you say his name.'

I stand. Fold my arms around my body. 'Leave it, Sean. This isn't the time.'

'Then when is? I'll be leaving for Newcastle soon. I don't feel happy going with these secrets between us.'

'He was controlling, all right? And because he was a police officer, no one believed me. I took Megan and left him. That's it. You know the rest.'

'Jesus. Why the hell did you never say?'

'Because I wanted to forget. I didn't want to be defined by him. It's taken years to get to a good place, Sean, and I don't need reminders.'

Sean sighs heavily. 'I understand that, but perhaps we should talk about this more when I'm back.'

'Perhaps.' But I know there's little more I can say about it without destroying everything we have.

Sean looks at his watch. He'll be leaving soon. 'Are you sure you're going to be all right here on your own?'

'I'm not on my own.'

'You know what I mean.' He reaches for my hand. 'I can cancel the trip if you want. Go another time. After what happened with Megan—'

'You don't need to. Now that Amity's here, I don't feel so worried about you not being here.' I have no intention of telling him it was she who'd made the phone call to the police. She who'd sent the article.

I want him to stay so very much, but I need him gone. It's the only way I'll be able to get rid of Amity quietly.

'Go, Sean. You're leaving later than you wanted as it is. I'll talk to Megan later and tell her I'm sorry for having a go at her. That it was only because I was worried.' I make myself smile. 'We'll be fine.'

It seems to satisfy him. Leaning forward, he kisses my lips, then gets up off the settee. 'I'm all packed. I'll say goodbye to Megan and Kitty, then be on my way. There's something I need to do first, though. Something I've been thinking of for a while. It will make you feel more secure while I'm away.'

I'm puzzled. 'What's that?'

'I ordered it a while back but never got around to setting it up.' He looks at his watch. 'It won't take long.'

He goes downstairs to the sunroom where we have a big sideboard that contains a lot of his surfing junk and returns a few moments later with a box in his hands. He puts it on the dining table and takes out the contents. Lays them out on the polished surface, looking pleased with himself.

'Just so I know you're safe. I can monitor the house from anywhere. Cool, eh?'

I stare at the small cameras lined up on the table. Feel the colour drain from my face. They look exactly like the ones Alex used.

As their unblinking eyes stare up at me, nausea rises.

Someone is always watching me...

FORTY-FOUR

ELISE

Now

The house is quiet. Since Sean left, I've been struggling to keep myself occupied: flicking channels on the TV, picking up my book and reading a few pages, scrolling through news items on my phone.

On the screen of the baby monitor, I can see Kitty is sleeping soundly, one arm thrown across her eyes, the other clutching the comforter that used to be Megan's. Turning my head, I look beyond the living area to the dark atrium where I can just make out my huge seascape on the right-hand wall – the one I know my daughter thinks is boring.

I stand, my book dropping onto the settee, and search out the strip of light under Megan's bedroom door. Hoping she's still awake. I haven't spoken to her since she stormed off to her room, wanted to wait until we'd both had a chance to calm down. While I've been sitting here, I've been thinking about the past and the future, and I know it is time – that I've left it long enough. However much I hate the idea, tonight is the night I need to explain why I've been so protective of her. That it's not just older boys she needs to be wary of, but a man called Alex. That I lied when I said he was a one-night stand.

I thought I'd never have to tell her, but now Sean knows, it's only fair she knows too. But what's really important is for her to understand what the man is like. What he's capable of. I need to impress upon her that, for both our sakes, she must never try to make contact with him. We're safe from him now, but we might not always be.

I get up, walk through the living area past the table where Sean had earlier unpacked the box of security cameras. After my meltdown, he'd hastily packed them away again, but the memory of them is still there. Of course, I'd had to explain why I'd left the room so suddenly, but I'd only given him a potted truth. I'd said Alex had been jealous, that he didn't trust me and liked to keep tabs on my whereabouts, even though I had nothing to hide. Eventually, I'd allowed him to put a couple up outside, as their presence would not be so intrusive. So invasive of my privacy.

The look of disgust on my husband's face is one I never want to see again. *The bastard*, he'd muttered as he'd put on his coat to leave. *The bloody bastard*.

Now I'm at Megan's door and, although every bone in my body is screaming at me not to do it, I force myself to raise my hand and knock. I've avoided this day for fifteen years, but it's time Megan knew the truth. Even if only part of it.

'Megan?' I say her name quietly, hoping she'll hear. 'Megan, can I talk to you?'

I wait. Through the door I can hear music playing, something with a deep bass beat I don't recognise. I knock again.

'Can I come in, Megs? This is important.'

She's clearly still sulking, pretending not to hear me. Or *not* pretending. Deliberately ignoring. Hoping I'll give up and go away. But I won't, because if I don't do this now, I never will.

'Leave her. You'll only make it worse.'

I turn. See Amity on the white settee under the sea painting. She's wearing a pair of my jeans and a jumper Sean bought
me last Christmas. In the dim lighting she looks just the same as
she did all those years ago at Earthbound. She has something in
her hand, and when I see what it is, my breath catches. I run to
her. Try to snatch it from her. But she waves it out of my reach.

'Where did you find that? Give it to me.'

Amity lowers her arm. 'You need to be more careful with
your things. El.'

'Give it to me,' I repeat, reaching out. 'Why does it matter to
you anyway? You know what it says. I told you I'd get you the
money. You can't let Megan see it or she'll think her father
really did care. That the bastard actually had a heart.'

Amity places the article on the coffee table in front of her.
Flattens it with her hand. She looks across to Megan's door, and
for the first time since she arrived at our house, I see worry
written on her face. 'She already has.'

'What? We agreed—'

'Don't look at me like that... I didn't show her. She found it
one day when you were out. Asked me not to tell you.'

I can't believe what I'm hearing. 'So why tell me now? If
Megan already knows about him—'

Amity lowers her forehead to her hands. 'Because, contrary
to what you might think, I do have a conscience. I've always
liked Megan, had a real soft spot for her at Earthbound, and to
be honest, I'm worried about her and what she's planning to do.
Worried for her safety.'

I stare at her. Wanting to ask yet terrified of the answer.
'What do you know?'

'He's been in contact with her, Elise.' Amity meets my gaze,
then looks away again. 'Alex has messaged her.'

'Oh God!' My gut lurches. 'He can't have. How?'

'Facebook apparently. Megan used Messenger to get in
touch with him.' She breathes in. 'Let's be thankful it wasn't

Instagram, which is where she's been posting most of her pictures... and how I managed to find you. At least she's taken down anything that would give your location away if he happened to look now. I checked.'

'She can't ever meet him.' Amity says nothing, but her face says it all. My eyes widen with horror. 'Tell me he didn't ask her.'

'He did.'

My fear turns to anger. 'And you didn't think to tell me earlier?'

'I tried to talk her out of it. Told her what he was like... what he'd done to you, though I didn't go into detail. She wouldn't hear a word against him, though. Said I didn't know him.' She stands. 'I'll try again if you like.'

'No. I'll do it. I have to make her understand.' Somewhere in the house, a floorboard creaks and a shiver runs through me. Even with Amity here, the place feels too big. Too empty. And to think that only a day ago, when I'd realised it was Amity not Alex who'd phoned the police, sent the article, I'd actually been happy.

How naïve I'd been to presume it would be Alex doing the searching not Megan. A terrible thought strikes me. 'You don't think she'll have told him where we live, do you? Where our house is?'

'I don't think so. She might play the stroppy teenager card at times, but she knows how you'd feel about that.'

It's small consolation. 'I'm scared, Amity. You don't know Alex. You think you do because of what I've told you, but he's worse than that. Far, far worse. You have no idea what he'll do to me if he finds me. I should never have stayed here so long.' I rub at my wrists, panic stopping me from thinking straight. 'He's out there. I can feel it.'

Knowing I can't leave it any longer, I hurry to Megan's door, and, without bothering to knock again, open it.

'Megan, I know you don't want...' I stop, the sentence slipping away from me. The door has opened onto an empty room.

'Megan?' But the word is redundant. It's clear she isn't here.

My eyes scan the clothes on the floor, the unmade bed, the mug that sits on the bedside table, desperate to have missed something, but even as I'm crossing the room to the fitted wardrobe, to see if anything's missing, I know she's gone.

My heart gives a lurch. Where is she?

The only things I can see are missing are her phone and her bag. A quick look in her wardrobe confirms that her denim jacket isn't there either. It doesn't look as though she'll have gone too far, but that's small consolation when I've no idea where she is.

I run back to Amity. 'She's gone.'

'What do you mean?'

'She's not in her room. She's not here.' I pass a hand around the back of my neck, trying to think, then turn on Amity, my face hard. 'You know where she is, don't you?'

'No.' Amity straightens. 'I promise you, El, I have no idea.'

'I swear to God, Amity. If you're lying to me—'

'I'm not. You have to believe me.'

'Okay.' Panic makes it hard to think. 'I'm going out to look for her.'

'I'll come too.'

'No, I need you to stay here in case Megan comes home before I do. Kitty should stay asleep, but the baby monitor is there so you can check on her. I'll have my phone if you need me.'

Amity nods. 'Megan will be all right, El.'

'You don't know that.' I stuff the newspaper article into my bag. 'Hopefully, I won't be long.'

I grab my coat and run downstairs to the lower floor. Let myself out of the sunroom doors into the cold night. The pool lights are still on, the palms and grasses that move in the breeze sending zebra stripes across the surface of the water. Our own little oasis.

When I reach the back gate, I slide the key into the padlock and open it. The gate clicks shut behind me, and I secure it. Megan has her own key, so there's no danger of her being locked out.

I'm on the boardwalk now, the weathered planks creaking beneath my feet. Nothing to guide me except for the few houses in the row that still have lights on.

I glance up at my own house. Only my studio and our bedroom, where Kitty is sleeping, is in darkness. The rest of the house shines out across the beach like a beacon. But as I set off along the boardwalk, the silver-laced sea and the flat, white moon my only companions, it gets darker. The shadows deeper. And when a cat jumps down from a fence on my right and runs across the weed-covered stones towards me, I almost jump out of my skin.

I take out my phone, meaning to message Sean to let him know what's going on, and see there's been a voicemail from him. I click on it and listen. Desperate to hear my husband's voice.

Hi El. I was thinking about what you said before I left about your ex, and it came to me that, recently, he seems to be always there. Not in our house, but, you know, in your head. Even when you aren't talking about him, I know you're thinking about him. Look, I get it that you haven't felt you can tell me much, but I'm not stupid. I know that something bad must have happened when you were with him, and, honestly, El, it's been eating me up.

I thought if we knew more about where he is now and what he's doing, then he wouldn't be this bloody great bogeyman from your past. He'd be real. Someone you could deal with better. Someone I could deal with.

*Anyway, I know a guy on the force up in Birmingham,
where you said you used to live, and I gave him a ring. He told
me that a few years back, Alex went for promotion, but despite
his good track record, didn't get it. Too much of a maverick and
they couldn't take the risk. Apparently, Alex isn't in the police
any more. After his setback, he stayed on for a bit but eventually left under a cloud... though no one seems to know for sure
what it was he did. Gossip has it he didn't play by the rule
book. Continued to deal with things his own way which made
a few of the top dogs nervous. What surprised me more, though,
was the support he had from his team. He was well liked, and
his leaving left a lot of bad feeling.*

*Lee thinks he's moved down south somewhere but doesn't
know where exactly. Anyway, what I wanted to say was with
him no longer in the police, if you wanted to make a retrospec-
tive complaint about him, it would be different this time.
Think about it, El. Love you.*

I stare at my phone. My blood runs cold. Sean thinks this is
good news, but it isn't.

With no job to focus on, no longer able to experience the
excitement of the chase, Alex will be restless. He'll have too
much time on his hands, and his resentment over having been
overlooked for promotion, then pushed out of the force, will
fester. Grow out of all proportion. Past slights coming to the
fore to be worried at like a tongue on a jagged tooth.

He's moved down south somewhere, Sean had said, but
where? When I'd thought he was nearly two hundred miles
away, I'd felt a little safer but now...

Alex will be ready to blame. To punish. He'll reason that
none of this would have happened if his bitch of a girlfriend
hadn't run off with his child. Humiliated him.

I walk faster. It's no longer *if* but whether he's *already*
found me.

FORTY-FIVE

ELISE

Now

I'm walking quickly, wishing now that I'd gone out the front door instead – kept to the well-lit roads and the pavements. But some sixth sense tells me Megan went this way. I just don't know where she was heading.

As I walk, I try to call Sean, but he isn't answering. I leave a message. *Megan's gone, and I don't know where she is. Will keep you posted.* Then shove my phone back into my bag.

I want to call out Megan's name, shout it as loud as I can across the beach, but I can't. As Sean and Amity have both said, she's not a child any more. Not really. All I can do is carry on walking, straining my eyes to catch a glimmer of light from a phone or a torch in the area of the rocks where I know she likes to sit. And when the boardwalk runs out, and the only things between me and the road are the beach huts, I check each covered deck. Look between each tongue-and-groove wall. Finding nothing.

Under my coat, goosebumps rise on my arms. The panic I'd hoped to keep at bay is rising. I'm aware of the hiss of the surf as it rushes up the stones. It's death-rattle as it pulls back. I stop, my hands resting on my hips, and stare into the darkness, the push of blood through my veins the only thing anchoring me to the present.

Where are you, Megan? Where the hell are you?

It's gone midnight when I get back to the boardwalk. I've looked everywhere I can think of and have found no sign of my daughter. As I hurry back, hoping that she'll be safely home by now, I think about my options if she isn't. I could call the parents of the few girls Megan has been friendly with at school. I could call the police and be told what I already know – that the chances are she'll be home soon or I could just wait.

God forbid she's gone to meet Alex.

Not for the first time, I wish Sean was here to advise me. Taking out my phone, I call again. Leave another message. *Couldn't find her. Hoping she's back at home now.* Why isn't he answering? Surely he'd have reached his hotel by now. Maybe there's been a hold-up on his journey. If he knew what was going on, I'd feel happier.

I walk faster. *Please be home. Please be home.*

When I'd left the house, the sky had been clear. Swept with stars. The rockpools flooded with moonlight. Now, a bank of clouds has covered the night sky, obliterating the moon and the red lights of the wind farm. Black sea and black sky merge into one. The darkness solidifies.

I feel a spot of rain then another. It's past midnight and the only house that's lit is ours. When the rain comes down harder, I pull the hood of my coat over my head and run, my feet slipping on the boards. Rain soaking through the material of my coat. Sticking my jeans to my legs. I think of Megan's denim jacket. If she hasn't already come home, she'll be drenched.

As though wanting to keep the rain company, the wind that

had been absent only a couple of hours ago, has whipped up and I hear rather than see the resulting rush of waves onto the shore. The settling of stones in their ebb. Ahead of me, above the wall, the palms on our patio thrash as the wind catches them, their undersides lit citrus green from the pool lights.

Clutching my hood to keep it up, I run the rest of the way, stopping when I get to the gate. It's still padlocked, but that doesn't mean Megan hasn't come home. She might have locked the padlock behind her or come in the front way.

The padlock is cold. Slippery wet. I fumble with the key, cursing when the lock doesn't open straight away. It's a relief to be back, the lit windows welcoming compared to the dark beach behind me, and I pray that Megan has come home, tail between her legs, ready to apologise for worrying me.

But there's something different about the house. I can see it now as I open the gate and thread my way between the ornamental pots, the leaves of the plants whipping at my arm as I go by. There's a light on in my bedroom, the one where Kitty's sleeping. She must have woken.

There's a movement at the window, seen through the whipping hashtag of the palm leaves. Megan, if my prayers have been answered, or Amity. The person moves closer to the window, and, at the same time, the wind drops. Stilling the leaves momentarily. Giving me a better view.

I stand paralysed, my eyes fixed on the figure at the glass. The padlock key pressing its cold shape into my palm. Because what I've just seen is my worst nightmare.

The person at the window, holding Kitty, is neither Megan nor Amity.

It's Alex.

FORTY-SIX

ELISE

Now

Blood hammers at my temples as I stand rigid, the rain pattering a staccato rhythm on the surface of the pool. Alex has my baby! There's a constriction in my chest that makes it hard to breathe. How did he get in when the gate was padlocked?

As the seconds tick by, dread tightens its grip. The sight of him, even after fifteen years, is terrifying. The way he's standing, the angle of his head, dragging me back. Threatening to turn me into that person again... the one I was then. Scared of doing the wrong thing. Scared of making him angry.

But I'm not that person any more. I'm Sean's wife. This is my family and I have to do something.

As I slide the sunroom door open, glad that Amity hadn't locked it behind me, I start to shiver uncontrollably. My clothes are soaked through, but it's not that... it's the fear. I have no idea what Alex plans to do. I'd always imagined it would be me he'd go after. Ready to pick up where he'd left off. Ready to punish. But he has Kitty. He has my baby.

Alex is in my bedroom on the second floor, but where are

Megan and Amity? Has he hurt them? Are they even here? Taking off my shoes, I tiptoe in my wet socks through the sunroom to the stairs. When I reach the first floor, I wait and listen. The lights are on, but my eyes are fixed on the next set of spiral stairs that continue up to the second floor where Alex is. I can hear him moving around. What is he doing? What is he planning?

A sound over by the settees makes me turn my head, and now I see what I hadn't before. Amity is kneeling on the floor, her hand covering her face. When she lowers it, her palm is covered with bright red blood. Her nose clearly broken.

I give a sharp intake of breath. 'Jesus.'

Amity looks up at me through swollen eyes. 'I didn't recognise him. He was in uniform and had a warrant card.' She stops, studies her bloodied hand as though seeing it for the first time. Her face white. 'I thought he was a regular police officer – that his coming here had something to do with Megan. I should never have opened the door. He said he's going to take the baby. That it's his right.'

My eyes slide from her to the stairs then back again. 'Was that all he said?' Panic makes me hiss out the words. 'Please try and remember.'

'There was something else.' Her voice is thick. Nasal. 'He said, "*An eye for an eye.*"'

A tremor of fear runs through me. 'I have to call the police.'

With one eye on the stairs, I take my phone out of my pocket, steadying it with the other hand as I'm trembling so much I'm afraid it will slip out of my fingers. The screen lights up with a message, but I ignore it, my finger hovering over the emergency services button. But, in that action, all the insecurities of my past come rushing back – bringing their terrible pictures with them. Me sitting in Corinne's car as I told her what Alex had done to me – each painful word forcing me to relive it. Then watching her through the window of the police station as she moved closer to Alex. Laughing. Downplaying what I'd just told her. Diminishing it.

I feel again the hot twist of betrayal. Alex had been right all along. People thought I was unstable. No one believed my story.

Maybe no one will now.

It would be my word against his. His against mine.

The baby monitor is on the settee next to where Amity is kneeling and on the small screen, I can see Alex pacing. I stare at the black and white image and tell myself that this time it's different: the evidence of what he's like present in Amity's bloodied nose. An injury caused by a man who was made to leave the police force, who entered my house under false pretences and who, at this very moment, has my child in his arms.

I jab the button. Press the phone to my ear. *Emergency services. Which service do you need?*

But the fear that the past will repeat itself has made me hesitate too long. Alex is standing at the bend in the stairs, looking down at me, Kitty pressed to his chest. Not the Alex from my nightmares but worse, because this Alex is real. Flesh and blood. My hand drops to my side, the phone slipping from my trembling fingers to the floor.

'Hello, Elise.' He says it as though it was only yesterday he saw me. As if we have unfinished business.

I stare at him, unable to tear my eyes away. He's in his early-fifties now, but if anything, he looks fitter, more athletic – time spent working out evident in the muscles of his forearms, his biceps. There's a sprinkling of grey around his temples and his jawline isn't as clean as it once was, but it's his eyes I can't stop looking at. Eyes that haven't changed one bit. They're fixed on me now, making me feel we're the only two people in the room. It takes me back to when we first met.

But, as he turns to Kitty, his eyes hardening, I see something new and terrifying in them. The steel glint of the fanatic.

It breaks the spell.

'Give me the baby.' I hold out my arms. 'Give her to me, Alex.'

He throws his head back and laughs. 'Really? I don't think so, do you?'

My stomach turns as he lowers his lips to her head, breathes her in. I want to run at him, gouge at his eyes, his lips, so he can't see her. Can't touch her. But I don't. He has Kitty and who knows what he might do.

Behind me, I hear Amity trying to stand. 'You're an arsehole. Deranged.'

Alex's attention turns to her, his eyes narrowing. 'If I were you, I'd shut the fuck up.'

'Or what? Break my nose?' Amity points a blooded finger at him. 'I know what you are.'

I stare at her in shock, try to convey with pleading eyes that I want her to stop. She'll only make things worse.

He's standing at the bottom of the stairs now and Kitty, knowing the arms that hold her aren't ones she recognises, starts to cry. Her arms stretching for me as Megan's used to.

The memory is strong. Megan's eyes on mine as I'd fed her. Her milky breath soft against my neck as I held her against my shoulder to burp her. The weight of her. The smell of her. My love for my baby had been so perfect, so powerful, it had given me courage. Made me strong enough to leave Alex when I didn't think I had the strength.

The thought of her releases me from Alex's spell. I run at him, but he's quicker. He pushes me roughly aside and, with Kitty's cry echoing in the large room, heads for the patio doors. As he yanks the nearest one open and runs across the balcony towards the spiral staircase, the bright security lights that Sean fixed, pick him out.

I run after him, feet slipping on the wet tiles, rain plastering my hair to my face.

Alex is below me on the patio now. I think he's going to make a run for it through the back gate to the boardwalk, but he doesn't. Instead, he walks towards the pool.

The rain falls through the beam of the security lights onto the dark leaves of the palms, making them shine. It bounces off the surface of the pool, giving the patio a tropical look. But it's an illusion, the night is cold and I'm chilled right through to the bone. Only the adrenaline coursing through my veins stops me from giving in to the rigours that are making it hard to climb down the twisting metal steps.

'Give Kitty to me, Alex.' I step towards him. 'She's frightened. She needs me.'

Alex turns, holds Kitty to his chest. 'Fifteen years I've waited to teach you what it feels like to lose your baby.'

I want to laugh. Alex can't teach me anything. He's nothing. Nobody.

'Give her to me. You never cared about your daughter, so you can stop the act.'

I take another step forward, but Alex just smiles.

'You grew a set of balls. I like that.' He jerks his head towards the pool. 'Teach the kid to swim yet?'

I stare at the water then back at him. 'Please don't do anything stupid, Alex.'

Lifting Kitty under her arms, Alex swings round. Holds Kitty out in front of him over the water. Sensing danger, she cries louder.

My tears are mixing with the rain. I don't know what to do. He'll do it. I know he will. I reach out my hand, my eyes beseeching him.

'Please.'

I'm so absorbed, so horrified by what is playing out in front of me, that I don't hear Amity. Don't see her until it's too late. She's by Alex's side, trying to wrestle Kitty from his grasp.

'Amity. No!'

With the ease of swatting a fly, Alex's free arm lashes out. Catches her on the side of the head. Dumb with shock, I watch as she falls back, her head making contact with the side of the pool with a sickening thud.

I start to go to her, but Alex holds out his hand. 'Leave her.'

'She's hurt.'

Alex looks down at her. 'She slipped... What can I say? Clearly not enough safety measures. You ought to look into that.'

There's blood around Amity's head, the rain diluting it, washing it into the joins between the slabs. Alex is a monster. Caring for nothing except exacting his revenge.

An eye for an eye.

He'll take Kitty from me, and I'll never see her again.

I watch in horror as he walks over to Amity, shoving her with his foot until her body's balanced on the edge of the pool. As if in slow motion, she topples, water sluicing onto the paving as her body breaks the surface of the ghostly blue. She's face down, just as she was the first time I saw her, strands of dark hair streaming out around her. As I watch, her body slowly sinks, and I drop to my knees and scream.

'Shut the fuck up unless you want this one to join her?' Alex's voice breaks through my terror.

I force my eyes up. He's holding Kitty over the water again.

'Please. No!'

The white chevrons of the epaulettes on his navy jumper are picked out by the bright security lights. 'You want her?' He lets go of Kitty, then catches her again before she falls. Kitty laughs through her tears, thinking it's a game.

'Yes.' I can barely form the words. 'Please. Please, Alex.'

I'll beg him on my knees if I have to.

Alex turns away from the swimming pool, holds Kitty to him. 'Then I want something in return.'

He slides his hand into his pocket and immediately I know

what he's going to do. Muscle memory makes me rub at my wrist. Makes my heart clench.

The handcuffs glint as he holds them out. Jangles them. 'Come here.'

I push myself back across the wet concrete. 'No.'

'I see. So that's how you want to play it.' He places Kitty on one of the sunloungers. Both hands are free now. 'I would have been a good father. You know that, don't you?' He considers the metal cuffs. 'You took that from me. From Megan.'

I shake my head. 'You're deluded. A narcissist. You never loved Megan. You loved nothing but yourself.'

Alex takes a step towards me. Draws his phone from his pocket.

'Is that so? Then how do you explain the messages between me and Megan? The bond we have. She confided in me, you know. Told me how you stifled her. Wouldn't tell her anything about me or let her try and find me. Here...' He shoves the phone in my face. 'Read them for yourself. Our daughter will be sad I never made it to our rendezvous tonight. Angry when I tell her it was you who stopped me. I forgive you, Elise, of course I do. It isn't your fault that your mental health issues cloud your judgement. But Megan...' He smiles. 'Megan will *never* forgive you. Not when she knows how you stole her from me. When she finds out what a selfish, evil bitch you were and still are.'

He grabs me by the arm and my self-control breaks. I'm shaking uncontrollably. Hate him with such a passion that I would rather die than be under his control again.

'The girl you've been messaging isn't Megan. Megan is *dead.*'

I choke on the last word, knowing I'm putting myself in more danger, but no longer caring. Chloe, the daughter he knows nothing about, will be back soon, and I have to save her from him. Just as I did when she was a baby.

Alex's face is inches away from mine. 'You're lying.'

But he can see from my face I'm not.

His face darkens and he raises his hand. The blow knocking me to the ground. 'What did you do to her? Tell me?'

But I can't. I won't. Not before I've told my daughter.

'Hold out your hands.' Alex grabs both my wrists, and I feel the cold metal snap into place around them. First one then the other.

The surface of the pool moves as the wind strokes it, and I think of my three daughters. The one I lost, the one I found and the one I share with Sean. Each so precious to me.

I can hear him reading me my rights, a gross parody of his former life, and close my eyes. Knowing he'll never let me get away with it. Praying for the end to come quickly.

Kitty gives a sharp cry, and I open my eyes again. As the leaves of the cordyline move in the wind, I think I see Chloe, but maybe she's just a vision. Conjured up by my love for her. By my acceptance that I'll never see her again. Alex's back is to her. He's kneeling in front of me, his hands sliding around my throat. Kitty's cries are louder now, and it gives me the strength to fight back. But he's too strong. It's a fight I can never win.

On silent feet, Chloe moves towards us. She raises her arms above her head and in the patio lights the heavy stone Buddha glows white against the night sky. With a cry, she brings it down on her father's head. Steps back in horror as he falls backwards.

Neither of us move. Alex is lying on the concrete. His lifeless eyes staring up at the starless sky.

Chloe is trembling. Hands pressed to her face. Pieces of the stone Buddha scattered around her. Some painted with Alex's blood.

'Come here, Megan. You're safe. He can't hurt us now.' I need her to know that before the shock sets in. Consumes her.

Slowly my daughter lowers her hands. Her face deathly white. She picks Kitty up from the sunlounger and sinks down beside me on the wet ground. Lays her head on my shoulder, her body shaking.

In the distance, a police siren wails.

She turns wet, scared eyes to me. 'Who am I, Mum?'

And in that moment, I know she heard everything. That the life I've lived for the last fifteen years is over and we can never be those same people again.

FORTY-SEVEN

ELISE

Then

I stood in Kristen's narrow hallway, listening as your cry became louder. A cry that said you needed your mother's arms around you and nobody else's. It invoked in me a primitive instinct to comfort. To succour. I'd made the right decision... I couldn't just leave you here.

I looked back at the living room door, surprised your cries through the baby monitor hadn't woken Kristen. Surely, even a tired mother would wake to a baby's cry. But, of course, you weren't her baby. You were mine. Maybe that simple fact enabled her to sleep when I would have woken.

I'd thought that I'd just leave, take you from the cot without a word, but now I saw how unkind that would be. Kristen deserved better. Not caring if it was the wrong thing to do, I went back into the living room and shook Kristen by the shoulder. She might be angry that my being here had broken our agreement, but I was equally angry with *her*. However tired she was, she should have woken to comfort my baby.

'Megan's crying, Kristen. Didn't you hear her? Wake up.'

I shook her again, but Kristen's eyes didn't open. Instead, her head slipped sideways off the cushion. It was only then I noticed how pale her face was. Saw the strange purple patches that bloomed on her skin.

'Kristen? Are you ill?' I pressed a hand to her forehead. It was warm but something wasn't right. She was so still. I took a step back. The awful truth of it dawning on me. What if all this time, Kristen hadn't been asleep? My hand shot to my mouth, and I doubled up, my other arm folding across my stomach. It couldn't be true. This couldn't be happening.

You had been quiet for a moment, but now, through the monitor, your cry came again, forcing me into action. I straightened and moved closer to the settee, my hand trembling as I lifted Kristen's arm and felt for the pulse on the soft skin of her wrist. Finding none, not even a faint flutter, I laid my head against her chest, but there was no movement.

She was dead.

'Oh my God! Oh my *God*!'

What terrible thing had happened here? There was no sign of an accident, or a fight. No sign of Alex. No reason to believe either mother or baby had been ill. I couldn't think straight. In front of me was the airer where Kristen had hung the baby clothes to dry in front of the heater. The *faulty* heater she'd wanted her landlord to fix or replace. I'd heard of people dying through carbon monoxide poisoning. Is that what had happened? On the coffee table in front of me was a letter headed Lambert Letting Agency. I picked it up, hardly able to read as the page was shaking so much. It was an advisory notice to remind Kristen that the landlord would be making an inspection visit to the property at nine o'clock the next day. Maybe she'd decided not to mention the heater to him until she saw him at the inspection. That error of judgement could have been the last one she made. The thing that killed her.

Pushing the airer aside, I switched the heater off, then went to the window and opened it, letting in the cold night air. My thoughts were in turmoil. I should try mouth to mouth, chest compressions, but I couldn't ignore the baby who was lying there next to Kristen. I hadn't even checked to see if she was all right. Whether she was alive or dead. I had to know if there was any hope.

As I bent to Chloe and lifted her from her mother's arms, cradling her head so it wouldn't fall back, I uttered up a silent prayer. *Please let her be okay.* But even as my lips formed the words, I knew it was useless. The child was lifeless. Her skin showing the same mottling as her mother's.

I pressed the baby to me, tears streaming down my face. 'Not Chloe too. Please, please not Chloe.'

And as I said it, I tried to ignore the irrational thought that at least the baby would not be left without a mother. At least Kristen would never know what it felt like to lose her child.

I held the baby close. My tears dripping into her hair. Feeling the weight of her. A weight my arms recognised. Responded to. Felt how her body fitted mine like the missing piece of a jigsaw. Without thinking, I ran a finger down her smooth cheek, the curve of her jaw. Knowing the shape of it.

The baby monitor barked out another cry, but this time my body didn't respond to it in the way it had before. The cry sounded different to me now. Higher pitched. Missing the hiccup that usually punctuated the sound.

I no longer recognised it.

Why didn't I recognise it?

I gasped at the sudden pain in my sternum. A deep, blunt pain like a wooden stake had been forced through it. I knew I had to look at the child in my arms, but the fear was a physical weight on my chest. I didn't want to do it because every minute I stood there with my eyes closed was another minute of not knowing. Another minute separating the before from the after. For once I let my eyes rest on her face, her hands, the tiny dimple in her chin, there would be no going back from it. That one look would shape my future. Drain the colour from it. Take me to a hell I didn't know if I would ever recover from.

But I had to look. What else could I do? Even though I think I already knew.

Over the last fifteen years, I've tried to bury the memory, and now that I've pulled it back, the image is ragged, faded at the edges. As I draw it towards me, I see the woman more clearly. See her as she stands in that small living room, the television now showing an advert of an expensive car driving along a mountain pass. Still feel the pain of recognition as she looks down at the baby she's holding. The one she gave birth to five months earlier.

I remember how she'd have given her life to change that fact.

And I want you to believe me, Megan. I still would.

What came next I can't explain. The air in the room felt a little thinner. A little more unreal, as though I'd stepped onto a film set without knowing my words or what action should come next.

My head knew you were gone, but someone had forgotten to tell my heart. All I could think of at that moment was that you were back where you belonged in my arms. I held you tight and rocked you. In a parallel universe to the one I'd been in moments before. All reason having left me.

'It's all right, Megan. I'm here now. I've come for you.'

You were cold that was all, the thin blanket you were wrapped in no substitute for the warmth of the cot. Never a good sleeper, you would have been unsettled in that strange bedroom... cried out for me. Kristen would have reached in and lifted you out. Taken you into the living room to comfort you. My eyes travelled to the half-drunk bottle of milk that had rolled under the coffee table. Pushed the image away.

All I needed to do was warm you up, then you'd be fine.

I pressed my cheek against yours, curled your small hand in my palm, hoping to transfer the heat from my body to yours. Whispering words of love. But you were so still. Your face a strange luminous white. Your lips tinged with blue.

Yet, the room was so warm. Uncomfortably warm even though I'd opened the window.

And although I fought against it, reality came galloping in. Wielding its sword. Unwelcome. Forcing me to surrender to the truth of what had happened. I placed the palm of my hand to your tiny chest, my cheek to your lips to feel for a breath that didn't come, and my heart was already breaking.

I wanted to die too, Megan. Wished that the malignant fumes had taken me as well. Grief swelled until there was no space left in my chest to breathe. Yet, still, I grasped at anything that would save you. Save *us*. If I could just hold you tight enough, close enough, and tell you how much I loved you, then maybe I could persuade you not to be dead. As I pressed you tight to my chest a feral keening escaped my lips. It was hopeless. You were gone.

I could no longer function. No longer think straight, the terrible thing that had happened unearthing a tsunami of feelings I couldn't control. Heartache. Despair. Hopelessness.

I had no idea what to do. Panic overwhelming my already tortured brain. A voice in my head was telling me I should phone for an ambulance, the police, tell them of the terrible thing that had happened inside this flat. But, if I did, Alex would know where I was. Would find out what I did... how I'd lied when I'd said you'd been taken from the playground. A trick to get away from him. I felt again the crushing pain of your death, but now another emotion was forcing its way in. Terror at what Alex would do if he knew. How he'd twist it. Make it look as though I'd been involved in your death somehow. It would be his revenge for having snatched you from him.

My body began to shake. I couldn't go home. Not now. Not

without our baby. But even if I left, went far away, it didn't mean Alex wouldn't find me one day. My body turned cold at the thought of what he would do if he found me without you. Alex's face was there in my head. His eyes beneath his officer's cap, steel-hard. I imagined him moving towards me. Slipping his hand into the pocket of his jacket. The clink of metal on metal. *An eye for an eye.* I gave an involuntary gasp of fear. My eyes searching the room for him as though he was already there.

He could never know.

Never.

The crying through the baby monitor had got louder. *Chloe* – the child Alex never knew he had. If he found out about her, would he try to claim her? I turned my head to the monitor's screen. The baby was lying on her back in the cot, her face looking up at me. Wanting her mother. Wanting comfort from someone who was no longer able to give it. Alone now. As *I* was alone.

However much I was hurting, I couldn't leave her to her fate. To Alex.

I wanted to blame Kristen for what had happened, but how could I when all she had done was try to help me? It was an accident. Taking you into her home had been a selfless thing. An act of mercy. She had done nothing wrong, her sole reason for doing this, her desire to save us from Alex. It was only right that I saved Chloe in return.

And, even then, with the pain of loss expanding until there was little space left for any other feeling, I knew what I would do. What I *had* to do.

Placing a kiss on your cold cheek, my tears running into your hair, I settled the blanket around you and placed you back in Kristen's arms. Then I left the room and went into the bedroom at the end of the hallway.

At the bottom of the wall by the cot was a nightlight. In its glow, I could see Chloe's face, red from crying. Her arms reaching up for me.

'It's all right, Megan. I'm here now.'

Grief and fear hadn't sent me mad. Despite how it might seem, I knew you weren't my child, but for my plan to work I had, from now on, to tell myself you were. Had to try to believe it. If I could save Chloe, then maybe the terrible accident that had caused your death wouldn't have been in vain. The landlord would visit the flat in the morning – let himself in if he thought Kristen wasn't there. When he found you both, he'd presume you to be his tenant's child. Why wouldn't he? And when the police arrived after he'd called them, there would be no reason for them to believe otherwise.

The baby I held now would no longer be Chloe but Megan. Not just because by then we would be far away from here. Far away from Alex. But because, with that name, a little part of you would live on. Stay with me always, keeping your memory alive.

A bizarre and unforgiveable thought, I know, but it was what I had to do.

That's what grief can do to you. Fear too.

That's what it did to *me*.

FORTY-EIGHT

ELISE

Then

The police station looked very much like the one Alex worked at, except that it was larger, the reception area wider with more seating. More noticeboards on the walls.

The desk officer frowned. 'You say you want to speak to someone about a missing baby?'

My heart was racing, and I folded my arms around the sling strapped to my body. Trying to take comfort from the weight of it and the warmth of the baby's body through the canvas.

'Yes.' I nodded at the man, even though it took all my strength not to sink to the floor. Sob until there were no more tears inside me. But what good would come of that? I had to stay strong. I had to stay focussed – not give in to the tide of emotion that threatened to sweep me away with it every time I thought of my child.

'Your own baby?'

'Yes.'

His eyes slipped to the baby in the sling. 'You have another?'

'No, this is my baby. I reported her missing last week, but now I need you to see that she is safe. Unharmed. I need to explain why I did it.'

'So the baby was never missing?' His frown deepened.

'No.'

The man pushed his chair back. 'I see.'

I turned as the door opened behind me and a female police officer walked in. The desk sergeant stood. 'Ah, PC Wells. Just the person. I have a Ms James with me. She'd like to have a chat to you about her baby.' He pointed his pen at Chloe. 'This little one was reported missing, but apparently it was just a hoax. Could you take over?'

The woman looked at the sling then at me, her face not giving away her thoughts. 'Of course. Come this way, Ms James.'

I hesitated, unsure now whether I had done the right thing. It was a dangerous move coming here, but I'd had no choice. If I'd left without a word to anyone so soon after reporting Megan missing, and the abduction case still open, the eye of suspicion would turn on me and I would become nothing less than a fugitive. Even though I'd wasted police time, I had to let them know that the baby was safe. Let them see for themselves that no harm had come to her. I would tell them why I'd done what I did. Tell them...

Alex's words were in my head again. *Nobody will believe you*. But this time I wouldn't let it stop me. I needed to give them a reason for why I'd done it, and the truth was as good as any. They could believe it or not, I no longer cared. I just needed them to know the baby was fine and that I was sorry.

When I'd finished my story, PC Wells looked up from her notebook. 'Does your partner know that the baby is safe?'

I shook my head. 'No, I don't want to see him. I don't have to, do I?'

'No, but we will have to let him know.' She breathed in,

looked out of the window, then back at me. 'I want you to reconsider your decision not to make a formal complaint against him.'

I shifted in my seat, swallowed down the lump of fear that
lodged in my throat at the thought of what might happen if I
did. 'I don't want to do that. I just needed you to know why I
made it all up. I thought it would help me get away from him.
Help *us*.'

I looked down at the baby strapped to my chest. Forgot for a
moment it wasn't you. And when the realisation hit with sledge-
hammer force, the raw pain was impossible to bear. The tears
arrived, hot and sudden, and I bent forward consumed by a
paroxysm of sorrow and fear for a future without you.

PC Wells stood. Poured a glass of water from the plastic jug
on the table and pushed it towards me. 'Have a drink, Elise.
Take a moment.'

I pressed the palms of my hands to my eyes, wondering if I'd
always feel like this. If the ache of my grief would ever go away
or if this would be my life.

Sensing my despair, Chloe started to cry, and my mother's
instinct kicked in. 'I need to go.' I dragged a tissue from my
sleeve and blotted my eyes. Blew my nose. 'She needs her feed.'

PC Wells nodded. 'I understand, but before you do, I'd like
to check the little one over, if that's okay with you.'

'Of course.' I unwrapped the sling, lifted the baby out and
handed her to the officer. Not wanting to sit there any longer, I
walked to the window and looked out. A bird alighted on the
roof of one of the police cars. Preened its feathers. 'Will you
take this any further... the false abduction?'

'I'll need to speak to the officers involved in the case.
Wasting police time is a serious offence, but I'll recommend that
we don't.' Her voice was neutral, but there was sympathy in her
words. 'There were, after all, mitigating circumstances.'

I turned back from the window. 'It was stupid of me.
Thoughtless... and I'm sorry.'

'The important thing is she's fine.' She smiled at the baby and handed her back to me, dabbing at the wet patch on the arm of her navy fleece where Chloe had been sucking it. 'Give your baby a feed now. You're right, she's hungry.'

Chloe kicked her legs. Struggled as I tried to get her in the sling. Was it obvious to the woman who was watching me that I wasn't her mother or was I being paranoid?

'We have your number. We'll be in touch.' PC Wells came round to my side of the desk. 'Here let me help.'

She was a mother herself. I could see it in the confident way she took Chloe from me. Waited until I'd arranged the material of the sling across my shoulders before handing her back. As I held her to me, she slid the baby's legs through the wrap and pulled it up over her bottom.

'Won't be long before she's too big for this,' she said, with a smile.

It was true. Chloe was a month older than you and already I could feel her weight pulling at my shoulders, making them ache.

'Yes, it might be the last time I take her out in it.'

In the back of the car was your pushchair and a bag of your clothes as I couldn't risk taking anything of Chloe's. Before I left Kristen's flat, I'd shut the window and turned the faulty fire back on, then I'd driven back home terrified Alex would be there. Thankful when he wasn't. I couldn't be bothered to wonder where he was; all I could think about was grabbing some things and getting out again as quickly as I could. I never wanted to set foot in that place again.

I hadn't gone to the police station that night – I was too tired. Too traumatised. My mind going back, again and again, to the moment I'd realised you were gone. Your blue lips and pale face ever present. And then I'd weep again, my forehead resting on the cold steering wheel. Wishing I was with you. Wishing I was dead too... until Chloe's cry would drag me back to the present and I'd reach for her. Lift her from your car seat and give her what little comfort I could.

Two lost souls.

Alone now except for each other.

'Have you somewhere safe to go?' PC Wells's voice pulled me from my thoughts.

'Yes,' I said, lifting my bag onto my shoulder. 'You don't need to worry about me.'

I didn't tell her where, just thanked her for her time and left the room. Walked out of the police station and into the street where my car was waiting. It wasn't that I thought I couldn't trust her. I simply couldn't trust anyone. Alex would worm his way out of this as he did everything else. If life had taught me anything, it was this: if I was to stay safe, I could only rely on myself.

The police station was in a town a few miles from our flat. By now Alex would know I hadn't come home, but, still thinking Megan was missing, I doubted he'd care. Once he was told that she'd never been abducted but was safe and with me, it would be a different story. I had no real plan, but I knew that I couldn't let him find me.

I strapped Chloe into the car seat and drove to a quiet street a mile or so from the station. With the spotlight on Alex, the chances of him coming after me for a while were slim... but what about later when everything had calmed down? It wasn't as though I'd made a formal complaint against him and, as I said, Alex had a way of talking his way out of things.

Lifting the baby from her seat, I held her in my arms and took the lid off the bottle of milk I'd made for her. Found myself smiling when she took the teat in her mouth and sucked greedily. When she'd had enough, I unscrewed the lid of the jar of baby food I'd found in Kristen's cupboard. I hadn't started you on solids yet, but Chloe was a month older. I would need to buy some more. Some larger stretch suits too with the cash I'd taken out of the bank earlier.

I looked down at Chloe, glad we had each other. And, as she looked up at me, trust in her eyes, I made a vow. I'd love this baby as my own. Love her like I'd loved *you*, Megan. And if, God forbid, in the course of time Alex ever found me, her resemblance to you was so strong he would never know the difference. Would never know what had happened... to you or to her.

I looked down at Chloe and thought of you, Megan. The life you'd lost and the one I had to save. In my bag was my burner phone and the one Kristen had used, taken from her bag when I'd been at the flat. I'd need to get rid of them but not yet. Using my own phone, I punched in the number on the scrap of paper I'd taken from my purse. Waited for Tanya's brother to answer.

It was time to start again. It was time to disappear.

FORTY-NINE

ELISE

Three Years Later

The moon is full tonight. Picking out the white edges of the waves as they recoil from the shore.

Sean takes my hand and I let him. Sense rather than see his relief.

'Okay?' he asks.

'I think so.'

'The food at Tosca was just as good as last time. Better if anything, don't you think?'

He's filling the space between our thoughts and I'm grateful. He's right. This has been our first night out since everything happened, and although I hadn't been keen on going, I'd agreed to it to please him.

I have to remember that Sean's been through a lot too. That if it wasn't for him, I don't know how I'd have got through the last few years. I try to calm my nerves with thoughts of the delicious pizza we shared. The tomato and mozzarella salad. The Prosecco – a glass more than I should have had, but one I'd needed.

We've been looking at the flecks of silver on the water, the twinkling of the wind-farm lights on the horizon, but now, as if knowing it's the right time, we both turn. Look up at the house with its wide windows. The light from the upstairs rooms casting a faint glow on the boardwalk.

'Okay?'

That question again. One he's asked a lot recently, worry etched into the furrows on his brow. I'm not sure I'll ever be okay again, but Sean's trying, and I force a smile. I owe him that much.

'Strange to be back,' he says, turning his attention to the plot next door which had once been a building site, but where now a three-storey concrete and steel house stares out at the beach like all of its neighbours. 'A lot has changed.'

'I know.' I look back at the house that used to be ours. 'It might sound odd, but would you give me a moment, Sean?'

His surprise changes to uncertainty. 'Sure. I want to have a look at the front of the new build. But will you be all right out here on your own?'

'I will. There's just some stuff I need to work through.' I squeeze his hand. 'Honestly, I'll be fine.'

'Fifteen minutes then, yeah?'

'Thanks.'

I kiss him. Wait until he's disappeared around the side of the last house before stepping off the boardwalk onto the beach. In my bag is the notebook I've been writing in, on and off, since we left Alex. I take it out and, by the light of the moon, read the final entry. The one I wrote last night.

When I think of you now, Megan, the pain of loss is still there, but it's a pain that's been tempered by time. The sharp edges of it blurred and softened, leaving more space for the love it never quite managed to smother. It weighs heavily on me that I've never been to see your final resting place, but I can't bring myself to, for fear of what it would do to me after all this time. Besides, I carry you with me every day in my heart.

Even though I gave your name to someone else, I never forgot you. Not ever.

I place my hand on the cover of the notebook. It's always given me relief to write down your story, so I'll tell you what I wrote earlier. How the story ends and how our new chapter will begin.

We're managing – that's the simplest way of putting it. Your namesake, Megan, is, despite everything, doing well. She's in her first year at Plymouth University, studying marine biology. She's enjoying her studies, has made friends and, at the end of each term, comes home to be with us. The counselling she's been having has helped a lot, and the nightmares she had, in the year after her father's and Amity's deaths, have been fewer and less vivid.

Her decision not to tell anyone how she came to be my daughter should have surprised me, but somehow it didn't. After I'd told her about her mother, about you, about how I'd done what I did to save her from a life in care or, worse still, a life with her father, she'd clung to me. We'd clung to each other. Adrift on an unknown sea. I'd been her mother for fifteen years and nothing could change that. She knew that I would go to prison if anyone knew what I'd done, and the question she'd asked herself was would that have been the right outcome for someone who had acted out of desperation? Out of compassion for the baby who had lost her mother?

Would it have been the right outcome for someone she loved?

My baby died and I never told anyone. I took someone else's child and pretended she was mine. She accepts all that. Accepts *me* for the person who brought her up and loved her. And, even now, I'm taken aback by her understanding. Her maturity.

Something she never inherited from her father. My only regret is the secret we keep from Sean.

When the police had arrived, they'd had no option but to charge Megan with Alex's death, but our statements had been backed up by evidence from the outside security cameras I'd never wanted Sean to put up. It had been a clear case of reasonable force being used in the defence of others and she'd been acquitted.

I try not to think of Alex too much, but it's hard not to remember the room they'd found in his flat – the one covered in photographs of me and our baby. I'd been right. Losing his job had left him with too much time on his hands. No longer able to get his thrills from apprehending criminals and meting out his own particular brand of punishment, finding me and his child had become his mission. His project.

When Megan had discovered the newspaper article Amity had sent, she'd made it easy for him by seeking him out. She may not have told him where we lived, but he must have seen her Instagram photographs before she deleted them and, like Amity, they were all Alex needed to locate us.

How close Alex had been to getting his revenge. Teaching me a lesson. If Megan hadn't been so upset after he'd failed to turn up at the meeting place she'd suggested. Hadn't spent the time walking home in the rain, searching for more information about him and finding it – I might have been another of his statistics. The information she'd found about his dismissal from the force had been enough to alert her. Make her think there was some truth in what Amity had told her about him. That he might not be the poor, heartbroken man she'd imagined him to be when she'd found the article. A man wronged by her mother.

What she'd found as she'd let herself onto the patio that night had proved it. Amity dead. Alex's hands around my throat.

Poor Amity. Sadness and guilt fight for space when I think

of her. At the waste of her life. In the end, she'd stood up for what she believed was right. Recognised the evil in Alex and I love her for it.

That newspaper article Amity sent to me... I still have it, folded into the back of the notebook. I slip it out and read again the false headline: I STILL MISS HER.

What had Alex felt in the moment I told him you were dead and the teenage girl he thought was you was someone else entirely? Had he even cared? It's something I often wonder. Yet, the irony isn't lost on me that the girl who'd once been known as Chloe *was* his daughter.

Alex had gone to his grave never knowing it, and, for everyone's sake, I'm glad.

I'm not sure why I kept the newspaper article. Maybe it's because it's the only picture I have of you. With a last look at your face, I place the article, along with the notebook, on the stones, then take out the cigarette lighter I bought in town for the purpose. Clicking it until the flame burns bright before touching it to the corner of the notebook's cover. I watch as it blackens and catches. Flames licking their way up the edges of the pages, the edges curling.

'I'm sorry, Megan,' I whisper. 'I'll never forget you.'

I straighten. Put the lighter back in my bag, then hurry back up the stones to the boardwalk. Sean will be back soon, and I don't want him to know what I've been doing. I look back at the smouldering ashes, the edges of the sea already licking at them. Soon the tide will wash them, and the past, away. It's a strangely comforting thought.

When Sean reaches me, I'm standing, head tipped back, watching the upstairs window of the house that used to be ours.

A young woman, around the age I was when I moved here, moves closer to the window, her baby on her shoulder. Someone joins her, her husband I presume. He walks to the side of the window, raises an arm and the blind moves slowly across the glass shutting them from our view. It's not the only change they've made to the property: the swimming pool is now filled in and paved over, a hot tub in its place, and the palms and potted plants have made way for a wooden pergola and a patch of artificial grass.

I feel Sean's arm around my shoulders. Lean into him. 'I hope they're happy here.'

'I hope they are too.' Sean's arm slips down to my waist. It's been hard for him: he loved this house. 'Ready to go now?'

'Yes.' I nod. 'I'm ready.'

I needed to come back here to see the place for myself. For closure. Soon we'll be back in our Victorian house in the pretty little village the three of us chose together. A house in a street of other similar properties where, at night, I can light the fire and draw the thick velvet curtains against the world. I feel safe there.

Before, it was Alex I was running from. This time it's the ghosts of my past. Maybe, in time, I can put those ghosts to rest. It's what I want. What I need.

Last time I had no choice.

This time I do.

A LETTER FROM WENDY

Firstly, I would like to say a huge thank you to everyone who has read *The Night Out*. I still have to pinch myself that this is my seventh psychological thriller! A reader really is an author's best friend, and I hope you enjoyed reading my book as much as I loved writing it.

If you did enjoy *The Night Out* and want to keep up-to-date with all my latest releases, just sign up at the following link. Your email address will never be shared, and you can unsubscribe at any time.

www.bookouture.com/Wendy-Clarke

Setting always plays an important role in my novels and this book is no exception. If you'll allow me, I'll tell you more about it. Some readers may already know that my husband and I are very lucky to own a beach hut on the south coast near Shoreham-by-Sea. It's where I write in the summer and (when not writing) it's where I go to swim, read, and relax.

The beach is beautiful whichever way I walk, but if I step out of my hut and walk to the east, the stones will eventually turn into a boardwalk. If I carry along this and look to my right, I'll see the beach and the sea where, at night, the red lights of the wind farm flash pinpricks of red lights into the darkness. Turning my head the other way, I'll see the backs of the eclectic mix of large houses that back onto the beach – all of them different except for one thing... the large windows that look out across the sea. As I've walked along the boardwalk in the direction of the fort, I've often wondered what those seemingly unadorned windows would look like at night when lit up like a stage.

The perfect setting for a thriller. The perfect setting for *The Night Out*.

Rather than set my story in one of the existing houses, I decided to create my own beachside residence using a pick-and-mix of elements taken from several of the homes I'd pass on my walk: a swimming pool from one, the spiral metal staircase linking the different outside areas from another, the palms and exotic shrubs from a third. The rest is from my imagination... as are the people who live in that large modern house with its open-plan living area, wide verandas and gated patio leading straight onto the beach.

I hope you loved *The Night Out,* and if you did, I would be very grateful if you could write a review. I'd love to hear what you think, and it makes such a difference helping new readers to discover one of my books for the first time.

I enjoy hearing from my readers – you can get in touch on my Facebook page, through Twitter, Goodreads, Instagram or my website.

Thanks,

Wendy x

www.wendyclarke.uk

facebook.com/WendyClarkeAuthor

twitter.com/WendyClarke99

instagram.com/WendyClarke99

ACKNOWLEDGEMENTS

This is my seventh book and the sixth I've worked on with my brilliant Bookouture editor, Jennifer Hunt. Writing a book is a two-way process and I am always grateful for Jen's patience, openness and skill in making suggestions that will without doubt improve my stories without demanding I accept them. She's with me every step of the process and I'm very lucky to have her. Someone once called us the dream team and I think they might be right!

It's not just my editor who gets a book to publication though, there are a lot of others who work behind the scenes at Bookouture, doing their best for our precious babies. In particular, I'd like to thank the fabulous publicity team of Kim Nash, Noelle Holten, Sarah Hardy and Jess Readett for making sure my book gets in front of as many readers as possible.

Thank you to my family for their continued support of my writing and to my friends – especially my writing buddy, Tracy, whose monthly meetup means a slice of delicious coffee cake as well as a huge amount of laughs, book chat and support. Thanks, too, to my Bookouture sister, Liz, who knows exactly when a sea walk and a chat are in order, and the lovely Friday Girls: Carol, Linda, Helen, Barbara and Jill, who've known me so long they keep my feet on the ground.

Thanks also to Graham Bartlett who so very patiently answers my police procedural questions. Any mistakes are my own.

My family are always there in the background cheering me

on and for this book, I must give a special acknowledgement to my daughter, Eve, who sowed the seed of the idea for *The Night Out* and my mum for suggesting my psychological thrillers for her book group!

The online reading community is a fabulous place to hang out as an author and I'd like to give thanks for their amazing encouragement and support. The same to the book bloggers who give their time to share their reviews with readers, helping them to make informed choices.

Finally, as always, the biggest thanks have to go to Ian, who supports me when my writing is going well but also when it's not, for thrashing out plot problems with me and for being the best husband any writer could wish for.

Before I go, I'd just like to say that without readers there would be no books so a huge thank you to everyone who has bought and read mine... especially you!

Printed in Great Britain
by Amazon